RACHANEE LUMAYNO

HEIR OF
CROWNS
AND
CURSES

KINGDOM LEGACY BOOK FOUR

Editing and proofreading by Tom Loveman

Cover art by Fiona Jayde Medi

Thank you for reading, I hope you enjoy Heir of Crowns and Curses!
If you have the time, please leave an honest review on Goodreads or wherever you
purchased this book! Thanks!

— · —

ALSO BY RACHANEE LUMAYNO

Kingdom Legacy
Heir of Amber and Fire
Heir of Memory and Shadow
Heir of Magic and Mischance
Heir of Crowns and Curses
Heir of Secrets and Spectres
Heir of Illusions and Others
Heir of Immortals and Empires

CONTENTS

Join the Newsletter

Hello Dear Reader!

Here's a fun fact for you—the first book in the Kingdom Legacy series, Heir of Amber and Fire, was inspired by a character in a Dungeons and Dragons campaign that I never got to play. Even though the game never happened, the character's backstory stayed with me, and became the basis of Jennica's story.

Since the first book had such strong ties to tabletop gaming, a friend suggested I create a campaign set in the world of the Kingdom Legacy series. And so *The Mysterious Magical Emporium* was born, and I'd love to send you a FREE copy! Just sign up for my newsletter at www.rachanee.net/newsletter, and your new campaign will be sent to you right away.

So grab your friends, grab some dice, and grab a copy of *The Mysterious Magical Emporium*, and get ready to spend some time in the kingdom of Calia with your new friends, Jennica, Beyan, and Taryn!

1

—:—

CHAPTER ONE

"I can't believe it. They want me to be a *what*?"

I stared in dismay at the fancy script gracefully inscribed across the thick cream paper.

You are cordially invited to the dedication of Crown Prince Coran of Calia, to be held in our capital city on the third day of our annual Haerfest Celebration, in honor of the autumn season ...

And underneath, in the blocky handwriting I recognized as being from the hand of one of my best friends:

Dear Rhyss,

Jennica and I would be honored if you would stand as Coran's godfather. We can think of no finer person to be his future mentor.

The handwritten part of the note was signed by both my friend King Beyan and his wife, Jennica.

The rulers of the northern kingdom of Calia.

"Did you get one of these too?" I held out the paper.

Across the table, Farrah reached over and plucked the ivory invitation from my unresisting fingers, narrowly avoiding her mostly full mug of mead. I grabbed mine up and took a drink.

Or tried to. It was empty. I turned it upside down, just to make sure. Yep, nothing there. Of course. Just my luck.

"Would you like some more mead, Rhyss?"

I looked up, sighing in relief. "You're an angel, Sylvie. That's why you're my favorite barmaid here at the Dragon's Tail."

Sylvie grinned as she refilled my mug. "I'm the only barmaid here at the Dragon's Tail. And you two—" she nodded at Farrah, who was reading the letter but looked up to give a brief nod of acknowledgement "—are in here often enough that I can tell when you're running low on drink even before you know."

"That's why you're the best barmaid in the best tavern in Orchwell."

Sylvie rolled her eyes. "It's the only tavern in Orchwell."

She topped off Farrah's cup, although it didn't really need it. "And I may be an angel, but don't think that flattery means I forgot your tab."

I groaned. Just add that to my already unlucky day. "I'll get it to you soon."

Sylvie snorted. "That's what they all say. You're lucky I like you. And that Farrah's been nice enough to pay down your bill from time to time." With that, the barmaid left to attend to another table.

Farrah, meanwhile, had finished reading the invitation, and was going over it again carefully, running her finger from word to word as if she needed to make sure she was really seeing what was written there. She burst out laughing. "Well, Rhyss. It looks like you've acquired yourself a baby."

I frowned as I ran a pale, freckled hand through my bright red hair. "Not like that, gods forbid."

"The chances of you actually becoming Coran's parent are slim. But that's not what gets me."

"What, then?"

Farrah laughed even harder. "The part about being his mentor."

Even if I was unsure about the whole godparent thing, her comment made me feel defensive. "Hey. I'd make an excellent mentor."

Farrah laughed so hard she couldn't speak for several moments. "Uh-huh, sure. You keep believing that."

I toyed briefly with the idea of pushing the issue, and then decided to drop it. This was Farrah, after all. She knew me too well, and was too often right about, well, everything.

"Well, what are you going to do about it?"

Farrah was waving the cream-colored paper in the air at me. I plucked it from her hands and stared at the fancy script again.

"Do I really have a choice?" I stared morosely at the invitation in one hand, and with the other, picked up my mug of mead and downed it one swallow. "I'm going to be the godparent to the heir of the Calian throne."

A few weeks later, Farrah and I traveled from our homes in the kingdom of Orchwell to its nearest neighbor, the kingdom of Calia. It was a trip we both knew well; as a Seeker, Beyan had been our former employer, and one of our dearest friends, before his marriage to the Calian princess, Jennica. He was still one of our dearest friends, as was Jennica. But instead of roaming the Gifted Lands Seeking out dragons, he now spent his time helping rule a kingdom.

Even after all this time, it still took some getting used to.

As if reading my thoughts, Farrah asked, "How long has it been since Beyan got married to Jennica and moved away from Orchwell?"

I scrunched my brow in thought. "Two years? Three? I lose track of time."

Farrah shook her head. Her violet hair, indicative of her half-Fae heritage, fell in front of her ebony face, and she tucked it behind her ear. I thought she was going to make a quip about *time's not the only thing you lose track of*, or something similar, but instead she was marveling about something else. "I honestly never thought I would have seen the day when Beyan got married, much less had a child. Never mind marrying into royalty. It had just been the three of us, for so long. I guess I thought things would never change."

"You've known him longer. I suppose it did come as a bit of a shock when it happened. But things can't stay the same forever."

"That's true." Farrah looked ... sad? Wistful? I couldn't quite read the expression on her face. For some reason, it worried me. Farrah was usually the calm, logical, competent one. *Sentimental* was not a word I'd ever use to describe her. She turned that indecipherable look on me. Now I was *really* worried. "One day the same thing might happen to you and me."

"I hardly doubt I'll go off and marry a princess."

Farrah shrugged. "You could. But that's not what I meant. Ever since Beyan left the field, it's been harder to find work. We were lucky with Kaernan's commissions, but it's not like he takes them all that often—"

"But he did recommend us to his other Seeker friends."

"Who had their own established teams and only hire us if their regular team can't do the job. It's not like it was before. We might end up working for different Seekers instead of being hired together. One of us could move away from Orchwell. Or maybe one of us decides to leave the help-for-hire business entirely. My point is, things are changing, but it feels like we're not choosing the changes, the changes are choosing *us*, and I hate feeling powerless about it all."

Farrah looked away. I was too stunned by her outburst—so unlike her—to have a response, and for a while the only sound was the *clop-clop-clop* of our horses' hooves as we traveled the well-worn road north to Calia.

Finally, I ventured, "Are you okay, Farrah?"

She sighed heavily. "Yes, I am. Or, I will be. Don't worry about it." Her tone told me the conversation was over. At least, for now. Quite possibly, permanently.

Farrah changed the subject. "What did you get as a dedication gift?"

Fine by me if she wanted to talk about something else. Dealing with emotions was never my strong suit, anyway.

I patted the satchel attached to my saddle. "Just a little token, really. Baby's first sword."

"Rhyss. You didn't."

"Well, he might need to go out in the world adventuring one day. Rescue princesses, stop evil sorcerers, slay dragons. Well, forget that last part. He'd be disowned by his parents if he did that."

"But what is a baby going to do with a sword? Is it a magic sword?"

"Um. No. It's just a regular sword. But really, what is a baby going to do with anything? It's not like he'll remember his dedication, anyway. Someday his godfather Rhyss will teach him how to use that sword, so really, I'm ensuring we'll have a strong bond in the future."

Farrah snorted. Miffed, I asked, "What did you get him?"

"I bought a simple necklace with a small golden sun for a pendant."

Now I snorted derisively. "Sounds impressive. I'm sure a newborn baby will *love* jewelry."

Farrah ignored my comment. "And then I enchanted it so when he wears it, it will mark him as a Friend of the Fae. It will keep him safe from the tricks and glamours of minor faeries, protect him from the Fae who might inhabit the woods and waters of the Gifted Lands, and its status will be recognized by the Faerie royals, King Finvarra and Queen Oona of the Seelie Court, should Prince Coran ever visit."

I swallowed the witty comeback I had been preparing, and instead repeated, "Sounds impressive."

This time I truly meant it. Farrah's gift would definitely be useful for a royal child and future ruler.

Farrah must have caught my changed demeanor, because her face changed from smug to sympathetic. "I'm sorry about my earlier comment. A sword is a great gift. He'll grow into it, and I'm sure he'll love training with you when he's old enough."

"It's really a silly thing to give him. I mean, Coran is the Crown Prince of Calia. He can have hundreds of swords made for him, much finer than the one I'm giving him. Magic to boot, if that's what he wanted. He doesn't need the absolutely worthless one I'm giving him."

Now it was Farrah's turn to ask, "Is everything okay?"

I laughed, but it wasn't a happy sound. "You're worried about things changing. I'm wondering ..."

"Wondering what?"

I sighed as the words came out in a rush. "Why Jennica and Beyan picked *me* to be the godparent for their child. For the heir to the throne, of all things! It should have been you—you have magic, after all. Or I'm sure Beyan has a Seeker cousin or knows someone in Orchwell who is still an active Seeker. But aside from being a friend of the royal couple, I don't have anything extraordinary to offer Coran. It just doesn't make sense to me, that's all."

We rode on in silence. I pretended to admire the scenery around us—the green of summer was beginning to give way to the reds and golds of the coming autumn.

Inwardly I chastised myself. Now who was being all emotional? But, I realized, it was a sentiment I had been harboring for a while, since we had gotten our invitations to the dedication. I just hadn't allowed myself to fully face my feelings about the situation until just now. But as long as Farrah and I were getting personal ...

When Farrah finally did say something, it was with her usual unflinching honesty, the trait that seemed so harsh and yet, over time, I had learned to appreciate. "You're right, Rhyss. At first blush, you do seem like a surprising choice. But Beyan and Jennica wouldn't have wanted you specifically without a good reason. And sometimes traits like bravery and honesty and trustworthiness are more important than having magical powers or an inherent ability like Seeking. You're important to the royal couple, and therefore you'll be important in the life of their child. And that's all that matters."

I hope so. I didn't say the words out loud, but Farrah gave me a gentle smile, as if she had heard what I'd been thinking.

"Is there anything else bothering you?" she asked.

"Yes, actually," I said, smirking. "Shouldn't it be godsfather, not godfather? Although godsfather is harder to say." I tried out each word. "Godsfather. Godfather. What do you think?"

Farrah groaned. "I think you should spare me your superstitious nonsense."

Talking about the gods never failed to get a rise out of Farrah. The religious beliefs in the Gifted Lands were as varied as its people—some believed in the old gods, as I did, that were rumored to have founded our kingdoms. Some worshipped the Fae, whose ancient magic permeated our human realm to varying degrees, depending on where you lived. And some people didn't believe in anything at all, unless it was something they could see with their own eyes and create with their own hands.

Farrah's half-Fae heritage made her uncomfortable with the idea of Faerie worship. "I believe in myself, but not like that," she would quip whenever the subject came up.

I grinned. "I haven't yet, and I don't plan to, ever."

Farrah grimaced and sighed. "Lucky me."

We fell into a companionable silence. We passed a few farms and single homes along the way, then reached the modest-sized town on the outskirts of the Calian capital city. From there, it wasn't much longer until we reached the open gates to Calia's capital, with its cool gray stone palace rising in the distance.

We passed through the city gates, which were, as usual, bustling with merchants, traders, visitors, and Calian citizens entering or leaving the city. Farrah scrutinized everything as we walked by—the city walls, the gates, the cobblestone streets, buildings, and even the majestic fountain in the city square.

"Would you stop gawking? You're acting like you've never been to Calia before, when we both know you've been here dozens of times."

Farrah stopped examining everything and gave me an exasperated look. "That's not why I'm looking, silly. I'm just impressed at how quickly the capital was repaired after the recent attack. You can hardly see any damage at all."

Oh, yes, that was right. Several months ago, Rothschan, a fellow Gifted Lands kingdom, had caught Calia off guard with a surprise magical attack. That Rothschan wanted revenge for the overthrow and subsequent death of King Hendon, who had been a beloved knight of Rothschan before becoming a not-so-loved king of Calia, was not a surprise. That the kingdom used magic—which they outright mocked, feared, and despised—to attempt that revenge was a surprise. One that had nearly succeeded in ruining Calia, and had definitely caused significant damage to her fair capital city.

Looking around, I saw that Farrah was right in her assessment. "Queen Jennica and King Beyan must know how to inspire their subjects. A generous treasury doesn't hurt, either."

"I wish we had been there to help," Farrah said. "Although it sounds like they had things under control. For the most part."

I chuckled. "I think that was the first time we missed all the action. Who would have thought going on a Seeker commission would be less exciting than staying home and going to visit friends?"

"Not only was I surprised when we came home to find out the news about the attack on Calia, we got a second surprise when Jennica and Beyan announced her pregnancy." Farrah chuckled as well, remembering. "Although, with everything that happened, it was smart of them to wait until they could be sure Rothschan wouldn't try to attack again."

I thought for a minute. "That's right; Beyan mentioned they were just about to announce it when all the chaos with Rothschan erupted. But are they sure Rothschan won't retaliate in some way? That's a kingdom with a long memory that holds even longer grudges."

"Didn't Beyan tell you?"

"Tell me what?"

"They have an ally from Rothschan now. Several, in fact, and some of them had been refugees living in Calia for a long time. But this new ally has the magical ability to overthrow the kingdom's current royal family and rule in their place, if she chose to. And the Rothschan royals know it. So there's a sort of stalemate between the two kingdoms right now. A rather reluctant truce, if you will."

"Really?"

"Honestly, Rhyss, don't you remember? It's pretty big news; Beyan had to have mentioned it."

I frowned, trying to recall my last conversation with my friend. I had been so surprised by his "Jennica and I are having a baby" announcement that I may have missed out on the rest of what he had been saying. I'm sure as King Beyan, his subjects hung on his every word, but my friend Beyan knew exactly what I—his longtime friend and former traveling companion—was like.

But I had always paid attention when it counted. Like if our group was under attack by bandits. Or we had to tread quietly because a dragon was near. Things like that.

Farrah shook her head at me, like she was annoyed, but it was more from force of habit than anything. After all the years of traveling together, she knew what I was like, too. She gave a heavy sigh of fond exasperation. "Well, at least you remembered that Rothschan attacked Calia, even if you didn't recall the details. That's something, at least."

"Don't worry, if Jennica and Beyan talk about it, I'll act like I know what they're talking about."

Farrah laughed. "Beyan will see right through that. Besides me, he's the only other person who knows you all too well."

Our conversation had taken us into the heart of the capital, past the Merchants' District, beyond the Academy of Magical Arts that Queen Jennica had founded a few years ago, and right to the palace gardens. Just beyond was the fountain-lined walkway leading to the Calian palace. The shimmering blue-and-green cobblestones in the palace courtyard always gave me the feeling I was underwater. No matter how many times I had been here, the palace never ceased to impress me.

Farrah giggled at me. "Now who's gawking?"

I playfully poked her—no easy feat, since we were both atop horses. "Still hard to believe rough-and-tumble Beyan lives in this fancy place."

Her grin softened as she stared at the majestic building before us. "Changes," was all she said.

As we approached, the door to the palace flung open dramatically. A musical voice proclaimed, "Lord Rhyss and Lady Farrah have arrived! Welcome to Castle Calia!"

2

— · —

CHAPTER TWO

FARRAH AND I LOOKED at each other and shrugged. "When did we get titled?" she asked.

"I have no idea," I answered, dismounting. "But you have to admit, it has a certain ring to it."

I helped Farrah dismount and then motioned to a waiting page, who sprang forward and led the horses away to be stabled. Gallantly, I offered the crook of my arm to Farrah, who grinned broadly as she placed her fingers lightly on my offered arm. "Shall we, my lady?"

"Certainly, my lord."

The page with the melodic voice scurried ahead of us as we entered the palace, headed for the Great Hall. Farrah and I followed at a more leisurely pace. The page flung open the doors to the Great Hall with the same dramatic flair he had shown earlier, loudly announcing, "Lord Rhyss and Lady Farrah are here, to request an audience with Her Majesty, Queen Jennica Allayne Kenet—"

Queen Jennica stood, effectively cutting off the rest of whatever the young page had been about to say. "Thank you, Sielan. You may go."

Sielan stopped mid-royal name recitation, looking confused. He opened and closed his mouth several times, like a fish gasping for air, then finally spluttered, "O-of course, Your Majesty."

As he turned to go, Jennica added, "And next time, don't forget to knock. Please close the door behind you."

Sielan, now bright red with embarrassment, bowed repeatedly as he backed out of the doorway. The impressive wooden doors of the Great Hall shut, the sound echoing off of the room's stone walls. The fading sound was replaced by the sound of laughter from Farrah, myself, and the three figures on the dais at the other end of the room.

Queen Jennica, lovely and intelligent, commanded the room with her, well, queenly demeanor. Her black hair flowed loose under the simple golden circlet on her head. When we had first met, she had been a bit headstrong, yet uncertain of herself. Then again, she had been a princess on the run, traveling with Beyan, Farrah, and me under false pretenses. But now, she was a wholly confident and self-assured woman, as befit the ruler of the most renowned magical kingdom in the Gifted Lands.

Standing behind the queen's throne was Taryn, a bubbly blonde former lady-in-waiting turned Royal Advisor. Although advisor was a bit of an understatement. Taryn not only advised the king and queen, she also assisted Jennica with any number of activities, some officially sanctioned, and many more in secret.

And finally, sitting in the throne next to Jennica, was King Beyan of Calia. Even after all these years it still felt odd to call him King Beyan or Your Majesty, although I made sure to use his titles and honorifics in public. To me, he was still just Beyan, the dragon Seeker and my friend and traveling companion of many years. Fortunately, Beyan was a level-headed sort, and didn't let his newfound royal status go to his head.

Still laughing, Beyan stood and held out his arms to us. His circlet, a matching twin to his wife's, lay slightly askew on his brown hair, making me grin. Some things really didn't change. "Rhyss, Farrah. We're so glad you could make it!"

After hugs and greetings were exchanged, Jennica looked around and frowned. "I'd say you two should sit so we can all catch up with each other, but frankly, the chairs here are uncomfortable."

"I can have Sielan fetch some other chairs, Your Majesty," Taryn said, moving toward a nearby bell pull.

Jennica stopped her before she could summon the young page. "No, don't bother. Sielan would probably faint from the excitement of it all, and I'd rather not sit on these thrones again, anyway."

"Is Sielan the page who showed us in?" Farrah asked. When the queen nodded, Farrah added, "He did seem rather ... excitable."

Jennica laughed. "'Rather excitable' is a nice way of putting it. He loves the formalities of palace life, and being around so many people of high rank. I think it bothers him that half the time his own queen would rather things around here were more casual."

"Is he new here?"

"He is. We hired him as a favor to his mother, who's served in the palace for a long time. She hoped being a page would help temper some of his boundless energy."

Beyan laughed. "Instead, he's just refocused all of that energy on being the kingdom's most perfect page. It's a bit trying."

Jennica stepped down from the dais. "Ah, well. He'll grow out of it. Eventually. Maybe."

"Why did he think we were nobility?" I wondered as the rest of us followed the queen, gathering around the closed doors to the Great Hall.

Jennica turned to us and smiled, her hand resting lightly on the door handle. "Sielan thinks anyone who comes in through the front, formal entrance is a lord or lady. After all, everyone else uses either the servants' or commoners' entrance." She opened the door and strode into the hallway.

"There's a commoners' entrance?" I whispered to Farrah, who shrugged. "I never knew that."

"Also, we may have decided to bestow some courtesy titles on our dearest friends." Beyan winked at Farrah and me. "Kind of comes with the territory of ... some other things."

Some other things most likely referring to the one thing that the royal couple had requested of me—namely, becoming Crown Prince Coran's godfather.

"Thank you, I think," I said. "Um ... not to be rude, because it is a great honor, but ... does it come with added responsibilities?"

"Only if you want them," Beyan said. "We were thinking the status change would really just be in name only. Although you would be entitled to land, a modest stipend from the Calian Crown for living expenses, and a seat on the kingdom's Council."

The financial part sounded enticing. And, hey, I would finally be able to pay off my tab at the Dragon's Tail. I imagined the look on Sylvie's face when I casually plunked down a hefty purse on the counter. *Keep the change*, I would say, as if I did this sort of thing all the time.

That would be fun.

As for the rest of it ... "Can I think about it?"

Beyan laughed. "Of course, my friend. I completely understand. After all, you're not the only one to suddenly find himself a lord, thanks to your connections."

Queen Jennica chuckled. "Connections? Darling, you earned that title."

Beyan laughed again. "I may have earned it, but it doesn't mean I wanted it."

The queen led us to the private chambers she shared with Beyan. "We'll be more comfortable here, plus it will be easier to visit without being overheard."

Upon opening the door to the bedchamber, a young girl of perhaps thirteen or fourteen instantly sprang up from her seat, then sank into a deep curtsy. "Your Majesties!"

"Hello, Leandra," Jennica said. "How's little Coran doing?"

"Excellent, Your Majesty. He's been sound asleep for a good hour or so."

"Good. Let's hope he stays that way for a little while longer." Jennica crossed over to where a simple white bassinet stood in one corner of the room, looked down at her sleeping son, and smiled. "We'll be here for a while, Leandra, so you may go."

"As you wish, Your Majesty. Will there be anything else you require before I go?"

"Yes. Please send someone from the kitchen up with refreshments for our guests. No need to hurry."

Leandra curtsied again, then left the room. Jennica and Beyan settled themselves in a settee by the fireplace, while Taryn, Farrah, and I settled ourselves in various chairs nearby.

"It's always lovely to see you two," Jennica said. Then, to me: "And I bet you were surprised when you received our note."

I laughed. Then, afraid of appearing disrespectful, I quickly turned it into a cough. "You could say that, Jennica."

"Would it surprise you more if I told you that I was the one who suggested you?"

Beyan reached over and grasped Jennica's hand. "I completely agreed with my lovely wife's judgment, but yes. She was the one who put forth your name as the best person to be Coran's godparent."

I was stunned into silence. I had assumed Beyan had suggested me, and that Jennica had—reluctantly—agreed.

Farrah smiled at me encouragingly. "I think it's an excellent choice."

Beyan grinned. "Glad you think so. And don't feel left out of anything, Farrah. We'll get you on the next round."

"Next round? Does that mean ...? Are you and Jennica ...?"

"Oh, goodness, no," Jennica said. "Let me get used to motherhood with Coran first."

We all laughed. I had finally gathered my thoughts enough to say, "Thank you, Jennica. I ... I'm honored you think so highly of me."

"Of course," she said. "I always have. But now, to a bit of business. The Haerfest Celebration starts tomorrow, with the dedication on the third day. It's always a lovely festival, but it can get a bit chaotic, so once it's underway, we won't have much time to prepare for the dedication."

"Prepare?" Was I supposed to give a speech or something? "Prepare what?"

Seeing the distress on my face, Beyan hastily said, "Nothing too scary, my friend. We just need you to stand with us and the baby during the ceremony, respond to a few questions at the right times, and be recognized by the Sword of the First King."

"Questions? What kind of questions?" Then my brain caught up with my mouth. "Wait a minute, did you just say I will get to see the Sword of the First King again?"

Farrah remarked, "That got his attention. You should have mentioned that on the dedication invitation."

"It definitely is a perk." The sword in question was an absolutely beautiful weapon. I had had the chance to, ahem, borrow it several years ago when Calia was in danger from a deranged, magic-drunk king. Afterwards, the former queen, Melandria, had been kind enough to have a similar sword made for me as a reward. It was a wonderful copy, but the original had been something special. Magical.

The Sword of the First King used to hang above the twin thrones in the Great Hall, but since my short-term theft of it, it had been locked away in one of the castle treasuries. The space was now occupied by a magical illusion that was sure to disappoint any would-be weapon thieves.

"What do you mean by, the sword will 'recognize' me?" I asked.

"It's a crucial part of the ceremony," Beyan said. "Just like it was used in Jennica's coronation, and our wedding. It binds us either to the kingdom, to each other, or both."

"Wait. Does this mean I'm giving up my Orchwell citizenship?"

"Not unless you want to. But it will bind you to Coran as his godfather, and thus, indirectly, in service to the kingdom of Calia."

"Oh. That's all right then." I'd never do anything that would harm Beyan or Jennica, and since anything that harmed their kingdom would obviously hurt them, I practically was in service to the kingdom of Calia anyway.

"You're sure?" Beyan searched my face anxiously. "I know what a free spirit you are. You'd be bound to the Crown Prince of Calia. It could potentially be a big responsibility, gods forbid."

"No more than saving your hide time and time again," I quipped. "Like when you fell into that snowy crevice while we were looking for that ancient ice dragon. Or when you were still developing your skills as a Seeker, and stumbled into that nest of baby earth dragons, with the mother nearby. Oh, and do you remember the time—"

Beyan held up a hand. "Say no more, friend. Standing as godfather to a baby, even if he is a prince, will be much easier than any commission you ever accompanied me on."

3

CHAPTER THREE

THE FIRST DAY OF the Haerfest Celebration went by in a blur. As Queen Jennica had predicted, the myriad of sights and sounds to experience were fun, but exhausting. Being the northernmost kingdom in the Gifted Lands, Calia often had harsher winters than its neighbors. Perhaps that accounted for the overwhelming frenzy that was the country's Haerfest Celebration. From sunup to well after sundown, Farrah and I attended various games and entertainments, and sampled a wide variety of Calian cuisine. By the end of that first day, my purse was much lighter, and my body a lot heavier.

That night, Beyan, Jennica, Farrah, and I had a private dinner together. Taryn was nearby, acting as nursemaid to baby Coran. I wondered why, since I was sure there were servants dedicated to that role.

After the food had been served, Taryn shut and locked the door behind the exiting servants, then joined us at the table while still keeping an eye on the baby.

"What's with the secrecy?" Farrah asked, indicating the locked door.

Beyan lifted his glass to his lips and took a long sip of wine. Almost like he was gathering the courage to say something. I grew nervous, and downed some wine myself.

"There was one more thing we needed to tell you, before the dedication ceremony," he said. "We didn't tell you when you first arrived, because we knew you had a lot to think about already. But remember when I said that becoming Coran's godfather could potentially be a big responsibility?"

I took another long swallow of wine. This wasn't sounding good. "Go on."

Beyan and Jennica exchanged glances before Jennica spoke. "There's one other thing that being the prince's godfather would entail. We would like you to serve as Regent, if the need ever arose."

I had either had too much wine, or not enough, because I was pretty sure I hadn't heard Jennica correctly. "Did you say, Regent?"

Farrah laughed. "Now that was not what I was expecting either of you to say."

Jennica said, "Neither Beyan nor I have any siblings. My parents have a new life, outside of Calia. They've spent the last few years traveling around the Gifted Lands and have accepted an ambassadorship to the kingdom of Graenir, in the southeast. They were here for Coran's birth, but moved to Graenir afterward. One of the rules surrounding their new position was that they can't travel outside Graenir for one year. Calia's never had relations with the mysterious kingdom—I don't think any of the other countries in the Gifted Lands have, either. It was an amazing opportunity to make an ally, one that we—as in, the kingdom of Calia—couldn't pass up."

Farrah put her hand on Jennica's arm. "While I'm sure you're happy, as queen, for the chance to ally with Graenir, I'm sorry—for you as Jennica—to hear that your parents are so far away. I'm sure you miss them."

Jennica shrugged, but she put her hand over Farrah's and squeezed it in an unspoken thank you. "I would have loved to have them around for the first year of my firstborn. Not a day goes by that I don't want them around for advice or assistance. But as queen, Calia is my first duty, always. Ruling a country means you often have to put duty above desire." She sighed. "But that means they are unable to help easily, should something happen to Beyan and me. You, Rhyss, and Taryn are the only ones we trust the most."

"Then why don't you have Taryn or Farrah stand as Regent?" I asked.

Farrah vehemently shook her head no. Queen Jennica said, "While Farrah would make an excellent godmother, we wanted Coran to have an additional positive male influence in his life, besides his father."

Taryn added, "Besides, I can serve the royal family and the kingdom better in my current position. Rhyss, you really are the best choice."

"Me? How?"

"You'll already be part of the prince's life. You'll be someone he can trust completely."

"And, since you're not part of the Calian court, he'll know you truly have his best interests at heart," Farrah said.

I looked at her, surprised. "You really think I can do this? I mean, I hope it never happens, but if it did ... you honestly think I'm the best person for it?"

The look in Farrah's eyes took my breath away. Genuine sincerity, and ... something else I couldn't quite decipher. "Yes, Rhyss. I don't think it. I know it."

There was a collective silence as everyone awaited my answer. Then, finally, I said:

"All right, then. I'll do it."

My answer was met with a crying sound from the nearby cradle. Taryn started to stand, ready to attend to the baby, but Jennica waved at her to stay seated and walked over, picking up her son and rocking him slightly to calm him down. She brought Coran over to where I was sitting at the table.

"See, little one? That's Rhyss. He's going to be your godfather. What do you think of that?"

Coran's answer was to keep crying. He reached out toward me.

"Would you like to hold him?" Queen Jennica asked me.

"Uh, I don't know ..."

"It'll be fine. Hold him like this." She demonstrated briefly, then handed the squirming little bundle to me. His crying grew louder.

"I don't think he likes me."

"Nonsense. Just give it a moment."

I did, holding my breath all the while. Eventually the little prince settled down, staring at me with his big brown eyes.

I dared to breathe again. Waggling my fingers in front of Coran, I laughed in surprise when he grabbed my fingers with a surprisingly strong grip.

"Ah, see?" Jennica said. "He likes you."

Looking down at the little Crown Prince, I knew at that moment my heart was given.

4

CHAPTER FOUR

By the end of the second day of the Haerfest Celebration, completely drained from the day's events, I wondered if I would have enough energy to make it through Crown Prince Coran's dedication. As I crawled into bed, I thanked the gods that the ceremony wasn't until midday. I could sleep in a little, I hoped.

But my hopes were dashed the next morning when a loud knocking sounded on my bedchamber door. I cracked open one eye. The sun was peeking through the curtains, letting me know the day had already begun. But it still felt way too early to me.

I groaned and turned over in bed, pulling a pillow over my head for good measure.

I was just drifting back to sleep when—

—The pillow was yanked unceremoniously from me.

"Hey!" I turned and blinked groggily, my brain and mouth both fuzzy.

"Good morning." Farrah's brisk voice cut through my fuzziness. So did the sharp sunlight that pierced my closed eyes when she pulled back the curtains.

"Go away. 'M sleeping," I mumbled.

"Not anymore. Get up." She whacked me lightly with the stolen pillow, then yanked the bedcovers off me. Cold air hit me, adding to the unwelcome wake-up.

I groped for the covers, but Farrah held the edges out of my reach. Finally, I gave up. I sat up and rubbed my eyes. "You're lucky I don't sleep naked."

Farrah snorted. "I've traveled with you for how many years now? No Seeker's companion would be so foolish. Bandits aren't usually polite enough to wait for you to put your clothes on before they attack."

She was right, as usual. I yawned. "Still, is there some reason you're up so early, and you felt like inflicting that on me? We've been through the fair twice over. My feet are swollen and ready to fall off, and I couldn't eat another thing even if I wanted to."

"That's surprising, coming from you. But no, we're not going to the fair. Have you forgotten already? Today's the day of the baby prince's dedication."

"That's not for another few hours."

"And there's much to be done before it happens. You can't just roll out of bed and walk into the ceremony." She eyed me, clucking her tongue. "Well, maybe *you* can, but you shouldn't. Come on."

She tugged on my hand, pulling me from the bed. Knowing that it would do no good to argue and delay things, I let her. She pushed me toward the door. "There's a servant waiting outside for you, who will assist you in the baths. I'll meet you after you're done getting ready; I have to get dressed myself."

Now that I was more awake, I realized Farrah was clad only in a white dressing gown; as she'd pointed out, we'd traveled extensively together in the wilderness of the Gifted Lands and I had seen her before in various stages of undress. But for some reason, seeing her in a full-length lacy dressing gown made me embarrassed, as if I had caught her in a private moment.

Why was I embarrassed? It was only Farrah, after all.

"All right." I spoke quickly to cover my embarrassment as I looked at a random point over Farrah's shoulder. "I'll see you later, then."

Farrah crossed to the still-open door and left, stopping briefly in the doorway to give instructions to someone unseen standing in the hallway. "Don't let him go back to bed, we're running late as it is."

I heard a murmur of, "Yes, m'lady," and then Farrah's footsteps echoing rapidly down the hall.

Sielan's tousled blond head poked around the doorframe. "My lord, I have come to escort you to the baths."

Inwardly, I groaned. Already the day was turning out sideways, and it had barely begun. Sure enough, Sielan yapped my ear off while escorting me to the men's bathing area, which normally wasn't that far away, but under Sielan's incessant chatter, felt like it was in another kingdom entirely.

"Ah, here we are, my lord," Sielan announced as we finally reached the baths. I hadn't bothered to try to curb his constant usage of my new title. Being "my lord"-ed every fifth word was kind of growing on me.

The page opened the door for me. "Thank you," I said.

"Of course, my lord. I believe your bath has already been prepared. Do you require assistance? Should you need anything—"

Before Sielan could say—or do—anything else, I pulled the door firmly shut behind me. I'm not entirely sure, but I think the poor page jumped back at the last second before the door clipped his nose.

I slipped into the waiting warm water and closed my eyes.

A discreet knock on the door alerted me that, unfortunately, it was time to get on with my day. I reluctantly pulled myself out of the water and dried off quickly with the linen towel that someone had thoughtfully laid out earlier.

Another knock sounded just as I pulled my nightshirt over my head. I yanked open the door, surprising Sielan, whose hand was raised mid-knock. "Ah, Lord Rhyss! I'm glad you're finished. If I may escort you back to your chambers?"

"It's all right, I know the way." I hoped I wasn't being too obvious in my attempt to get rid of him.

"It's no trouble, my lord."

I sighed. It was probably faster to just give in and let him escort me. It was his job, after all, and he seemed very determined to do it. I started walking, Sielan on my heels. With more endless chatter.

When we reached my room, Sielan said, "I understand you journeyed here without a valet. Allow me to—"

"No, no, that won't be necessary," I said hastily. "Why don't you tell Farrah ... er, I mean, Lady Farrah ... that I'm ready? By the time you find her and relay the message, I will be."

Sielan looked confused, probably because I was decidedly *not* ready, but merely replied, "Of course, my lord." He turned on his heel and walked away.

Thank the gods that he's used to the odd whims of the nobility. Breathing a sigh of relief, I entered my bedchamber and started to dress for the day.

It wasn't long before Farrah returned. By herself, thank the gods. I peered behind her. "No escort?"

Farrah was staring at me in dismay. "What are you wearing?"

I looked down at my outfit. It was my usual traveling garb—a plain, cream-colored linen tunic and brown homespun pants. "What's wrong with it?"

Farrah clicked her tongue in disapproval. She looked around, her frown deepening. Crossing to the wardrobe, she flung it open and started rummaging through its contents.

"What are you doing?" I asked.

"You can't wear that to the dedication." Her voice was muffled, since her head and half of her body was in the wardrobe. "Sielan was supposed to help you dress."

"No, thank you," I said vehemently. "Even the short walk to the baths was too long with that boy."

"If you're going to be godfather to a prince, you have to start acting like one. And for today at least, dressing like one." Farrah withdrew from the wardrobe, several items of clothing in her hands. She tossed them at me. I just barely caught them. "Put these on."

"No."

"Rhyss, we don't have time to argue—"

"I mean, you're just standing there staring at me."

Farrah let out an exasperated sigh and turned around. "Fine. Are you happy?"

Well, not really. I could already tell the clothes were going to be stiff and uncomfortable, and I hadn't even put them on yet. But it definitely wasn't the thing to bring up to Farrah. I quickly changed into the new outfit. "You can turn around now."

Farrah turned, scrutinizing me. I had traded my practical traveling clothes for Calia formal wear: dark gray pants, topped by a crisp white shirt and a sky blue jacket with a high collar. While my new clothes were of a fine cut and fabric, I still felt silly, standing there in my finery.

Especially since Farrah was frowning at me as she studied me and my new outfit.

Now that I wasn't so distracted—and Farrah's arms weren't overflowing with clothes—I was able to look at her. Really look at her. She was resplendent in a light lavender gown that enhanced the purple color of her hair, which had been half pinned up, with gentle curls framing her face. With the way the fabric shimmered in the sunlight, and the low-cut bodice and full skirt of her formal dress, she truly looked like a Lady Farrah.

She looked breathtaking. Even if her frown had deepened.

"What? What's wrong now?" I asked.

Farrah came closer. My breath caught. Her hand reached out, tugging and straightening my jacket.

"I believe the current fashion is to wear it like so." She expertly adjusted the collar and buttoned the middle part of my blue coat. Stepping back, she looked over her handiwork. "Beyan will know for sure, but I think that's right."

I fought the puzzling wave of disappointment that suddenly swept over me. Bizarre. It was probably just tiredness, from being woken up so early and abruptly. "Do I pass your approval?"

A slight smile bloomed on Farrah's face. "I think so." She turned toward the door. "Come on, we need to get going."

If you're going to be godfather to a prince, you have to start acting like one. With Farrah's comment still ringing my ears, I sprang forward, reaching the chamber door ahead of her. Gallantly, I pulled it open. "After you. My lady."

The smile on her face grew wider. "It really does have a nice ring to it, doesn't it?"

Together, we left the room.

5

— · —

CHAPTER FIVE

"... AND ON THIS momentous occasion, we gather to celebrate the birth of Coran, prince of Calia, and to present him to his people as their future sovereign and servant."

The vicar continued his dedication speech. It took all I had to stand still on the dais and look—I hoped—dignified. What I really wanted to do was scratch my neck. The fancy sky blue coat looked pretty, but was also made of pretty scratchy wool.

Unthinking, I reached up to my neck just as I caught Farrah's eye in the assemblage. She shook her head ever so slightly. I sighed and put my hand back down.

To distract myself from ripping the hateful jacket off and giving into a scratching frenzy, I looked over the crowded area.

I was standing on a makeshift platform in the main square of Calia's capital, near the large public fountain and the gates to the city. The palace was in the distance, and my decidedly evil wool jacket matched the beautiful day overhead.

On the dais, standing next to me, were King Beyan and Queen Jennica. The vicar, who was still droning on, stood on the other side, opposite the three of us. Baby Prince Coran lay in between, in a cradle that took up the center of the dais.

The area in front of the dais was crowded, with every available seat taken, and many more onlookers standing on the sides and in the back. All the area shops had closed for the dedication, not that anyone could have gotten through such a large mass of people easily. I could just imagine the headache this event was causing the city guards.

Farrah sat at the front, with Royal Advisor Taryn on her right, and some other Calian dignitaries I didn't recognize. The former dragon Seeker Kye, Beyan's father, was sitting on Farrah's other side.

While the vicar continued his extremely long speech—seriously, how much was there to say about a baby that was only a few weeks old?—I noticed some slight movement in the back of the crowd. Two figures in dark greenish-blue cloaks had joined the crowd and were slowly threading their way to the front, presumably for a better look. They stopped halfway, probably unable to gain any more ground amidst the throng of people.

"... And so, it is my solemn and joyous duty to dedicate our beloved Prince Coran to you, the people of the kingdom of Calia. May he and Calia both grow together in strength and wisdom."

I smirked as I pondered the vicar's words. *How can one be both solemn and joyous at the same time?* I caught Beyan's eye, as well as the faint smile forming on the corner of his lips. My friend was thinking the same thing.

Jennica looked at me pointedly, and ever-so-slightly nodded her head toward the vicar. I blinked, confused, and then Beyan surreptitiously nudged me.

"Rhyss of Orchwell, do you accept this responsibility?"

Oh. While my mind had been wandering, the vicar had moved on to the part that included me. The part where I officially pledged to be Coran's godfather, and tied myself to both him and Calia.

"Yes." The weight of what I was accepting suddenly fell on me, and I'm afraid my voice might have squeaked a little. I cleared my throat and tried again, louder. "Yes, I do."

The vicar stepped back to allow Beyan to cross the dais. A page standing nearby approached, holding a rich blue velvet pillow with the Sword of the First King lying across it. The king took the sword, holding it aloft for all to see. The sword gleamed in the sunlight. Although I carried its twin—indeed, the specially commissioned double was hanging at my side—there was nothing like the original.

"Come forward, Rhyss of Orchwell." Beyan's voice rang across the square.

As I crossed to the other side of the dais, I took a quick peek into Coran's cradle. The baby prince had been sleeping peacefully during the vicar's entire boring speech—I would have too, if I were in his place. But as I passed, his big brown eyes opened, and he cooed and gurgled at me.

I couldn't help smiling back, and briefly reached into the cradle to touch his tiny hand. There were more cooing and gurgling sounds from the baby, and a collection of sighs and happy murmurs could be heard from the assembly.

But nothing made me feel better than the smiles on my friends' faces. Looking at Beyan and Jennica, I could practically hear what they were thinking: *We made the right choice.* It made me feel a lot better about what was to come.

I stood before the king. Beyan said, "Rhyss of Orchwell, you have been chosen to act as Crown Prince Coran's godfather due to your steadfast heart and deep dedication, to both the queen and I, and to our kingdom. Do you pledge to serve our son with the same love and dedication, guiding him as he grows, and to serve as Regent should the need arise?"

I took a deep breath. This time there was no squeak of worry to betray me, and no hesitation. "Yes."

The murmurs in the crowd started up again, but this time they took on a different tone. Beyan and Jennica hadn't announced their plan to have me serve as Regent before today, and I would have bet my sword that many of Calia's councilors and nobles were upset to hear that they had been passed over for such an important position by a commoner from a foreign country.

"Then kneel, my friend."

I knelt down. Beyan placed the flat of the Sword of the First King on my shoulder. "Queen Jennica and I, King Beyan, along with the kingdom of Calia, recognize you, Rhyss of Orchwell, as godfather to our son, Crown Prince Coran of Calia."

The sword started glowing, an icy blue color a few shades paler than my coat. I felt a slight shock as tingles ran from the sword into my shoulder, spreading through the rest of my body. I felt lightheaded, and a bit detached, like my soul had separated from my body for a brief instant. Beyan was still talking, but I was so focused on the odd sensations, I didn't register what he was saying.

And then the tingling feeling was gone. Beyan lifted the sword from my shoulder, and held his hand out to me. "Rise, Rhyss."

I took his hand and started to get to my feet.

And then the ground shook, the dais rocked underneath us, and a large cloud of green smoke filled the square, obscuring the area entirely.

6

—·—

CHAPTER SIX

THE GREEN SMOKE WAS so thick, I couldn't even see Beyan, who I knew was standing right next to me.

Around me, I could hear screams in the crowd, punctuated by coughing.

"I can't see, I can't see!"

"Irien? Irien, where are you?"

"This smoke is making me dizzy!"

And then, louder, the voices of the guards trying to keep the crowd under control: "Everyone, please remain calm and stay where you are! This smoke should go away shortly!"

"Rhyss?" I jumped at how close that voice was to my ear. Beyan. I reached out, my arm getting smacked by a hand flailing about in the haze.

"Yes, I'm still right next to you."

The hand stopped flailing and grasped my arm. "Good. I'll keep a hold of you so I know where you are. Jennica!"

There was no response. Beyan called again. "Jennica!" Still no response, although I thought I heard coughing from where she had been standing. "We need to get to the queen."

"What about the baby?"

"Jennica first, then Coran. He's in his cradle, he's not going any-where." Beyan coughed. "Go slowly, and cover your mouth and nose if you can. There's something odd about this smoke, it's making me disoriented."

"I thought I was just still feeling the effects of whatever the sword did to me." My voice was muffled now, as I was talking with my left shirt sleeve in front of my mouth.

"No, I'm feeling it too," Beyan said. We started to slowly move sideways, trying to find Jennica in the confusion. Somewhere in front of me, I could hear baby Coran wailing, along with the cries of the other babies and children in the crowd who had been in attendance at the dedication.

Our slow side scuttle in the green fog felt excruciatingly slow, but I eventually bumped into someone. Or, I should say, my foot bumped into someone. Lying on the floor.

"Jennica? Is that you?"

Whoever my foot had found didn't respond.

"Beyan?" I resisted the urge to yell, knowing he was right behind me, still holding my arm. But it was unnerving not to be able to see him. This fog was playing tricks on my mind, making me think my friend was far away. "There's someone lying here."

Beyan and I both slowly sank to our knees, feeling around on the ground. The person before us was slender, their skin smooth and soft. *That rules out the vicar*, I thought. Then I heard a strangled cry from Beyan.

"It's Jennica," he confirmed. "I felt the crown she was wearing, tangled up in her hair."

I swallowed, my heart sinking. "Is she—"

I heard a rustling, then Beyan said, "She's alive. She's breathing, but barely. I think she's unconscious."

"You stay here," I said. "I'll go get Coran. I'll call out once he's secure."

"All right."

I backed away from Jennica and started crawling toward the area where I thought the cradle was. Afraid of walking off the edge of the dais, I moved forward slowly, using my hands to test if I was near anything, be it a piece of furniture, a person, or a drop off the platform. As Beyan had said, this haze was disorienting. It hadn't dissipated one bit, despite the hollow reassurances of the guards. The screaming beyond the dais had grown louder, and I worried about Farrah, Taryn, and Kye possibly getting hurt in the midst of a scared and panicked crowd.

Finally, my hand struck against something solid and wooden. My hands climbed up the wood as I stood up slowly, my limited senses confirming that the mystery object was, indeed, Coran's cradle. *Thank the gods.* Now fully standing, I grabbed the edge of the cradle with both hands, then reached into it to pick up Coran.

The cradle was empty.

Coran wasn't there.

I felt around the entire inside of the cradle. No baby. He hadn't curled up into a corner, not that the cradle was that big anyway. I felt all around the sides, like perhaps the baby prince had crawled over one of the cradle walls. Nothing.

I dropped to my knees and felt around the floor at the cradle's base. Maybe he fell out? Not likely, but I didn't want to rule out any possibility. Not that it mattered. Coran wasn't outside his cradle, either.

"Rhyss?" Beyan's voice pierced the fog. "Do you have Coran?"

"No," I said, trying to keep the panic from my voice.

"No?!" Beyan's voice was definitely laced with panic.

"He's not here. I can't find him."

"Can't find him? But he's a baby! Where could he—"

"How's Jennica?"

"I still can't wake her."

I cursed mentally. Jennica was a powerful magician, and would know how to rid the area of this cursed fog. I had no doubt it was magical in nature. But if it could render her unconscious, then whoever had caused this fog was perhaps a more skilled and powerful magician than even the Queen of Calia.

And then suddenly, the green fog lifted. Completely. As quickly as it had covered the main square, it disappeared like it had never existed. The sun still shone overhead, the sky still a beautiful blue.

However, the scene in the square was pure chaos. Chairs had been overturned, some broken, in the crowd's frenzy to try to get away. Those who had stayed looked stunned, either by the disorienting fog, or from injury inflicted by their fellow citizens. A few scared souls came out of various hiding places. The guards hadn't fared much better, having been hurt or nearly trampled in their attempts to keep the crowd under control, despite their temporary blindness.

I looked to where Farrah had been sitting with Taryn and Kye. The three of them were still there, but now there was a slight shimmer in the air around them. Farrah had her hand outstretched, concentrating on her upraised palm, and Taryn had her hand on her shoulder, eyes closed. The sudden dissipation of the fog and the equally sudden reappearance of daylight caught Farrah's attention, and she glanced up toward the dais, catching my eye. She raised an eyebrow quizzically. I took a deep breath, taking in the fresh, fog-free air. I nodded at her, and she dropped her hand. At the same time, the magical shield she had constructed dropped, and the shimmer around the trio disappeared.

She murmured something to Taryn, who opened her eyes and blinked, as if coming out of a deep trance.

On the dais behind me, King Beyan was cradling his still-unconscious wife. Tears shimmered in his eyes, and my heart broke at the sight.

I turned to the cradle, hoping against hope that baby Coran would somehow, miraculously, be lying in it. But the cradle was still empty, with no sign of the little prince.

Although, now that I looked closer, there was something …

The straw that had lined the cradle was all askew, evidence of my frantic searching. Sticking out from one corner was a small bit of paper, which had been easy to miss in the dense fog. Curious, I plucked the paper from the crib, unearthing a letter with a deep green wax seal.

7

CHAPTER SEVEN

"THE QUEEN SEEMS TO be stable, although without her awake and able to communicate, it's hard for me to assess the extent of her injuries. For now, I can only suggest we continue to watch her, and wait for her to wake up. I'm sorry I can't do more, Your Majesty."

King Beyan nodded his head in acknowledgment. "You've done what you can, Pendt. Thank you."

Healer Pendt bowed to the king, then left the Great Hall. Beyan slouched in his throne, distractedly running a hand through his messy brown hair. His hand snagged on the golden circlet still tangled in it, and he pulled the circlet off his head, turning it over and over in his hands.

Next to him, Queen Jennica's throne sat empty, a stark reminder of who was missing from the room.

Taryn reached over and gently plucked the golden circlet from Beyan's hands. "I'll take care of this for you, Your Majesty. Also, I've sent for the magician Limande. He might be able to heal Jennica's soul, whereas Healer Pendt can only treat the body."

"I hope so. Thank you, Taryn."

Farrah was studying the letter I had found in Coran's cradle. More specifically, she was studying the green seal on the paper.

I was ready to burst from inaction. It had been several hours since we had returned to the palace with the unconscious queen. All we could do was wait. Wait while Healer Pendt looked Jennica over, then rendered his verdict. Wait now for another person to come and examine the queen. Wait while Farrah poked at that green seal and decided the best course of action.

I hated the waiting because with each passing moment, Beyan's face grew more shuttered and dejected. I couldn't stand to see the pain on my friend's face. If there was something I could do to erase it, I would.

Except I couldn't do anything.

I hated feeling so useless.

Finally, I had to ask, "So, what do you think? Is it safe to open?"

"As safe as something tainted by foul magic can be, yes," Farrah said mildly, not reacting to my outburst. "From what I can tell, anyone who wields magic should be very careful opening it. Or, better yet, not open it at all."

"That leaves Beyan and me, then."

"In theory, I could probably open it too," Farrah said. "Fae magic might have some resistance to whatever enchantment is on this seal. After all, my Fae magic protected Taryn, Kye, and me earlier today. But it doesn't always play nicely with other types of magic ... so I should be one of the last options."

"Like I said before, that leaves Beyan and me."

"We shouldn't risk the king of Calia, who right now is the only person able to rule the country." Farrah handed me the letter. "So that leaves you."

"Great." I eyed the letter suspiciously, suddenly loathe to open it. Farrah *said* I should be all right, and I trusted her judgment, but still ... "Should we set some wards?"

"A good idea." Farrah muttered a quick spell, and the air around her, Taryn, and the king shimmered.

"What about me?"

"You can't break the seal if you're shielded," Farrah said. "And there's no sense in including the letter inside your shield. That defeats the purpose entirely."

"Okay, but don't blame me if I have to throw this thing across the room and it takes out a wall or two."

"Just throw it toward the west wall," Beyan said. "I wouldn't mind redoing that section of the castle."

"Ha ha," I said to him, but I was glad the idea of opening the mysterious letter was enough to bring him out of his depression, even temporarily. "All right, here we go."

The green seal was slightly smudged, but I thought I could make out the depiction of a snake and a butterfly impressed into the wax. One of the butterfly's wings was caught in between the snake's mouth. As I stared, the wax animals seemed to move—the butterfly fluttering rapidly, trying in vain to escape the snake as the reptile twisted sinuously. I blinked, and the image stilled. I looked at Farrah. "Did you see that? When you were looking at the seal?"

"Did I see what?" She looked confused. "What are you talking about?"

"The animals in the seal. The snake, the butterfly? Did you see them move, too?"

She took the letter back from me, looking hard at the green circle of wax. "Rhyss, there's nothing there. There are no symbols in the wax. It's completely blank."

Farrah passed the letter to Taryn, who shook her head before she passed it to Beyan. Beyan frowned. "I don't see anything either."

"I swear I saw something," I insisted.

"Maybe you did, Rhyss, but whatever it is, it's hidden to the rest of us," Farrah said.

I took the letter back from Beyan and glared at the green seal. The snake and its butterfly captive were still inlaid in the wax, completely still now, mocking me. I slipped my finger under the seal and broke it. There was a slight tingle in my hand from the seal's magic, but after I flexed my hand a few times, it disappeared.

I unfolded the letter.

To the King and Queen of Calia:

What an absolute delight to attend such a beautiful and auspicious event! We thoroughly enjoyed ourselves. Please forgive us for not stopping to offer our felicitations. We were rather busy, as we're sure by now you know. And, do not worry about your son.

He will be well taken care of until the proper time arises.

The deafening silence that had descended over the room as I read aloud was broken by a timid knock at the door of the Great Hall. An unsure voice said, "Pardon me, Your Majesty. But ... there's a growing crowd outside the castle, wondering ... is there still Petitioner's Court today?"

"Oh, goodness." Beyan frowned. "I completely forgot."

"I'm sure if you announce that it's been postponed, they'll understand," Farrah said.

Beyan sighed as he shook his head. "One of Jennica's hard-and-fast rules is that certain things that connect us to our people, such as Petitioner's Court, should never be canceled, unless all three of us are unable to be present." He waved a hand, indicating Taryn, himself, and Jennica's empty throne. "And after what happened today, the people are going to want reassurances that only their sovereigns—sovereign—can provide. No, I shouldn't cancel."

"We should still have it, but it will be shortened today," Taryn said. "That should be a fair compromise." She turned to the waiting page and said, "You may let them in, but please inform them of today's changes." The page nodded and left.

Beyan reached for the simple crown Taryn held in her hands and tiredly placed it on his head. Taryn adjusted it for him while he smoothed his clothes out and sat up straighter, steeling himself for the task ahead. To Farrah and me, he said, "Taryn and I have to be here, but if you two want to leave, that's fine. I'm sure you both could use a rest after today."

Beyan's statement seemed more like a command than a suggestion, and as I looked at the stiff-backed man before me, his face set in a resolute court mask, I was reminded that my old friend was now a king. There would be parts of his life that would forever be foreign to me. Shoving the letter in my pocket, I nodded, and clapped my hand on Beyan's shoulder. "I know you have a myriad of servants at your beck-and-call, but ... if you need anything ..."

He reached up and squeezed my arm. The sheen of unshed tears in his eyes made a lump form in my throat. Farrah leaned over and hugged Beyan, and then the two of us left the Great Hall, just as the first person entered the room for Petitioners' Court.

The castle guards were herding the Calian citizens who had turned out to bring their concerns before the Crown. And there were many of them. The line of people extended down the hallway, around the corner, ultimately disappearing through the door where no doubt more people were waiting.

I said to Farrah, "What do you think? Are you going to go back to your room?"

"Honestly, I have too much pent up energy to rest," she said, echoing my earlier thoughts. "What about you?"

"I won't be able to sit still, either," I said. "Want to take a walk around the castle grounds?"

Farrah nodded, and we started walking past the waiting crowd. As we neared the doors leading to the outside, one of the people in line called out. "Rhyss?"

I turned toward the voice as its owner stepped out of the line and hurried after Farrah and me. "Rhyss, it's your cousin, Enlar."

"Enlar!" I looked him over. "You're taller than I remember."

"Well, it has been a while—over ten years. We were barely in our teens when your family moved to Orchwell."

I laughed and embraced him. "It's good to see you. Are you here to speak to the king?"

"No, actually. I'm here to see you."

I felt vaguely guilty; shortly after Enlar had decided to make Calia his home, he had written to me to tell me the news. But I hadn't yet had the chance to visit him. I hadn't even told him I was going to be here. "How did you know I was in Calia?"

"I saw you at the dedication. Or, what was supposed to be the dedication."

Of course. That made sense. "Well, Farrah and I were going to step outside the castle for a walk. We could use some fresh air. Would you care to join us?"

Enlar nodded, and after I made introductions, the three of us left the castle.

When we got outside, I whistled. My guess was right—the line of people waiting to attend Petitioners' Court wrapped around the castle wall. Even though the king had announced it would be a shorter day, I doubted it would be. Poor Beyan.

Seeing the line, Enlar commented, "I'm glad I saw you before I entered the castle and the Great Hall. I might not have found you in that crowd."

"It's good to see you, cousin," I said. "How have you been?"

"Quite well, thank you. And thank you for your recommendation to come to Calia. My magic has really flourished since I came here to study."

As we started to walk away from the castle, something small, solid, and moving very fast smacked right into me. The little boy of about four or five who had accosted my legs landed on his bottom and started wailing.

"Allston! What have I told you about running, especially here at the palace?" Coming up the walkway was his mother, who was rushing after him but unable to move as quickly as Allston due to the infant she was carrying on her hip. "I'm so sorry, sir."

"It's all right," I said, kneeling down so I was at the little boy's level. He was still crying. If anything, his mother's scolding had set him off more.

I dug into my pockets, turning everything out to find what I wanted. "Here you go."

I handed the little boy a paper-wrapped wafer. That did the trick. Pretty soon he was surrounded by shreds of paper, not to mention his harried-looking mother and baby sibling.

"Thank you, sir," Allston's mother said. "What do you say, Allston?"

Allston merely grinned at me, showing off a crumb-covered mouth full of food. I grinned back. Allston's mother took her son by the hand. The little family disappeared into the castle.

"That was kind of you," Farrah said. "Also, when did you pick that up? I don't remember stopping by any of the stalls at the festival today before we went to the dedication."

"I snuck a few from the kitchen after we finished breakfast," I said. "I figured the dedication ceremony would take a long time, and I thought I might get hungry."

Farrah laughed and shook her head, but Enlar was staring at the ground. At what had been the contents of my pockets. "What's that?"

Crumbs were everywhere, and not all of them were from Allston's treat. Suddenly, I was grateful for my scratchy sky blue coat which was—thank the gods—on loan from the Calian royals. Some poor servant would have to clean out the messy pockets, not me.

"Mostly food," I said.

"No, this." He bent down and picked up the letter that had been left in Coran's cradle. I picked everything else up—including the paper shreds that Allston had left behind—and shoved it all into my pockets. Honestly, I felt sorry for that future servant who'd be responsible for my formalwear. I stood up, brushing off my pants.

Enlar was gazing at the letter's broken green seal, a mix of horror and fear on his face. "Where did you get this?"

I hesitated. Beyan hadn't given me explicit instructions not to talk about the letter, but I also didn't want to be indiscreet. But something about the letter had kindled recognition in my cousin, so ...

"Do you know whose seal that is?" Farrah asked Enlar.

Enlar tore his gaze away from the letter and met our eyes. "Yes. Yes, I do."

8

CHAPTER EIGHT

"THEY CALL THEMSELVES THE Emerald Order. Or, more simply, the Order. They don the green cloak in honor of the late Lord Indwere, who was the son of a minor Faerie nobleman and a Bomorran woman. Indwere taught the first members of the Order how to tap into Fey magic through nature. Their goal is to tie all of the Gifted Lands closer to the Fae. Publicly, they say their purpose is to strengthen relations with the Fae, but their true aim is to steal the magic from the lands of Faerie until there is nothing left."

Enlar took a sip of his drink and sat back, studying Farrah and me. We were in a public house just past the Merchants' District in Calia's capital. Farrah and I had wondered at the wisdom of sitting in a tavern to talk, worried about who might overhear us. But the place was surprisingly empty; the majority of the capital must have gone to the palace for Petitioners' Court. The Dancing Star was one of the few businesses actually open. Fortunately, the owner left us alone after serving our drinks, and we had the place to ourselves. Still, we kept our voices low.

"Steal Faerie magic?" Farrah looked horrified. As well she should. Being half-Fae herself, this would affect her Fae father, and any of her relatives on her father's side. "How is that even possible?"

"You know of Valdonne's Treaty, yes?"

We both nodded. Valdonne's Treaty had been enacted close to two centuries ago, between the whole of the Gifted Lands and the land of Faerie. Named after a former ruler of the kingdom of Shonn, it was meant to protect the seven kingdoms of the Gifted Lands from the machinations of the Fae.

It was one of the few times that all seven kingdoms were united on something; for the most part, each autonomous country focused solely on its own issues. But the land of Faerie—and all its citizens—touched all of the Gifted Lands, with its strongest control in Shonn, Farrah's home country, where the Veil between the two worlds was the thinnest.

Nearly two hundred years ago, a war had broken out between the Fae and the Gifted Lands. Jealous of the magic that was beginning to bloom in the Gifted Lands, the Fae sought to suppress it or eradicate it entirely from the human world. The Great War lasted for five years, with neither side gaining an advantage until close to the end. For although the mages of the Gifted Lands were new to their power, their magic was so foreign to the magically superior Fae that eventually the Fae didn't know how to overcome it. With the Great War's end came an uneasy truce between humankind and Faerie.

The kingdom of Shonn, being the closest in proximity to Faerie, had suffered the most damage in the Great War. So the other kingdoms allowed Valdonne, the then-king of Shonn, to be the one to draw up the terms of the treaty between the worlds, with the other six kingdoms' input, of course.

Since Valdonne's Treaty had been enacted, our otherworldly neighbors usually left us alone, with the exception of the kingdom of Shonn. Indeed, Farrah's half-Faerie heritage was proof of the Fae mixing—or as some would say instead, meddling—with humankind.

"The Emerald Order is actively working to weaken Valdonne's Treaty," Enlar continued. "Completely get rid of it, if they can."

"But what are they doing? And why?" Farrah asked.

My cousin made a face. "They're doing the Fae's dirty work for them. Under Valdonne's Treaty, some of the most reprehensible acts of the Fae are outlawed. If one of the Fae were to do them, it would mean immediate death. But if a human does it ..."

Farrah's eyes widened. She whispered, "Like what?"

"Do you recall the Faerie custom of changelings?" At Farrah's gasp, Enlar nodded grimly. "The Fae can't steal human babies outright anymore, but there's nothing to stop them from buying them from humans willing to sell them. Indeed, there's quite a market for human children."

"That explains the what. Now, what about the why?"

Enlar looked around, even though the tavern was still empty. Well, except for the three of us. No sign of the tavern owner. Still, Enlar motioned for us to lean in closer and lowered his voice even more.

"There's talk that some of the other kingdoms are calling for war with the Fae again. Notably Shonn."

"Really?" Farrah frowned. "This is the first I've heard of this."

"It's very hush-hush," Enlar said. "And speaking of hush-hush ... the Emerald Order is trying to make that war happen, although they won't admit to it publicly."

"How do you know all this, if they aren't letting their reasons be known widely?"

Enlar's eyes dropped, ashamed. "I ... I was part of the Emerald Order for a while."

"*You* were part of this Emerald Order?"

"At one point. Not anymore." Enlar looked deep into his mug of ale, as if the right words to say would magically appear in the frothy liquid. "It's the reason why I left Bomora. Why I wrote my cousin Rhyss—" he nodded at me "—and asked him if he knew of anyone who could teach me how to tame my magic, as far away from my home country as I could get. It's a talent that's hard to come by in Bomora, and those who do have it are exploited by the Emerald Order so the group can get their grasping, greedy fingers on more."

"What do you mean?"

"Bomora, as a whole, doesn't have a lot of magicians. No one knows why for sure, but it may be because we're so far away from where most of the magic seems to be centered in the Gifted Lands. If someone does have magical ability, they very rarely carry that talent into adulthood. It usually fades away by then."

"That's awful." There was a look of deep sympathy on Farrah's face. "As I am half-Fae, magic is in my blood. I've never known what it's like to be without it. To have magic available to you, only to wake up one day to discover it's gone, would be an incredible tragedy. Like losing a limb, or having your soul torn away."

"You understand, then." Enlar sighed heavily. "I believe the Emerald Order started as a way to help the Ungifted—those who had magical talent, then lost it—cope. There were so few of them that they just really needed the support of those similar to them. But recently, more and more Bomorrans have become Ungifted. And the aims of the Emerald Order have changed from support to something more ... sinister."

We all fell silent, nursing our drinks and our troubled thoughts. Then, abruptly, Farrah said, "I just realized something. Enlar, you saw the decoration in the seal, correct?"

He nodded. "It's the Emerald Order's emblem. Very distinctive."

"Yes, but you *saw* it. No one else in the throne room did, we all just saw a green circle of wax. Except for you, Rhyss." She turned a suspicious eye on me. "You said you saw a snake and butterfly emblem in the wax. How are both of you able to see it, but none of us could?"

Before I could speak, Enlar said, "It *is* a Bomorran group, after all. The emblem is probably enchanted so that anyone from Bomora can see it, regardless of whether or not they're a member of the Emerald Order."

Farrah frowned. "There's no special induction ceremony into the Emerald Order? Don't you remember when you were suddenly able to see the secret picture in the seal, when you weren't able to before?"

Enlar shrugged. "The Order does have an induction ceremony; I've attended many. I've always been able to see the hidden emblem, as far as I can remember. But then again, I was in the Emerald Order for a long time."

Farrah didn't seem completely convinced, but she let the topic drop as we heard bells chime over the city. "Oh! Petitioner's Court should be over. We should get back to the palace."

"Would you want to come back with us?" I asked my cousin. "I'm sure the king would be interested in hearing your tale."

Enlar shook his head. "I've told you all I know; it's easy enough to relate my story to His Majesty. I should get back to the boarding-house."

We stood up and left the tavern. Enlar's boardinghouse was just a few streets away from the palace, so as we walked together, we turned the talk to lighter topics, such as what life was like in Orchwell, or his studies at Calia's Academy of Magical Arts. Enlar mentioned that the students were in a frenzy over examinations; he could barely enjoy the Haerfest Celebration because the tests were only a week away.

When it came time to part ways, Enlar asked us, "How much longer will you be in Calia?"

"I'm not sure," I said. "Originally we were going to leave a day or two after the dedication, but now ... We'll stay as long as Beyan needs us." Farrah nodded in mute agreement.

"Well, then. I hope to see you again before you leave, Cousin," Enlar said, embracing me briefly, then bowing over Farrah's hand.

"Good luck with your exams," I said.

He grimaced, then looked over my head at the looming silhouette of the palace. "Thanks, but I somehow think you'll need luck more than I will."

9

–·–

CHAPTER NINE

WHEN FARRAH AND I returned to the palace, I expected that we'd find King Beyan still in the Great Hall, perhaps discussing the recent petitions with Taryn, or just taking a moment for himself.

But he wasn't in the Great Hall, nor was he in the dining hall for the evening meal. Instead, we found him in the private bedchambers he shared with Jennica, looking worn as he slumped in an uncomfortable wooden chair by their bed. A full tray of food—closer scrutiny made me think it held dishes for both the king and the queen—lay untouched on a small table nearby.

The king was understandably too worried to eat. And as for Queen Jennica?

She was still unconscious.

An uneasy feeling settled over me. If Jennica wasn't waking up, the magic holding her in its thrall must be very strong indeed. The queen was a master magician; very few spells could hold her for long.

Except for this one.

I cleared my throat, a subtle way of alerting Beyan to our presence. "Beyan ... there's been no change?"

He looked up at us, his face streaked with tears. He shook his head. "No. Nothing."

Eyeing the abandoned tray, Farrah said, "Come over here. You need to eat."

"I'm not really that hungry."

She clucked her tongue at him. "Doesn't matter. You need to keep your strength up. And so does Jennica. While you're eating, I can try to feed her."

When Farrah used that tone, it was best not to argue, even if the fate of an entire kingdom was in question. Beyan stood up numbly and allowed Farrah to switch places with him, then went over to the table and woodenly picked up a bread roll.

I brought Farrah some now-cold soup, and then went back to the king to see how he was doing. He hadn't put any food in his mouth; instead, there were large crumbs and pieces of bread all over his plate. The shredded roll was a sad testament to his anxiety.

Gently, I took what was left of the bread roll from his hands. "You're really worried, aren't you?"

Beyan didn't answer me immediately. His attention was on Farrah, who had propped Jennica up to a semi-sitting position and was now attempting to pour small spoonfuls of soup down the queen's throat. He whispered, "I hate seeing her like this. And I hate that I can't do anything to help her."

To distract him—and also to give him a bit of hope, maybe—I said, "Farrah and I may have some insight on who's taken your son."

Beyan's attention snapped back to me, his eyes boring holes in mine. "Who? And where?"

I quickly relayed the conversation Farrah and I had had with Enlar, finishing with, "Now that you know where your son's been taken, you could go get him."

But I had barely finished speaking when Beyan shook his head.

Farrah said, "He can't leave Calia, not while Jennica is in this condition."

"It's not just that," Beyan said. "Even if I was willing to leave Jennica while she's like this—not that I am—I wouldn't be able to leave her side for too long. I may not be an active Seeker anymore, but it's still in my blood. Staying near her is what keeps me from going insane. If I left her behind while I traveled to Bomora ... it would only be about three or four days before I started to lose my mind."

He sighed, studying Jennica's inert form. "Before we got married, I was able to hold the madness back much longer, but now ... my Seeker magic has gotten too used to being around her."

"What do you propose to do, then?" I asked.

Beyan rang for a servant. "If your cousin can help get my son back, then he can have anything he wants in the kingdom."

It wasn't long before a knock sounded on the door. Beyan called out, "Enter!"

The person who opened the door wasn't a page, but Royal Advisor Taryn. She sketched a quick curtsey. "I told Sielan I would answer your summons. I figured it would be best for the queen to have some ... privacy."

Meaning, the fewer servants who were around to gawk and gossip about the queen's health, the better.

Beyan nodded distractedly, obviously less aware or caring of court intrigues than Taryn, who, as a former lady-in-waiting, had grown up working in the palace and knew quite well about servants' wagging tongues. "Yes, yes, good idea. Taryn, I'm glad you're here. It'll save us time."

Taryn's confusion, which she was too polite to voice, was mirrored on both Farrah's and my faces.

"Rhyss's cousin Enlar has some information on who kidnapped Coran. You remember Enlar, he was here when Rothschan tried to destroy Calia a while back? He's studying at the Academy of Magical Arts now. Call him up, will you?"

Any other time, I would have laughed at Beyan's recollection of how he knew my cousin. *When Rothschan tried to destroy Calia? Which time? You'll have to be more specific than that.*

I swallowed the joke that threatened to spill out of my mouth. Catching Farrah's glance, I saw the twinkle in her eyes and knew she was thinking the same thing.

Taryn was already reciting the spell that would allow her to magically connect with Enlar. His image appeared over her open palm. He looked a bit bleary-eyed, and I guessed the long hours of studying had already started back up.

"Madame Advisor. How may I help you?"

Beyan leaned over so he could face Enlar. "Enlar! Good to see you again."

Enlar sat up straighter at the sight of the king. "Your Majesty! To what do I owe the honor?"

"I understand you may know where my son has been taken, and by whom."

Enlar looked uneasy. "I'm fairly certain that it was the Emerald Order, Your Majesty. From what Rhyss and Farrah told me, and from what I saw—their secret emblem in the seal—I would say it's very likely."

"Since you know this group, would you be willing to go back to Bomora and find my son? I'll give you whatever you ask. The kingdom of Calia would owe you a debt beyond measure."

But Enlar shook his head. "I'm sorry, Your Majesty. As much as I would like to help you, I can't go back. No one ever leaves the Emerald

Order, except through death. Death in service to it—or death as the penalty for choosing to leave. My life would be forfeit the minute I stepped foot in Bomora."

Beyan took a breath, ready to argue or to persuade him. Or perhaps to order him to go. Beyan was the king, after all.

"I'll go."

My statement surprised everyone, including myself.

"Are you certain?" But I could see the hope in Beyan's eyes, and I knew I couldn't rescind my words.

"Yes, of course. I'll leave in the morning."

"I'll go with you," Farrah said immediately.

"You don't have to," I told her. "You might be needed here."

She shook her head. "No, you'll need my help on the road more than Jennica will need me here. She's got the finest healers here, as well as Taryn and Beyan."

"All right, then." Beyan sat back, relieved. "Thank you, Rhyss, Farrah. Enlar, that will be all. Thank you for your assistance."

"Before I go, Your Majesty, there is one more thing I should tell you. Well, actually, Rhyss and Farrah. Remember that secret seal you saw on the kidnapper's letter? Everyone involved with the Emerald Order receives a signet ring with that emblem engraved on it. If you can get a hold of one, it will make entry into the Emerald Order much easier."

"Do you have—" I began to ask my cousin, but he was already shaking his head.

"Sadly, no. I sold mine to a traveling peddler to get money for my journey. It seemed safe enough, since he couldn't see the seal and was traveling south, away from Bomora. He said something about how it would be more valuable melting it down than keeping it intact, so even if I knew where exactly he went, it's probably been destroyed by now."

Beyan sighed, frustrated. "Of course, you don't have your secret special ring anymore. That would just be too easy."

"It's all right, Beyan," I said, clapping a hand on his shoulder. "Farrah and I are resourceful. We'll figure something out."

"As I well know, my friend." Beyan reached up and squeezed my hand. Looking back at Enlar's image, he asked, "Is there anything else you wish to share?"

"No, Your Majesty."

"Then thank you for your time." After a quick round of farewells, Taryn closed her hand, ending the spell.

Beyan rang the bell again for a page. When one appeared, he instructed her, "Please have someone in the kitchens pack several days' worth of provisions for two."

"Yes, Your Majesty." The woman bowed, then left.

The room fell silent in the wake of the page's leaving, punctuated only by the occasional raspy breath from Queen Jennica on the bed.

Finally, to break the silence more than anything, I said, "Thank you, Beyan."

The king chuckled grimly. "It is I who should thank you. My gratitude to you and Farrah for going to find my son is immeasurable. I wish I could do more than just give you a few supplies for your journey."

Farrah handed the bowl of soup to Taryn and stood up. The bowl was still fairly full; Farrah had only gotten a few spoonfuls past the queen's unresponsive lips. "I guess I should start packing."

"Likewise." Sighing, I stood as well. "Although no amount of preparation may be enough. After all this time, I can't believe I'm finally going home."

10

CHAPTER TEN

FARRAH AND I SET off the next morning just as the sun started to peek over the horizon. Beyan and Taryn awoke early to see us off.

"If you need anything—food, supplies, extra horses, money—let Taryn know right away," Beyan told us. There was a slight emphasis on "money," and I knew what he was thinking. No ransom would be too high to pay to get his son back.

I just hoped it wouldn't come to that.

After we said our goodbyes, Farrah and I mounted our horses and rode away into the cold early morning. The sun overhead hinted at a pleasant day, but there was a chill in the autumn air reminding us that soon winter would have its snowy hold on the land.

Perhaps it was the weight of the mission before us, or perhaps it was because we were still somewhat sleepy, but both Farrah and I shared a subdued mood as we rode through the quiet streets of Calia's capital city, then through the gate and into the countryside. Our thoughtful silence lasted through the next town that lay directly south of Calia's capital, all the way until we reached the crossroads that would take us west to Bomora.

"How many years has it been for you?" Farrah asked, finally breaking the silence.

I blew out a breath, seeing it fog briefly in front of my face before blowing away in the wind. "I don't even know anymore. Ten years, at least. Maybe a little bit more?"

"Did your parents ever go back?"

"No. I think they intended to, a few years ago. But the accident happened before they could return."

I had moved from Bomora to Orchwell, where I lived now, when I was around thirteen or so. My parents had never expressed any desire to go back while I was growing up, although I know they missed their home country. A few years ago, they had discussed the idea of going back to Bomora for a visit. But, unfortunately, that wish was never realized.

A fire had broken out at my parents' bakery in Orchwell. By the time the fire had been extinguished, it was too late for the bakery. And too late for my parents, who had been trapped inside.

I had been on the road with Beyan and Farrah at the time, on one of Beyan's dragon Seeking commissions. When we returned to Orchwell—one day after the fire—I had been devastated to learn of their deaths, and even more devastated that I hadn't been there. If we had returned just one day earlier, I could have saved them from their fiery fate. Maybe. Maybe I would have perished with them. I don't know. But I hated myself for being too late, and for not being able to change the past.

Farrah gave me a small, sympathetic smile. "I'm sure they'd be delighted to know you're finally going back, then."

"This is not exactly a sightseeing trip," I reminded her.

"No," she agreed. "But we'll still be visiting different places in Bomora, by necessity. And it'll probably be easier to get this job done if we rely on any friends or relatives you still have in the area." When I nodded, she continued, "Speaking of which, *do* you still know anyone in the area? Besides Enlar, who doesn't live in Bomora anymore, so for purposes of this discussion, doesn't count."

I didn't answer Farrah right away, thinking over her question. "As far as friends go—I'm not sure. I mean, I had friends growing up there, but when my family moved to Orchwell, I didn't keep in touch with any of them. I suppose some of them might still be in Bomora. As for family—no. Enlar's mother—my aunt— passed away when we were young, from an illness. His father died a few years later. Fell off a horse, broke his neck. Died instantly. That happened after my family had moved to Orchwell. We offered Enlar a place to live with us, but he declined, and then he stopped writing to us for a few years. Until he contacted me and asked about Calia's magic school."

"That's sad," Farrah said. "To lose both parents ... I bet that's why he joined the Emerald Order."

"Probably."

"Which one was your relative by blood? Your aunt or your uncle?"

"My uncle, Enlar's father. He was my father's older brother. It was just the two of them, no other siblings." I looked at Farrah curiously. "You've certainly got a lot of questions today."

She blushed. "I'm not trying to be nosy. It's just—in all the years I've known you, you've never talked about your extended family, or what your life was like in Bomora before you moved to Orchwell. I just wondered about it, that's all."

"I guess there's not much to say. We left when I was a teenager. Mother and Father wanted to focus on our lives in Orchwell, and on me fitting in in our new country. I'm not one to dwell on the past, anyway. You know that, Farrah. I'm a live-in-the-moment kind of person."

At that, she laughed. "Yes, you are. Maybe a little *too* much."

We lapsed into a companionable silence. Then Farrah said, "I can't believe we never went to Bomora while on a commission with Beyan. Or any other Seeker, for that matter. You'd think at least Kaernan would have had a commission out there." She named another Seeker in Orchwell who employed our services as cook, healer, and muscle-for-hire regularly.

"It's kind of out of the way. And somewhat ... inaccessible. Not that you can't travel there, like any other kingdom in the Gifted Lands, but ... Bomorrans like their privacy."

Farrah sighed. "We're looking at what, up to a week of travel?"

"If we were going south, where the terrain is relatively easy, then yes," I said cheerfully. "But we'll be going through some wild country, not to mention the most mysterious haunted forest in all of the Gifted Lands. So it might take us a little longer to traverse."

Farrah shot me a dirty look. "You don't have to sound so happy about this."

"And you wondered why I didn't go back to Bomora much."

11

—•—

CHAPTER ELEVEN

DURING THE FIRST FEW nights of our trip, we stayed in various roadside inns. Money was no problem, thanks to the generosity of King Beyan and the Calian treasury, but we were still conscious of spending too freely. In part because we wanted to be good stewards of the purse we had been given, but also because it was never wise to flaunt a lot of wealth while traveling. Farrah and I could hold our own in a fight, but there was no sense in tempting fate—or curious eyes and unwanted attention.

One place we stayed at was a cozy roadside inn called the Blue Pony. Like the others, it was serviceable, but not fancy. We arrived as the sun was setting. Locals and travelers alike were rapidly filling the room. Farrah and I settled into the inn's public room for a meal before all the tables were taken.

Our dinners had just been served when two cloaked newcomers entered the inn. Surveying the room, they sat down at the end of our long table, near us.

"I guess this will have to do, there's nowhere else to sit," a light feminine voice said. She pulled back the hood of her cloak—an odd muddy brown color—revealing a young woman of perhaps twenty, with black hair and sharp blue eyes. The young woman sat down in the empty chair next to me.

Her companion—also dressed in a cloak the same ugly brownish color—followed suit, taking the empty seat across from her, next to Farrah, just as the innkeeper's daughter approached the table.

The young woman ordered for both her and her hooded companion, then sat back. "Mother, honestly. You're attracting more attention with your hood up than you would if you just showed your face."

The young woman's mother sighed, but put her hood back. Something gold glinted on her hand, but her movement was so quick that I didn't catch the detail of her ring. She was an older image of her daughter, but the worry lines between her brows suggested she had seen more hardships than her daughter had.

"A little caution never hurts, Yolinde."

"I think we're far enough away that you can relax a little. Besides, they're busy with other things right now. That poor babe."

Something about their quiet conversation drew my curiosity. Across the table, I saw Farrah stiffen and grow still, and I knew she was also paying close attention to what the two women next to us were saying.

The innkeeper's daughter brought the women their food. Yolinde's mother picked up her spoon, gloomily surveying their bowls of stew. Her ring glinted in the firelight. Now, if only she would turn her hand, just so ...

And then I saw it. My eyes widened.

Her ring bore the snake-and-butterfly seal of the Emerald Order.

I surreptitiously studied the two women more closely. The younger one made a slight movement as she got comfortable, and I saw a flash of brilliant green hidden just inside her cape that didn't match the rest of her dull brown cloak. Hmm. My guess? A hasty dye job to cover the cloak's true color.

"Enjoy, daughter," the woman said sadly. "We're spending the last of our coin on this dinner. It will be foraging in the woods for a while until we can find some work. Maybe in Orchwell, or perhaps in Shonn."

"But I thought we were going to Annlyn?" Yolinde said, naming the southernmost country in the Gifted Lands.

"Annlyn, Shonn, wherever. It doesn't matter. Just as long as it's far away from Bomora as possible." Yolinde's mother started in on her stew, eating slowly.

Farrah caught my eye and nodded ever so slightly. I nodded back, just as imperceptibly, and then leaned back to watch Farrah work her magic. Not in the literal sense, although I'm sure her natural ability to put people at ease may have been due in part to her Fae heritage. There's a reason the Fae are known as beguilers and charmers.

"Excuse me," Farrah said to the woman sitting next to her. "My companion—" she inclined her head toward me "—and I couldn't help but overhear your conversation. Are you two traveling from Bomora, by chance?"

"Why would that matter to you?" Yolinde's mother asked cautiously.

"We're heading there ourselves," Farrah said. "It's a long journey from there to here. Longer still for you two, from the sound of it."

"State your point, miss," the woman snapped.

"That ring you wear," I said. "It's got a very ... unusual ... design. Would you be willing to sell it?"

The woman looked torn between hope and wariness. "I might. It depends. What are you offering?"

I took out a small, worn leather purse and held it out in front of the women, jingling it a bit so they could hear the many coins inside. "Double this if you can give us information as well."

"No."

"Mother!" Yolinde protested. "If they're taking your ring, they deserve to know. And besides, we could use the money. They already know that."

The older woman didn't say anything, just bit her lip and looked at me, then Farrah, and finally her daughter. She sighed heavily. "All right. I accept your offer." She looked around the room. "I suppose you want to go somewhere private so we won't be overheard? So you can get the information you want, then get rid of my daughter and me as you see fit?"

I blinked in surprise, even as I put away the purse. "Madam, I assure you we have no evil intentions."

Meanwhile, Farrah muttered something under her breath. The air shimmered and thickened ever-so-slightly, then settled around the four of us. I could still see through the thin magic barrier, but the room beyond looked a little hazy, like everyone else was moving about in a fog. The sound beyond our bubble seemed muffled, as well.

Yolinde looked startled. "What did you just do?"

"I've enclosed us in a magic bubble that blocks our conversation to anyone outside it," Farrah said. "It has the added benefit of ... well, not turning us invisible, exactly. More like making people forget we're here for a time. Until I lift the spell."

Yolinde's mother reached out a hand experimentally toward the hazy barrier, then withdrew quickly, as if the magic had shocked her. Wonderingly, she examined her fingers briefly, then looked up at Farrah and me.

"Convenient," she said with grudging respect. "So no one will overhear us. But how do we know you won't betray us with the information?"

"We won't," I said. "Although I don't suppose our word alone is enough for you."

The woman shook her head. "When you hear our story, you'll understand why we have reason to be distrustful of strangers."

Farrah waved a hand over the table. Once again the air shimmered, tiny sparkles hovering above the food and drink arrayed on the table before settling into it and disappearing.

"What was that spell, now?" Yolinde sounded more fascinated than frightened.

"It ensures that those who break bread together cannot betray each other, under penalty of death. We will not hurt you with any information you share with us tonight, nor can you hurt us with anything you may learn from us."

Catching Yolinde's mother's wary look, Farrah said, "And no, I did not poison you." She leaned over and took the tiniest bit of stew from the woman's bowl and ate it. "Does that satisfy you?"

The woman snorted. "I suppose it will have to do. What is it you want to know?"

"Let's start with who you both are ... and what your connection is to the Emerald Order."

12

CHAPTER TWELVE

THE WOMAN TWISTED THE gold ring around and around on her finger. I couldn't tell if she was trying to take it off, or if it was a nervous habit. Eventually, she sighed and pulled it from her finger and placed it on the table in the center where all four of us could see it. There was a small length of twine wrapped around the bottom, a crude way of resizing the large gold ring to fit her smaller finger.

The woman sighed heavily. "Very well, then. My name is Aela. This is my daughter, Yolinde." Yolinde inclined her head to Farrah and me. Aela continued, "We hail from Bomora. Which is where the Emerald Order is located, although I suspect you already know that.

"My late husband was a member of the Emerald Order. This was his ring." Aela's fingers closed over the signet ring briefly, but then she released it and withdrew her hand. The ring glinted in the firelight. "He was a good man, but grew quite enamored of the group and their philosophies, ultimately joining them and engaging in their ... activities. I turned a blind eye to it. We had a good marriage, and I had my daughter to raise.

"You know the Emerald Order has a keen interest in all things magical, yes?" When Farrah and I nodded, Aela continued. "It didn't matter so much when Yolinde was younger. But then she began showing signs of magical ability. And instead of her magic fading out as she grew older, like most Bomorrans who show magical promise, my daughter's talent only grew stronger."

Like Enlar's, I mused.

"The Emerald Order started taking an interest in Yolinde. Wanting her to join, wanting her to pool her magic with other members' magic to do ... I don't even know what, nor do I want to know. They put pressure on my husband to make Yolinde join. My husband, bless his soul, refused. Saying it was Yolinde's choice, and he wasn't going to force her if she didn't want to join."

"Which I didn't," Yolinde put in emphatically. "The whispers on the street about the Emerald Order were enough to warn me away. And once you're in it, it's hard to leave."

"Which was another problem my husband was facing." Aela pursed her lips in barely concealed anger, although I didn't think it was directed at her late husband. "His refusal to cooperate and force Yolinde to join put him at odds with the Order's leader. He was still in the Order, of course, but it was very obvious that he was no longer held in favor. Any tasks the Emerald Order had for him were few and far between, and he wasn't privy to the knowledge he had had before.

"And then he was asked to assist on a very important assignment. One that, it was implied, if he helped with, would forgive his inability to bring Yolinde into the group. I didn't think he should participate—the less we had to do with that group, the better. But my husband wanted to do it—he seemed almost desperate to be a part of it.

"The Emerald Order intended to steal a magical artifact that was guarded by an oversized black dog. According to the tales, the hound was under an enchanted sleep, and would only wake if it sensed ill intent nearby. Humans are quite capable of lying, but even the craftiest person cannot hide their thoughts or deepest emotions. My husband was given a charm that was supposed to disguise his true intentions and let him get past the beast's guard."

Aela's face turned still and sad. "But the charm was a fake. My husband's intentions weren't masked at all, and the magical creature ripped him apart before he even knew what was happening. And even worse—the artifact he was sent to steal was already gone. It had been taken a few months prior, while the guard dog remained. My husband's death was completely in vain, a setup by the Emerald Order leadership."

"How are you so sure this is the truth?" Farrah asked gently.

Aela laughed bitterly. "The leader was only too happy to tell me all about his death—when the Order came to seize our house."

Yolinde took up the tale. "Those in the Emerald Order are expected to pledge something of value against the missions they carry out. A way of ensuring that they have incentive to complete their tasks successfully—and stay in the group. The leadership hoped Father would pledge me. Instead, he chose to stake our family's entire fortune."

"The one smart thing he chose, among a myriad of stupid decisions." Aela sounded fierce. "I'd rather be poor than turn you over to that hateful group, daughter."

Yolinde reached across the table and squeezed her mother's hand. "And now we're penniless, nameless, and on the run for our lives."

"Not penniless any longer," I said, tossing two money pouches on the table. The clink they made as they landed on the heavy wooden surface made both Aela and Yolinde smile.

"And for that, we thank you," Aela said gratefully.

I scooped up the ring and started to unravel the twine wrapped around its base.

Farrah said, "I'll remove the silencing spell."

She raised her hand. But before she could undo her spell, Yolinde said, "Wait! There's still more my mother needs to tell you."

Farrah put her hand down. As one, we both turned to Aela. She squirmed under our gaze.

"You now know our tale," she said. "What more do you need to know?"

At that, even Yolinde gave her mother a pointed look.

"Mother. They've been quite generous with us. We would be absolutely evil, no better than the Emerald Order, if we sent them on their way without telling them the rest of it."

"The rest of it?" I echoed.

"Yes," Yolinde said, turning to me. "True, that was Father's ring. But what Mother didn't tell you is that the ring is bound to its owner. Or it might be more accurate to say, the owner is bound to their ring. It's the ring that compels a member of the Emerald Order to finish their task, or keeps them loyal. It's extremely hard to break the bond; only a master magician might be able to accomplish that feat, but we know of no one who has."

"Really." I frowned, thinking of how Enlar had sold his ring before reaching Calia. If what Yolinde said was true, then my cousin shouldn't have been able to part with his ring. And he was no master magician; he had come to Calia to learn how to grow in his skills.

But he had told me he no longer possessed the ring, and he hadn't mentioned any magic binding him to it. Or breaking that magic.

So why had he omitted such an important detail?

"So if that was your husband's ring," Farrah said to Aela, "does it have any power over you? Or is it just a keepsake now?"

Aela shifted uncomfortably. "It is both. Obviously, with my husband's death, it is no longer bound to him. But when the Emerald Order came to claim our home, they offered us a way to 'pay off' the debt. They wanted me to assist in an important mission, of utmost secrecy. I brought Yolinde with me to help."

Yolinde snorted. "Hardly."

"Yolinde!"

"Mother saw it as our chance to escape Bomora. That's why I went with her. She didn't need me; her only job was to retrieve the baby and bring him back to Bomora."

"What baby?" I asked, although I had my suspicions.

Aela sighed. "Since my daughter seems so determined to spill all our secrets, here's the rest of it. The Emerald Order planned on kidnapping the newborn baby prince of Calia. There are few women in the Emerald Order—"

"That's true, since Mistress Fairweather died a year ago," Yolinde put in. "That leaves us, and—"

"Anyway," Aela continued on, "the leader thought I would be ideally suited to help take care of the child en route from Calia to Bomora. But I figured, in all the commotion of the kidnapping, it would be the perfect time for Yolinde and I to run. The Emerald Order would be too busy with the baby to come after us, at least for a while."

"Ah, that explains your cloaks," I said, nodding toward their outfits.

Both Yolinde and Aela looked sheepish.

"We didn't have much time—or the resources—to properly dye them," Aela said. "Perhaps it would have been wiser to burn them or even bury them, but we didn't bring extra clothing with us. Our money is needed for other things. And it's getting colder. So for now, we're keeping the cloaks, as much as I'd love to be rid of them."

She grimaced, indicating the ring between my fingers. "At least we can be done with that."

I had finished removing the twine from around the ring's band. Farrah held out her hand, and I dropped the ring into her waiting palm. Holding it between two fingertips, she turned it this way and that as she studied it in the firelight.

"So this ring is bound to you?" Farrah said to Aela.

"Yes," Aela admitted reluctantly. "I had to accept the binding in order to be able to participate in the prince's kidnapping. If I hadn't ..."

"Then our house would have been confiscated, you would be begging on the streets, and I would be in the Emerald Order's grasp," Yolinde said. "You did what you had to do."

Aela sighed. Words came pouring out of her in a rush. "Someone was in place in Calia a day or two ago to attend the prince's dedication, which was where the Emerald Order was going to make their move. After, we were supposed to meet that person, but we missed our rendezvous."

"Is there a penalty for missing that meeting?" Farrah asked.

"Not right away. But the rings are linked to their owner, and to the Emerald Order as a whole. A delay of a day or two means nothing, but if enough time passes, then a ring will let its wearer know. Burning, freezing, causing your finger to swell—those are minor inconveniences compared to some of the harsher tortures." Aela looked at her former ring with distaste. "I'd say in another day or two, that ring will start misbehaving."

"Hmm." Farrah turned her attention back to the ring, with occasional side glances at Aela.

"What else do we need to know? About this ring, or the Emerald Order?" I addressed Yolinde, sensing she would be more forthcoming with information than her mother.

"The Emerald Order's signet rings always find their way home," Yolinde answered readily. "Regardless if one completes their task, or dies in the process, the ring will, somehow, inexplicably, return to Bomora. So if you have one … it will guide you right to the Emerald Order's headquarters. Whether or not they'll allow you entry—that's another issue entirely."

"Huh. Interesting," I said. "You may not agree, but that's actually a useful feature. For our purposes, at least. Are the rings linked to each other? Can we use this ring to find whoever has the prince, currently?" It would be very handy indeed if the ring could just lead us right to the kidnapper, before he or she reached Bomora.

Yolinde frowned. "You can try. But our contact didn't track us down, which makes me think they were unable to do so through our rings."

"Or they were busy with other concerns," Aela pointed out. "Like a loud, fussy newborn."

"A fair point."

I turned to Farrah. She was practically cross-eyed from her intense scrutiny of the ring, and a bit of red showed at the corner of her mouth where she was biting her tongue unconsciously. I hid a smile. I always enjoyed seeing Farrah working at her magic, even if I didn't understand a bit of it.

"Farrah."

No response. That ring was, apparently, mighty interesting.

"Farrah!"

She startled and looked up, then frowned at me. "Don't interrupt me when I'm in the middle of a spell."

"As far as I could tell, you weren't spell casting. Just looking at that ring."

"I was studying the bond between it and Aela. I think I've figured out how to transfer the bond from her to you."

"Hey!" I yelped. "Who says I want that thing bonded to me?"

At the same time, Aela breathed a sigh of relief. "That will help us immensely. Even though you bought it from me, it's still linked to me and would keep leading you back to us. Which is something, once we all part ways, that my daughter and I definitely do not want. If you're looking for the Emerald Order, and the Emerald Order is looking for me ..."

"Don't fret," Farrah assured her. "It's elementary magic. May I see your hand?"

Aela held her hand out to Farrah, palm up, revealing a faint scar in the middle. "Do what you have to. It will be worth it to be rid of that burden."

Farrah nodded, as if she had expected either this response or the scar in Aela's hand. I wasn't sure which. "Thank you. Your cooperation makes things much easier." She pulled out her eating knife, whispering a quick spell as she did so. The blade glowed blue, and then Farrah slashed Aela's palm with the blue-tipped knife. Aela hissed briefly in pain. A small bead of blood bloomed in the middle of Aela's palm.

Farrah dropped the ring in the blood pooling in Aela's out-stretched hand, then motioned to me. "Give me your hand, Rhyss."

I recoiled. "No. I don't want you to slice into me, thank you very much."

She rolled her eyes. "I'll heal you both after I'm done, although the cuts will close on their own quickly enough. I can't transfer the bond to myself; the ring's power is incompatible with my own Fae magic. Plus, I don't really look or sound like a Bomorran. You're the only logical choice for this. So, come on, now. Give me your hand."

Reluctantly, I held out my hand, palm up, to Farrah. She whispered the same quick spell as before; the knife glowed blue again and Aela's blood disappeared off its edge. Once that happened, Farrah cut my hand as well.

"Ouch!"

She ignored my cry and guided my bleeding palm toward Aela's. "Put your hand on top of hers, with both of your open cuts touching the ring."

I did as instructed, trying not to grimace at the slimy feel of both Aela's and my blood coating the metal piece of jewelry. Aela's face was impassive, her demeanor calm, and I wondered if she had gone through a similar ritual when the ring was bound to her.

Farrah was muttering something fast and unintelligible under her breath, ending in a louder, "And so may it be. *Fiat.*"

Aela's hand pulsed once with a red glow, and then that light rose up and encompassed my hand. I felt a prickling sensation, like a bunch of tiny needles were pressing into my palm, with the highest concentration where the ring was in the center. Just when the pain reached a near-unbearable point, the feeling and the red light disappeared. At the same time, Aela let out a huge breath of relief, her face and bearing much lighter than when we had first started talking.

"It's all done," Farrah said. "I've transferred the ring's binding from Aela to you, Rhyss. I've also blocked the ring from being able to 'punish' you for any failed missions."

I removed my hand from Aela's, surprised to see the ring was clean and shiny, instead of being coated in blood. I gingerly took the signet ring from Aela's palm and placed it on my left hand, where it fit snugly on my index finger. Meanwhile, Farrah took Aela's hand and gently touched her open cut. It quickly sealed itself, leaving only the original faint scar that had been there before.

"Give me your hand," Farrah said to me, and she repeated the same process with my hand.

Aela flexed her hand in wonder. "Thank you, miss. Not just for the healing, but for ridding me of that." She indicated the signet ring on my finger.

"It is I who should thank you," I said. "For the ability to gain easy entry into the Emerald Order."

Aela's face darkened. "You may be grateful now for the help, but mark my words. Once you face the Emerald Order, you won't be thanking me."

13

—·—

Chapter Thirteen

Aela and her daughter Yolinde quickly finished their meal and made ready to head out into the night.

"Are you sure you want to leave now?" I said. "I'm sure the innkeeper has extra rooms. We'd be happy to pay for one, if you wanted to stay."

"You've been very generous already," Aela said. "But truth be told, we'd rather put as much distance between us and this place as possible. Anyone who may be tracking us would know we were here. It wouldn't be wise for us to linger."

Although Farrah and I didn't think it was wise for them to leave, either, we couldn't argue with their logic. The two women bade us farewell. As they walked out the door of the Blue Pony, Farrah whispered something and blew on her fingertips in the direction of the departing women, much as if she had blown a kiss to them. Aela slipped out into the night, unaware, but Yolinde turned back and looked at Farrah sharply before following her mother.

"What was that?" I asked.

"Just a small protection spell," Farrah said. "It only lasts for about a day or so, but it should protect them from most magical prying eyes and minor physical harm. Hopefully it keeps them safe for the night, and gives them enough time to get out of the area."

"Good idea," I said.

She shrugged. "It was the least I could do, since they weren't going to sleep at the inn tonight."

A big yawn escaped my lips. "Speaking of sleep ..."

Farrah yawned as well. "I agree. It's definitely time to turn in for the night. I'm surprised I'm only just feeling today's travel now."

The inn had mostly cleared out, with just a few late night dinner patrons in the main room. The innkeeper stopped by to clear our table, his arms already laden with dirty dishes. "Your rooms are upstairs, second and third doors on the right."

We thanked him and went upstairs, which was dimly lit by a few candle sconces.

"Which room do you want?" I asked Farrah.

"Whichever one will let me get to sleep faster," Farrah retorted.

I laughed and headed for the third door. "Good night, then."

"Good night."

Entering my room, I threw my pack down on the rough pinewood chair at the foot of the bed, twisting my neck and stretching my arms overhead, trying to work out the kinks from sitting on a horse for several hours. The room was plain, but serviceable. I sank down on the bed to remove my boots, enjoying its surprising softness. My ungraceful maneuver caused the lit, half-used candle on the nightstand to flicker briefly, although it still illuminated a fair amount of the small room. Through the pulled-back curtains, I could see the full moon and starry night sky lighting the shallow balcony outside.

I debated cleaning the dirt of the day's travel from my face using the basin by the door, but I decided I was too tired. I chuckled. Instantly I could hear Farrah's voice in my head: "Being tired is no excuse for not being clean."

Sighing, I quickly cleaned up and then fell into bed, still fully dressed in my traveling clothes. I barely noticed as I blew out the candle and my head hit the pillow.

I woke up feeling uncomfortable. At first I thought it was the shock of cold air and my not-made-for-sleeping clothes—after all, I had fallen asleep in my shirt, coat, and trousers on top of the bed's coverlet. But then I realized, while those things certainly were unpleasant, they weren't what had woken me up.

The shadowy figure currently sneaking around my room was responsible for that.

My first groggy thought was, *Farrah? What is she doing in here?*

But as my brain started to wake up, I realized Farrah would have knocked. And she wouldn't have snuck around my room, she would have just walked over and smacked me awake.

I tensed, quickly thinking through my options. I had some weapons in my pack, which was sitting on a chair across the room. My dagger was in my right boot, which was at the foot of the bed. My sword was in its belt, still around my waist, but twisted underneath me. I could reach it, but I just had to be careful not to betray the fact that I was awake to my unexpected guest.

I rolled over gently, letting out a fake snore for good measure. My right hand crept behind my back, grasping the hilt of my sword.

My visitor crept carefully to the side of my bed. The moonlight reflected off a sharp silver dagger in the intruder's hand. A gold signet ring—a twin to my own—glowed faintly on their little finger.

The person raised the dagger to strike.

I yelped and grabbed my sword from its sheath. The tip of my sword hooked the blade above me. It flew across the room, hitting the wall then clattering to the floor.

I sprang from my bed, holding the intruder at sword point. "Who are you, and what do you want?"

I heard a sharp intake of breath. "Who are *you*? You're not Aela." The high, light voice was decidedly feminine.

I jabbed my sword at the woman. "I think you owe me an answer, first."

Moonlight streamed into my room through the open window—*so that's how my visitor got into my room*, I thought—and glinted off the ring on my finger. The person saw it and, even though she had a sword poking at her chest, relaxed a little. "You must be taking Aela's place, then? She missed her rendezvous; I always suspected that woman was trouble."

I thought rapidly. If I played along—and played things right—I could potentially get some information. Also, I didn't want to kill anyone if I didn't have to.

"You're right," I said, lowering my sword slightly. "Everything happened so fast, I wasn't able to send word to the leader about the change in plans. But that doesn't explain why you tried to kill me, just now."

"When she didn't show, we had to go after her, to find out why," the woman said. "And to silence her if she planned on betraying us. We should have been halfway to Bomora by now. Set us back about two days."

We? Who else was with this person?

And how would I get her to stay here and keep talking long enough for me to rouse Farrah next door for help?

Come to think of it, how would I even wake Farrah up without arousing suspicion?

"Well, you have your answer now," I said. "I'm guessing you and your companion have a camp nearby? Let me know how to find it, and I can meet you there in the morning."

"No," the woman said. "We'll go now. We can travel for a few hours before stopping, and maybe make up some of the lost time."

I couldn't leave, not without alerting Farrah in some way first. "If we leave right at daybreak, that should be adequate, don't you think? I'm sure you could use a rest, especially if you've had to waste time tracking Aela."

The woman hesitated while I continued, trying to sound nonchalant. "Besides, I paid good coin for this room."

She eyed me suspiciously. "You're not truly with the Emerald Order, are you?"

Whoops. I had pushed too hard. "Of course I am." I waved my hand—the one sporting the signet ring—in the air. "Isn't this proof enough for you?"

Outside, a baby's wail pierced the air. I froze.

Coran!

I cursed myself mentally. I had been sure the woman and whoever she was traveling with had set up a camp nearby. But I had been mistaken. The crown prince was just outside the inn, and this was my best chance to recover him.

I just hoped I hadn't botched everything.

The woman backed up a step away from me, one hand slipping into a pocket. Seeing that subterfuge was now useless, I raised my sword and lunged, hoping to slow her down or cause her to fall. But before I could nick her, she withdrew her hand from her pocket. She threw a small object to the ground.

Pale gray smoke filled the room, burning my eyes and causing me to cough. I reached out, but my sword met empty air. My nighttime visitor had escaped.

Cursing, I hastily sheathed my sword. Shielding my nose and mouth with my sleeve, I moved through the dissipating haze to the window. Peering over, I saw the woman scramble down a rope secured to the balcony's railing.

Without hesitation, I was over the railing and giving chase. But in the back of my mind I wondered, *How did she secure that rope to my balcony? I should have done a thorough check of my room before falling asleep. Farrah will never let me hear the end of this.*

Speaking of Farrah ...

I glanced up at her window. It was decidedly dark, and it looked like she had drawn the curtains against the moonlight. I didn't want to call out, afraid of rousing the entire inn. I would have thrown rocks at her window to try to wake her, but with what rocks? And with what free hands?

A rustling below me caught my attention. The woman had jumped from the rope and was already moving away. I was halfway down the rope.

And then the rope shot through my hands faster than I could climb down, the friction chafing and scorching my fingers. I grabbed at the rope, at the wall, at anything, trying to hold on, to stop myself from falling, but the rope disappeared from my hands.

I started falling, twisting in the air to see the woman running away from the inn toward two horses. Atop one horse sat another shadowy figure. The rope trailed after the woman like a long, sinuous ribbon floating in the wind, even though the air was still tonight, until it rapidly coiled together in her outstretched hand, which she was holding high in the air above her.

Oh. A magic rope. That explains it.

I hit the ground hard, my bony backside taking the brunt of the fall. "Oww!" I groaned, not caring how loud I was. At least I hadn't landed on my sword. I scrambled to my feet, quickly shaking out my limbs. Thankfully, I hadn't broken anything, either. At least, I didn't think so.

In the distance, I could hear Prince Coran crying, when his cries were abruptly cut off. I suspected a magic spell had been used to either silence him or put him to sleep.

Although I tried to run after the two abductors, my body had definitely been shaken by the fall. All I could manage was a clumsy sort of limp-trot.

I hadn't gotten far when the intruder reached her horse and mounted it. The two figures rode into the night.

I debated getting my horse and going after them, but then realized how futile that would be. Since I could barely move at my normal speed, by the time I reached the stable, readied my horse, and rode after them, their trail would be cold. I also didn't want to ride off into unknown danger without Farrah. I'd need her help, not to mention she would be furious with me if I left her out of an adventure.

And I could definitely use her healing help right now.

I limped back toward the inn. I started to head to the front but stopped, realizing that now, in the dead of night, the place would be locked up. The innkeeper—and any guests—would not appreciate it if I created a ruckus trying to gain entry.

I looked up, gauging the distance between the ground and my room's balcony. Too high to jump, and the inn's walls were, unfortunately, too clean to climb. No snaking ivy or convenient trellises adorned the walls. I ran a chafed, bloody hand over the wall. *That's going to leave a mark. I hope the innkeeper doesn't come back here in the daytime.* The stone was cursedly smooth, too. No bricks jutted out at odd angles to make an attempt at scaling the wall easier.

Had I known the night was going to turn out like this, I may as well have gone with the mysterious stranger. Either way I wouldn't have gotten use of my rented room, but at least I would be less bruised and battered.

I was just about to take off my coat and bed down on the grass for the night when a window opened above me. Flickering candlelight silhouetted a shadow framed there.

"Rhyss? Is that you? What in the name of the Gifted Lands are you doing down there?" Farrah hissed as she leaned out and looked down. Unlike me, she had changed out of her traveling clothes to sleep. Her white dressing gown gave her an air of unexpected elegance, and I found myself tripping over my words.

"Well, there was this woman—" I started, then stopped, realizing how bad that sounded. "Never mind, I'll tell you later. Can you unlock the front door for me?"

She shook her head. "I can do better than that. Stand right under my window."

I did as she said. Farrah whispered something I couldn't quite hear, stretching her hand out toward me. I felt myself start to rise. Startled, I reached out both of my arms, trying to steady myself, but I needn't have worried. Farrah's spell was sure and steady, and pretty soon I was hovering just outside her window.

She reached out and grabbed my hands, then my arms, pulling me closer to the open window frame. "Get in here," she whispered.

I made a clumsy head-first dive through Farrah's window, even as she was pulling me inside. Her levitation spell faded halfway through my dive, causing me to go sprawling across the floor. And on top of Farrah.

"Oof!" she grunted softly.

"Sorry," I whispered. I propped myself up on my elbows to give her some space to breathe. Her lavender hair was haloed around her head as she looked up at me, her eyes dark liquid pools drawing me in, and for one random, wild moment I thought, *What would it be like to kiss her?*

And darn it all, now that that thought was in my head, it wouldn't go away.

"Rhyss?" Farrah whispered.

"Yes?" I leaned forward, holding my breath.

"Would you get off of me? This is extremely uncomfortable."

"Oh. Oh, yeah. Sure." I rolled to the side. Farrah sat up, brushing herself off and straightening her hair.

She reached out toward my face, and my breath caught again in anticipation.

Farrah plucked a dried leaf out of my hair and tossed it aside in disgust. "Why do you have leaves in your hair? And your clothes are all dirty. Don't tell me you missed camping when you had a perfectly good bed next door." She frowned. "And what's this about a woman?"

"Trust me, I'd rather I was in bed right now, and that what just happened was all a weird dream." I filled her in on the night's events, ending with, "It pains me to think that Coran was so close, but I failed to get him back."

Farrah squeezed my hand. "It's okay. We *will* get him back."

I sighed. "Thanks."

"One good thing came out of this, though. We confirmed the rings are connected to each other, as well as to the Emerald Order and to their owners. Maybe I can use your ring to find your mysterious visitor."

I gladly gave her my signet ring to experiment on, but when she had a chance to examine it for a bit, she sadly shook her head and handed it back. "If there was a way to use the rings' links to track her down, I can't access it anymore. She's blocked the connection, somehow."

"It's no matter." I slipped the ring back onto my index finger and breathed a barely audible sigh of relief. I had a growing need to have my ring near at all times, and it was troubling me. But I didn't want Farrah to know either of those things. "We know where they're going, eventually."

"True," she said. "I just don't like being surprised. It would be nice to know what awaits us in Bomora."

I stood up and brushed myself off, then held my hand out to Farrah. "Well, we can discuss it on the road. After getting a good night's sleep. Or, at least, a sleep for what's left of the night."

Farrah took my hand and let me help her up. I may have held her hand a little longer than usual before letting go. Did she notice? It didn't seem so.

I opened her door and stepped out into the hallway. "Goodnight, Farrah."

She quickly and quietly moved to the doorway. "Wait, Rhyss," she whispered.

I turned, that thought again of, *What* would *it be like?* running through my head, when Farrah leaned over and waved her fingers at the closed door to my room. I heard a quiet click as the door unlocked.

"There. Now you can get in."

"Thanks, Farrah," I whispered. I paused, and in that moment she shut the door behind me. I tried to ignore my rising feeling of disappointment, and quietly slipped into my room.

14

—·—

Chapter Fourteen

Despite the late night, I woke up at first light. I'd like to think it was due to my unwavering discipline when I'm on a job, but in actuality, it was the copious amounts of sunlight streaming in through my window that did the trick. But, hey, even if I hadn't bothered to close the curtains, at least I had remembered to shut and lock the window before falling into a dreamless sleep.

The other thing I had thankfully remembered to do was remove my sword belt before getting back into bed. I hadn't bothered to undress (again), so getting ready took hardly any time. I refastened my sword belt around my waist and checked my boots. My dagger was still hidden inside the right one, and my bag was still sitting on the wooden chair where I had carelessly thrown it the night before. A quick rummage through it showed that all my things were still there. Perhaps my nighttime visitor's only goal was to kill or threaten Aela, although I'm sure after she had done that she probably would have searched Aela's things at leisure.

Shouldering my pack, I opened my door and slipped into the hallway. I could feel last night's adventure with every slow step I took; my back was screaming in pain.

Next door, Farrah was also just exiting her room. "Oh. Good morning, Rhyss."

"Good morning, Farrah." My throat was unusually dry, but that was probably because I hadn't had any breakfast yet. Some mead or cider would definitely hit the spot.

Farrah's purple hair had been braided back from her ebony face in a hairstyle practical for traveling. Gone was the ethereal white dressing gown from last night. Everything about her outfit today spoke of practicality: plain cream linen tunic over dark brown pants, tucked into matching brown knee-high boots. It was an outfit I'd seen her in countless times—honestly, I'd seen Farrah herself countless times over the years—and yet I felt like I was seeing her, really seeing her, for the first time.

Farrah stared at me. "What?"

"Huh?" Have I mentioned I'm not a morning person? As my articulate way with words just proved.

"You're just staring at me. You all right?"

I blinked and shook my head to clear it. "Yeah. Uh. Just moving slowly today. I got a bit banged up from last night's fall."

She smiled sympathetically. "I should have healed you last night. Sorry about that, I wasn't thinking about it in the midst of everything else."

"It's okay, there were more important things happening. I'm still mad at myself for losing Prince Coran like that."

"You couldn't have known he was so close." She motioned toward the stairs. "Let's get a quick breakfast, then be on our way. Maybe it's not too late to pick up their trail. If you can wait a bit, I'll heal you when we've stopped for a rest."

"Sure." I followed Farrah down the stairs.

The inn was just stirring. We grabbed some leftover rolls from last night's dinner, then headed to the stable to get our horses. We were on our way within the hour, the morning air chilly enough that we could see our breath.

We headed west, on the main travelers' road that would lead us to Bomora. For a while, we just focused on waking up and staying warm.

"So, while I can't use your ring to directly find last night's visitor or her companion," Farrah said, "do you think it's worth it to try to track them and catch up to them today? They have at least half a day's lead on us, but even if they rode through the night, my guess is they would have stopped this morning for a few hours' rest."

"We can try," I said dubiously. "But even if they did stop, we don't know what they're capable of. Besides warding their camp, they could have set a bunch of mundane and magical traps around it. They could even have made themselves invisible. Without knowing exactly where they are, I don't want to chance blundering about to locate them. We could find ourselves in worse trouble if we're not careful."

"What do you mean?"

"What do you know of the western part of the Gifted Lands?"

Farrah paused, considering the question. "Not much, actually. My family never had a reason to travel outside of Orchwell, before they moved back to Shonn. You and I never really came out this way when we were working with Beyan. And, now that I think about it, even Kaernan's commissions were never this far west, either. The furthest we ever traveled this way was Rothschan." She was referring to the lost-loves Seeker that sometimes hired us, now that Beyan was retired from dragon Seeking, and our first commission with him that took us to the military kingdom of Rothschan.

"You never wondered why?"

She shrugged. "Not really. Like you, I just go where the job takes me."

I smirked. She and I did have that in common.

She smirked back at me. "I can tell you're dying to give me a history lesson, so go ahead."

I chuckled. "It's so rare I get to do it, let me enjoy the moment." I paused for effect. "Okay, I've enjoyed it. Now, then. You know Bomora's pretty isolated, right?"

"I just assumed Bomorrans are a very private people."

"Partly. But there's a forest on our outer borders that's very hard to cross."

"Really? What's so difficult about it?"

I smiled grimly. "They're called the Hwisprian Woods for a reason. The forest is haunted. If you spend any length of time in them, you might go insane. If you're lucky, and are able to return from them. Most people tend to disappear."

Farrah frowned. "Haunted? Faeries, or ghosts?"

"No one's really sure. Possibly both?"

"But people obviously leave or visit Bomora, so how can they if they have to cross this Hwisprian Woods?"

"You can go around them, and many people do. But it adds several days to your trip. If you go south, you have to deal with the hassle of crossing through Rothschan. If you go north, it's unclaimed wilderness, but dealing with regular beasts, though wild and ferocious, might be preferable to unknown monsters. A few years back there was a man who ran a business escorting people through the woods safely, but he closed up shop and moved away."

Farrah's frown deepened. "So we can go through Rothschan, which brings its own challenges. And we can't use our connections to Calia to ease our passage, since Calia and Rothschan aren't on the best of terms right now. If we go north ... it might be easier, but then we lose time that we can't afford to lose." She looked at the sun's position in the sky, considering. "How much longer until we reach this forest? And how long does it take to cross it, assuming we can do so unharmed?"

"We should reach it around midday. If all goes well, it will take a day and a half to cross it—one overnight stay, at least." I frowned. "And you can bet the Emerald Order will take the quickest route back to Bomora, even if it is the most dangerous."

"If all goes well," Farrah echoed. "Well, there's nothing for it. Through the Hwisprian Woods we go."

"Are we sure we're ready for it?"

She gave me a sidelong glance full of mischief. "Are we sure *it's* ready for *us*?"

15

Chapter Fifteen

As I had estimated, we reached the edge of the Hwisprian Woods just before midday. We stopped for a rest just a few feet away from the entrance to the forest.

And, looking upon it, it really felt like a formal, forbidding entrance. Instead of a gradual transition into the forest, such as scrub, or small trees here and there, the road we were traveling on disappeared into dense, tall trees, swallowed by darkness beyond.

The woods formed a stark contrast to the bright sun shining overhead, its heat burning off the edge of the morning chill. Farrah and I ate our cold lunches in just a stone's throw from the forest edge, both trying to be as quiet as possible. If we did speak, it was in quick, hushed tones. We both sensed that the forest was watching us, and we were trying to remain as unobtrusive and unthreatening as possible.

By unspoken agreement, neither of us brought up Farrah's earlier boast about the woods. If the forest was indeed observing us, then we didn't need to invite trouble.

I mean, any more trouble than we would already invite by entering the area.

Most of my aches from last night's fall had melded into the aches from traveling on horseback for several hours. After a quick examination, Farrah said, "It's not as bad as I thought it might be, considering. Time will heal you better than magic could."

I knew—from long experience—that doing the light bit of healing magic my aches would need would barely take anything out of Farrah. I sensed there was something else going on to explain her reluctance to heal me. "You just don't want to perform any spells right now."

"Exactly," she admitted. She glanced uneasily at the forest's entrance, then back at me. "Well, sitting around here won't get us anywhere. Shall we?"

I nodded. We remounted our horses and spurred them toward the Hwisprian Woods.

At the forest's edge, our horses stopped, snuffling in worry. After much urging, they started forward reluctantly.

The *clop-clop-clop* of our horses' hooves seemed deafening as we traveled down the road. After a few moments, I said, "Is it just me, or our horses walking louder than usual?"

Farrah said, "Haven't you noticed? There's nothing here, except the trees, and us. If there are any animals, they're either hiding or unnaturally quiet."

She was right. A forest would usually create some noise, even if it was just the occasional chirping of birds or insects, or the wind twisting through the trees. Since it was late autumn I would have expected to at least hear the crunchiness of dead leaves under our horses' hooves.

But here in the Hwisprian Woods, there was nothing. No sound. And no fallen leaves, either.

"It's not too late to turn around," I said.

Farrah bit her lip and looked about. "We really shouldn't take the longer route ... but part of me would prefer it."

As one, we turned our horses around and headed back the way we had come. We hadn't gone very far into the forest, so I figured we would find our way back to the open road beyond the treeline soon enough.

But we didn't.

We kept on the forest road, but we couldn't find the way out of the forest. The trees rose above us, tall and forbidding, blocking all but the faintest bit of sunlight. Since I couldn't see the sky overhead, I had no idea how long we had been traveling, or what time of day it was.

Finally, Farrah brought her horse to a halt. "Are we lost?"

"I don't think so." I looked around. This area of the Hwisprian Woods looked much the same as the part we had left. And the part we had entered. Maybe we were lost. But we hadn't strayed from the road, so how could we have gotten lost?

Farrah's face was troubled. "If we're not lost—and I agree with you, I don't think we are, either—then we're stuck in this forest. We can't go back the way we came. Something won't let us."

Hearing Farrah voice my own fears sent a shiver down my spine. After years of assisting various Seekers as help-for-hire, not much—while traveling, or in dealing with people—surprised me. But this dark, magical wood had me spooked.

"Well then, there doesn't seem to be much point in continuing this way." I hoped Farrah didn't hear the slight tremor in my voice. "We may as well turn back around and make our way to the other side of this forest."

Farrah nodded as we, again, turned our horses back around. We traveled on in silence for a while. The area didn't look any different, but it felt ... better. Like we were traveling forward, instead of going around in circles.

The lack of sound, with the exception of our horses' hooves against the dirt road, grated on me. Eventually I had to break the silence, if only to stop myself from going crazy. "Earlier you said something wouldn't let us leave the forest. What did you mean?"

Farrah didn't respond right away, and I had a sudden, worrying thought that whatever was dampening the normal forest sounds had stolen her voice away as well. I looked over at her. She was looking around warily. "You feel it too, don't you?"

I looked around too, but whatever had captured Farrah's attention was beyond my comprehension. "Feel what?"

"Look around."

I thought that's what I had been doing, but I did it again anyway. "I don't get it."

"It's nearly Samhain," Farrah said, touching on my earlier thoughts. "Back in Calia, or Orchwell, most of the trees would have lost their leaves already. But if you look around here—" she stopped her horse, pointing at a tree covered in bright green leaves, with a few red and gold leaves dotting its canopy "—these trees look barely touched by the change of seasons at all."

I frowned. "Well, we are further south. Maybe the leaves will change later."

"Perhaps, but we're largely straight west of Orchwell, and even the area around Orchwell looks like fall, heading into winter. Not like the trees are only just turning." She sighed. "And even though I know you don't know any magic, you can't help but feel it all around you in here. Can't you?"

I paused, concentrating. There was an odd, somewhat heavy feeling in the air. I had assumed it was just the jitters of the unknown on my part. I whispered, "Magic?"

Farrah reached out and touched the tree, closing her eyes. I realized she was trying to commune with the forest. "Whatever governs this wood, it's ancient. As old as these trees. Possibly older."

"Huh." I swept my eyes around the forest, taking in the imposing, stately boughs lining our path on both sides. "Is that a good thing or a bad thing?"

"Depends."

"On what?"

Farrah opened her eyes and met my gaze. "On whether or not it likes us."

I gave her a subdued nod. "Best not to light any fires when we camp tonight, then."

"Among other things, yes."

We fell into a mutual, grim silence, intent only on getting through this forest as quickly as possible. The never-ending sameness of the trees lining our path gave me the impression that we had gone nowhere, although the aches in my body from riding for hours told me otherwise.

Out of the corner of my eye, I thought I spied something pale and large paralleling us in the trees.

"Did you see that?" I hissed at Farrah.

She nodded, although I noticed she was careful to meet my eyes only, and studiously avoided looking in the general direction of whatever was following us.

"What is it?" I asked.

She shook her head, ever so slightly. "Whatever it is, don't give it heed."

It was on the tip of my tongue to ask her, *Why not?* But I knew Farrah well enough to know, if she was giving me a warning like that, she had a good reason for it. I swallowed my question and concentrated on the road again.

We continued on. It was only when both of our stomachs started growling that we realized it was dinnertime. And more importantly, we should probably make camp for the night.

We found a small, usable area just off the road. Neither of us wanted to venture too far into the forest. Nor did we want to go hunting for any game in this forest—if, indeed, there was any game to hunt. Instead, we dined on cold rations and just a bit of water from our water skins—because, again, we were both loath to leave the camp to find fresh water.

The daylight—such as it was in that oppressive forest—faded and gave way to a crisp autumn night. The chill of the upcoming winter lingered in the air, but since we had agreed to not light a fire, Farrah and I piled on extra pieces of clothing from our bags and bundled ourselves in our bedding.

Farrah surprised me by plopping down right next to me. Layered in all that fabric, she resembled a fluffy fabric worm topped with lilac hair.

"We'll have to huddle together tonight for warmth," she said.

My face instantly heated, and I didn't even have the excuse of being too close to a fire, since we didn't have one lit. I just had to hope in the darkening twilight, Farrah wouldn't notice. "Too bad we can't light a you-know-what."

"Come on, I'm not that bad," Farrah said teasingly.

I hadn't been thinking that. Quite the opposite, actually. *Where had that thought come from?* My face flushed more, if that was even possible. Ah, the joys of being a pale-skinned redhead.

Flustered, I asked, "Do you think it would be possible to at least cast some sort of heat spell? Surely that wouldn't be offensive to ... the forest?"

Farrah's blankets rustled as she shook her head. "I don't think it would be wise. Even though it's harmless magic, the forest might not view it that way. It might consider any unapproved magic a threat."

I had no idea that a forest could have an "approved magic" list, but then again, before today, I wouldn't have believed that a forest could be sentient, either.

I pitched my voice lower. "Speaking of viewing ... is whatever was following us earlier still in the area?"

Farrah's worried eyes met mine. "Yes. It never left us."

"Since we can't set a ward—" Farrah shook her head, confirming my hunch "—then we should probably take turns keeping watch tonight."

"A watch is always a good idea," Farrah said. She looked around furtively, although it didn't seem there was anything in the trees to notice. "But whatever it is, I don't think a mere night watch will be enough to guard against it."

We fell silent then, watching the light around us fade. Drawing closer together for warmth and comfort, we both felt that oppressing sense of something nearby, watching us.

Biding its time.

16

CHAPTER SIXTEEN

FARRAH OFFERED TO TAKE first watch, mainly because she was curious about the Hwisprian Woods and wanted a chance to try to commune with it further.

"Perhaps if I can connect with it," she reasoned, "it will view us as friendly—or at least, as neutral—and allow us to continue the rest of our journey through it unharmed." She shrugged. "It's worth a try, at least."

The adrenaline from being on constant edge earlier left me exhausted. Within moments, I was sound asleep.

Only to be woken, some undetermined time later, by Farrah shaking me.

"Wha—?" I asked groggily.

"Shh!" She put her hand over my mouth and leaned close to my ear. I caught a whiff of her vanilla-and-lavender scent. "There's something out there."

Instantly I came fully awake. I sat up, surveying the dark woods beyond our meager camp. The horses were still tied up nearby, resting. Their occasional snuffs punctuated the night. If they were spooked by whatever Farrah had seen, they didn't give any sign of it.

A flash of white caught my eye, and I turned sharply, hoping to catch a clear glimpse of whatever was watching us. There it was, to my right. No, my left.

How had it moved so quickly?

I stood, wanting to be ready to face whatever was coming. My blankets fell off my shoulders as I did so, slumping on the ground behind me. Next to me, Farrah stood as well.

I reached for my weapon, even as Farrah grabbed my arm and silently shook her head. I shrugged her off, but didn't draw my sword. Yet. Despite Farrah's earlier warnings to not anger the forest, or anything that lived in it, I knew I would feel better with a weapon in hand if needed.

The flash of white appeared again, solidifying into ... a presence of some sort. I'm not sure what to call it, honestly. It wasn't a ghost, or a monster. Nor was it an angel or even a demon. All of those have form, substance.

I couldn't make out an exact form as I stared at the white light that approached us. As it bobbed closer, it grew brighter and bigger, overpowering my light-starved eyes in the darkened forest. Blindly, I reached out for my sword, but even though I knew where it was, knew it was easy to grab, my hand slipped and closed over air.

And then, as the light touched me, I was frozen, and couldn't move, couldn't see anything, but that blasted bright whiteness. I heard a far off cry from Farrah—*why is she far away? She's standing right beside me!*—and then the light pulsed, surrounding me in a sparkling deluge, and winked out.

The signet ring on my hand stung my finger with unexpected heat, then turned chill with cold. I cried out in pain.

When my eyes readjusted to the darkness, I stood alone in the middle of a moonlit clearing.

I looked around wildly. Farrah was nowhere to be seen. The horses, our meager camp—all of it was gone. I knew I hadn't walked to get here, and I also knew, with a sinking heart, that I had no sense of where I was. Farrah and the camp—which was just off the road—could lay in any direction. Since we had entered the forest, we hadn't been using the sun or stars to mark our way, since the woods had effectively blocked the sky overhead.

Steeling myself, I picked a direction and started walking. But once I reached the edge of the clearing, I couldn't leave it. Puzzled, I tried another direction. The clearing wasn't that large, and I reached the opposite end quickly.

But I still couldn't leave.

A quick check of the entire clearing confirmed my suspicions: I was, indeed, trapped here.

The sensation of something sweeping behind me made me turn. The white light that had stolen me away appeared again, but this time, as it moved toward me, it solidified into something I could recognize.

A pale woman approached, her bare feet treading lightly on the forest floor. Her body seemed to be covered in vines; as she drew closer, I saw in the moonlight that she wore a gown made of moss, leaves, and flowers. A crown of tulips adorned her white tresses, worn long and flowing around a heart-shaped face with blue eyes so light they were nearly as white as her hair. She was radiant, lit from within, so that I could see every detail about her as clearly as if we were meeting under the high noon sun.

I fell to my knees, bowing my head. "My lady."

The pale lady spoke, her voice musical and rich. "Rise, Rhyss of Bomora."

I slowly rose to my feet, my eyes wide and wary. The pale lady laughed. "Oh, yes, I know who you are. Just as I know you bring one of the Fae with you."

I bowed my head. "Forgive me, my lady. You obviously know who I am, but I do not know who you are."

Her eyes flashed, changing briefly from their pale blue color to a cool silver. "My name is unpronounceable in your tongue, human. Not that I would be foolish enough to give you my true name. Know simply that I am the Heart of the Hwisprian Woods. I know everything that happens in my forest."

The silver faded, becoming an unexpected, frightening red glow. "What I do not know is your purpose. You wear the ring of my enemy, but although it is bound to you, it does not own you. As it often does, for other wearers. A most intriguing puzzle."

Her enemy? The Emerald Order?

"Your enemy is mine as well, Your Grace."

"Is it?" she mused. Her eyes flashed again. The eerie red of her eyes disappeared, replaced by the original pale blue.

Suddenly, vines snaked up from the ground, winding around my legs and holding me in place. The Heart stepped delicately toward me, peering into my face. She was so close that our noses practically touched. If she had a weapon concealed on her person and chose to use it at that moment, I would be powerless to stop her. "But how do I know you speak the truth?"

"I know of no way to prove myself to you, my lady. I can only give you my word. But I don't suppose that is enough."

Her eyes narrowed. "It is not. But at least you are wise enough to know that." She paused. "Do you know the full extent of the Emerald Order's crimes, Rhyss of Bomora?"

I shook my head.

"Let me show you." She pointed to the center of the clearing, where the moonlight shone down like a lone spotlight on a stage.

Two tall, ghostly figures appeared in the moonlight. Cloaked in dark velvet, they moved furtively, but with purpose, stopping in front of a stately tree just as translucent as they were.

While many of the trees in the Hwisprian Woods could be considered stately, there was something special about this particular tree that set it apart from the rest of its companions. Ancient and regal, an otherworldly sense emanated from it. The guardian and mother of the forest in which I stood, this was the Heart of the Hwisprian Woods.

One of the figures removed something from their belt, hidden just under their cloak. I sucked in a breath as I saw the moonlight glint off the sharp edge of a shiny silver axe. A strange green light dripped off the axe's edge: an enchantment of some sort.

I gasped and muttered, "What kind of fool brings an axe into a sentient wood?"

The Heart answered, "No fools, these. Just two men with evil intentions."

Even though these images were just shadows of the past, I could feel the collective anger and hostility from the forest around me, radiating the strongest from the ageless, white-haired woman standing near me.

The first cloaked man hefted the axe. The trees nearby moved, their branches reaching out to stop the man from chopping down one of their own. The ground shook as the land itself tried to trip up the two people. But the second man raised a hand, shouting something.

A gold signet ring glinted from his finger, and I knew, with sudden certainty, that the woodcutter also wore the same piece of jewelry.

The ghostly tableau didn't provide me with any sound, but from the continuous stream of words the second man was saying, and from the way the trees shuddered and were still and the ground ceased rippling, I could tell he was subduing the forest with very powerful magic.

Meanwhile, the woodcutter chopped away at the magnificent tree.

I watched, wide-eyed, as the two men wreaked havoc on the Heart. Within the tree, the image of the white-haired Heart appeared, over-laid on the bark of her tree. With each blow from the enchanted axe, the Heart's face contorted—in rage, in anger, in pain. Her mouth opened in a wordless scream. The woodcutter winced, but kept at his task. The magician broke off from chanting to clap one hand over one of his still-hooded ears. He reached out with his other hand—the one he wore his signet ring on—to touch the trunk of the tree, still chanting some incantation. The ring began to glow.

"What is he doing?" I asked, horrified.

"Stealing my lifeblood, and with it, my soul. And the very life of this forest." The Heart's voice broke.

Thankful this memory contained no sound, I shuddered at the sight. I could feel the intensity of the Heart's pain as the two merci-lessly worked to fell her tree.

All too soon, the woodcutter had worn away at the Heart's base. Heartsick, I watched as the tree began to fall. The woodcutter's com-panion finished his spell and hastily stepped back, out of harm's way.

But just before the trunk hit the ground, it disappeared, leaving only the stump of the Heart's former tree.

The two cloaked men looked around in confusion that rapidly turned into a shrugging indifference. If anything, the tree's myste-rious disappearance worked to their advantage: there was no sound of a falling tree to betray their position in the forest, nor was there a felled tree as evidence of their actions. The pair left, taking their evil enchanted axe with them.

And contained in the magician's ring, the Heart's soul.

The image faded. Moonlight still bathed the center of the clearing, where I could now see the dark shadow of a majestic tree stump. How had I missed that while I had been stumbling about in this area?

As if she had read my mind, the Heart said, "Yes, that is what remains of my tree. With what little magic I have left, I have hidden it from human eyes. Should those two men—or their associates—return to finish what they started, then the Hwisprian Woods would die even faster than it already is."

"Finish what they started? How?" I asked. Then the rest of what she said hit me. "The forest is dying?"

"They stole most of my magic, but they didn't completely kill me," the Heart said. "Outright death would have been kinder, but these heartless men did not care for my comfort. Given time, my tree might have grown back, but they cast spells to ensure it would not. I am now condemned to die a slow death, feeling my magic trickle away from me, powerless as I watch my forest fade away around me."

Her voice grew forlorn. "Already my trees are feeling the touch of autumn, where before my ageless ones were evergreen. Soon winter will come to my forest, but unlike the common woods of the Gifted Lands, when spring returns and awakens the trees, my trees will remain forever asleep."

The vines crept up higher around my body and tightened. I gasped for air as the vines squeezed my chest.

The Heart's eyes glowed red as she regarded me. "And now the Emerald Order sends another of theirs to harm me and mine, someone cloaked in strange magic. Even though you travel with one of the Fae, I do not trust you. Just a day ago, two of your company came through my forest, using my own magic to keep me at bay so I could not touch them. But you have no such protection."

She raised her hands. Crimson light crackled from her fingertips.

"Please, my lady," I cried, my voice hoarse with fear. "I swear to you I am not part of the Emerald Order, that they are our common enemy. Please. Allow me to prove this to you."

The red light continued to drip ominously from her pale fingers as she studied me.

Slowly, she lowered her hands. "Very well. If you speak the truth, then you can prove yourself to me in this way: Recover and return my magic."

"I will do my best. But how will I know who has that enchanted ring? All the Order's signet rings look the same, I think. And what if they've already used up all of your magic?"

The Heart smiled grimly. "The one who stole my magic is the Order's leader. Bring me his ring, or bring me him. I will find a way to recover my magic, whatever is left, from him."

I swallowed hard. "Dead or alive?"

Her smile turned feral. "It matters not. If he is dead, then his magic will leave him and return to me. If he is alive, then I will have the satisfaction of retrieving my magic from him."

The Heart approached me where I stood, still pinioned by her vines. "And to ensure you will do your best ..."

She stretched her hand out, her finger just grazing the unexposed skin of my neck, right above my left shoulder. I winced from the quick flash of heat from her fingertip.

The heat faded. The Heart stepped back, studying her handiwork.

"I have marked you with a spell to keep you true to your word," she told me. "Were you to look at it now, my mark would be barely noticeable, just another freckle in the sea of freckles upon your skin. But over time, it will grow, until it covers your entire body. If you do not fulfill your promise to meet me in the allotted time, it will turn into thorned vines similar to these—" she indicated the vines holding me captive "—to pierce your flesh and strangle the air from you, until you cease to live."

She snapped her fingers, and the vines holding me loosened and fell to the ground. Heaving a huge breath, I followed suit and fell on my hands and knees, gasping and wheezing.

A cool hand tilted my chin up. The Heart's eyes, now back to their original light blue, looked down on me. "You have three days. If you do not return by sunrise on the fourth day, then you will die."

Before I could respond, she snapped her fingers again. Suddenly I was no longer in the moonlit clearing with the Heart. I was still doubled over on the ground, but now Farrah's sleeping form was next to me, with the horses nearby.

Still shaky from my encounter in the deep woods, I sat propped against a tree and leaned my head back. Although I felt exhausted—and I now had a suspicion that Farrah and I didn't need to keep a watch anymore in these woods—I also felt that sleep wouldn't come easily.

But the whole thing had been so surreal. Perhaps I had dreamt it?

I touched the spot on my neck where the Heart had burned her mark on me. My fingers found a small, raised bump, about the size of a nail's head. While I did have a smattering of freckles on my face and my body, none of them were raised. Or warm to the touch.

So, not a dream then.

The Heart's words came back to me: *You have three days.*

Three days to reach Bomora, infiltrate the Emerald Order, get Crown Prince Coran, steal the Heart's magic back, and return to the Hwisprian Woods.

I sighed.

No one ever told me that this was what being a godparent would be like.

17

— · —

CHAPTER SEVENTEEN

I WOKE UP TO the feeling of someone poking me, repeatedly, too close to the spot of my new magical mark.

Groaning, I forced my eyes open. Farrah's concerned face hovered in front of me, close enough to kiss.

Heat rose in my cheeks. *Where did* that *thought come from*?

"When did you get back to the camp? Why didn't you wake me? What—"

I yawned and cut off Farrah's next question. "We had a visitor last night. Here's what happened ..." I quickly outlined my encounter with the Heart of the Hwisprian Woods, including her request for us to recover and return her magic. I didn't mention the spell she had placed on me to enforce it.

Farrah frowned. "When you left, I was too jumpy to sleep. But a few moments later, I opened my eyes, feeling well-rested, and it was daytime. And you were back, and sleeping against this tree. I suspect magic was involved, but I've never met any magic I couldn't counter. Or at least sense, and try to fight against." Her frown grew deeper. "I didn't even feel this magic coming over me."

"It's all right," I said. "I have a feeling the Heart watched over us last night." *Besides, if I die here or am injured before I leave her wood, I won't be of much use to her.*

Farrah stood, brushing dirt and leaves from her clothes. I followed suit, and we quickly packed up camp and got the horses ready to leave. Soon we were back on the road—one that seemed noticeably more straightforward than the previous day's meandering one. The forest's silence accompanied us as we rode. Still watchful, still wary, but less oppressive than it had felt yesterday.

After an hour's easy ride, we reached the western edge of the Hwisprian Woods. Farrah commented, "I didn't think we were that close to the forest's end."

"We're not," I said, recalling my last journey as a teenager through this forest. Perhaps the journey had felt longer to my younger self, but I didn't think that was it. "I think the Heart is helping us on our way."

Farrah nodded, and both of us spurred our horses to a brisker pace. Not that our speed mattered, but we both wanted to leave this haunted forest as fast as we could.

Once we cleared the forest, we were officially in Bomora, although it would be about a half day's ride to the country's capital city and civilization. Compared to the other kingdoms in the Gifted Lands, Bomora was fairly small. My home country didn't even have the small towns or villages that dotted the landscape around Calia, Orchwell, or Rothschan, our nearest neighbors. There were a few farms in the area, but as the Aentin Sea was the country's western border, Bomora mostly relied on the fishing trade to sustain it.

The silence that had pressed in on us during our time in the Hwisprian Woods stayed with us for a while longer, but eventually the clear blue sky and cheerful sun overhead chased away the oppressive feeling.

The horses seemed to breathe easier with each step away from the forest. I know I definitely was.

"Are you looking forward to returning home?" Farrah's husky voice broke the silence between us.

I shrugged. "It's been so long, I barely remember what it was like living there. My parents and I intended to go back, but then the accident happened.... It just didn't feel important to return, after that. It's not really home to me anymore, anyway. You know what it's like. We're rootless vagabonds. So how can I say Bomora is my home any more than Orchwell is home, or any of the other places we've visited?"

Farrah smiled gently. "You and I both know, your true home is where you make it."

I smiled back. "You're right, as usual, oh wise one."

Even though I teased Farrah, we both knew there was no heat behind it. She *was* a wise person, and often her level-headedness kept me out of trouble. Or, I should say, from getting into deeper trouble than I already had invited.

"Why did your family leave Bomora, anyway?"

Brow furrowed, I shot Farrah a look. "I told you."

"No, you didn't. You told me you moved when you were thirteen, and that you still had some family back there. But you've always been so closed about your past, and I've never wanted to pry."

I snorted. "Then why start now?"

She rolled her eyes. "Because you're finally opening up to me about this stuff, after all these years. Because it would be nice to know more about Bomora and what we might be walking into when we get there. But mostly because you're one of my dearest friends, and I care about you and your life."

I didn't respond right away, and the silence between us stretched out for several awkward moments. Finally, Farrah said, "Rhyss. If I offended you—"

"No." My voice came out hoarsely, as if I hadn't used my voice in days instead of just several minutes. I cleared my throat, willing it to be steady. "You haven't offended me."

Farrah didn't say anything, just waited for me to continue.

Slowly, I said, "What do you know about Bomora?"

Farrah frowned. "Honestly? Not much. It's rather remote, and it's not easy to get to." She waved her hand in the direction of the Hwisprian Woods, now well behind us. "None of Beyan's commissions ever took us there, and I remember Queen Jennica mentioned once that none of the other kingdoms really engaged in trade with Bomora. I always thought that was odd." She gave me a pointed look. "And the one person I *do* know from that country is quite tight-lipped about it."

I grimaced. "Well, with good reason. In the history of the Gifted Lands, Bomora has traditionally been considered the black sheep of all the kingdoms. It's where the other countries would send their criminals—the ones that they deemed beyond redemption."

"Really? I always thought that was just a myth." She tipped her head as she studied me. When she realized I wasn't joking, she raised her eyebrows. "Although I suppose every myth has a kernel of truth in it, somewhere."

"Indeed." I nodded. "Bomora eventually became a haven for those seeking to flee the law from their home countries, too. It's not big, compared to the other kingdoms. We're largely self-sufficient because of our proximity to the Aentin Sea. Fishing sustains our kingdom, and—on the rare occasions we do trade with other countries—is one of our major trades. Among other things."

"Other things?"

I cleared my throat. "Our ... colorful ... history lends itself really well to ... ah ... piracy."

To my surprise, Farrah laughed. A rich, hearty, uncontrollable sound. Even her horse pricked his ears at it, startled by its unexpectedness.

And when she kept laughing, I asked, "What's so funny?"

She didn't answer me right away. She was too busy still laughing. Finally, when her guffaws had simmered down to mere chuckles, she said, "It's just ... it explains so much about you."

"Hey! Thanks a lot."

She wiped tears from her eyes. "Not in a bad way. I mean, even if illegal activities are in your heritage, it's those very same skills that have gotten Beyan, you, and me out of several scrapes. So I'm not complaining. Or offended, if that's what you're worried about."

I wasn't. Farrah was one the most open-minded people I knew. In our line of work, you had to be.

She eyed me curiously. "So if the stories about Bomora are true, then what else is?"

I sighed. "Unfortunately, the Emerald Order. It was just a few years old when my family moved to Orchwell. You've heard the saying, 'Nothing good ever comes from Bomora'? If the kingdom couldn't earn a respectable reputation, then they would take it by unethical means. You know, the Bomorran way."

"No one can fault Bomora for relying on their tried-and-true skills," Farrah murmured, eliciting a small chuckle from me. "So, that's why your family left?"

"Yes. They wanted me away from the bad influences that pretty much make up all of Bomorran culture. The rise of the Emerald Order just solidified their decision."

Farrah nodded in understanding. "Well, no matter the reason, I'm glad you and your family moved to Orchwell when you did."

I smiled at her. "Thanks. But while we're in Bomora's capital city—such as it is—we'll have to stay sharp. As obvious outsiders, we'll be easy targets."

Farrah straightened in her seat, a hint of mischief in her eyes as a smirk played on her lips. "Targets, yes. Easy? Definitely not."

I laughed. "Gods help anyone who tangles with you, Farrah."

She snorted. "Well, since I don't believe in the gods ... I guess anyone who tangles with me will be in a lot of trouble."

18

— • —

CHAPTER EIGHTEEN

AROUND MID-MORNING, WE STOPPED for a brief rest about halfway between the Hwisprian Woods and Bomora. The horses didn't really need the rest, but Farrah pointed out that we should probably contact King Beyan back in Calia to give him an update. She politely refrained from also pointing out that, if anything, I was the one who needed the rest—after the bizarre events of last night, I was practically falling asleep in the saddle.

We had a cold—and belated—breakfast just off the side of the road while the horses grazed nearby. I hadn't realized how hungry I was until I held the food in my hands, and devoured it in about two or three bites. Farrah just raised an eyebrow at me and kept daintily chewing.

"You know, you could make yourself useful and call Beyan instead of just watching me eat," she eventually said.

"I can't do magic, you know that," I said.

"That's not a problem." She put her sandwich down in her lap—a half a sandwich! how did she still have half a sandwich left? …. and would she share it with me?—and rummaged in her pack. Pulling out an item, she handed it to me. "Here you go."

I took the smooth gray stone from Farrah and looked it over. It was small, no bigger than a coin. I had no idea what to do with it. "Uh, Farrah? This is a rock."

She smirked. "Very good."

I rolled my eyes. "Okay, but what am I supposed to do with it?"

"Call Beyan, of course."

I sighed. Farrah laughed, taking pity on me. "Okay, okay. Jennica and I were experimenting with infusing objects with easy magic. Spells like conjuring light, or calling someone. We thought it might come in handy, especially for people like you or Beyan who don't use magic."

I gave an approving nod. "Very handy indeed. Good thinking."

Farrah smiled, basking in the praise. "Thanks. We haven't done thorough testing yet, but the two stones we spelled should work for a dozen uses, at least."

"Great." I turned the stone over and over in my hand, but I didn't see any clues in how to use it. No runes, no sigils. Not even an arrow pointing to a certain spot with a plainly written "press here"—which would have made my non-magical life much easier. "Want to give me some hints on how to make this thing work?"

"It's easy," Farrah said around a mouthful of sandwich. "Just hold the rock in your hand, like so." She reached out and touched my hand, curling my fingers around the rock firmly. "Then concentrate on who it is you want to call. Think of their face, their voice, anything that reminds you of them. If it helps, say their name aloud, repeatedly. That should do it."

"Oh. Okay." I closed my eyes and concentrated. After a moment, I cracked one eye open to check my progress. Nothing had happened.

I closed my eyes again. Feeling a little silly, I said, "Beyan. Beyan."

"What?"

I nearly dropped the rock in surprise. Beyan's image floated above my hand.

Farrah clapped her hands. "Oh, good! It works!"

Beyan looked like he was squinting. I realized he was craning his neck around, trying to figure out where Farrah and I were. "Where are you two?"

"Near Bomora," I said. I quickly filled him in on what had happened since we had left Calia. Minus my encounter with the Heart of the Hwisprian Woods, of course.

"It's too bad you couldn't catch up with the kidnapper before she got back to Bomora," Beyan said, sounding frustrated. "But I'm glad you have that ring. Hopefully that makes it easier to get Coran back."

"I hope so too." I briefly toyed with the idea of adding something vaguely comforting, like, *Don't worry, we'll have your son back soon.* Or, *It will all be okay.* But this was Beyan, one of my best friends, someone I had even fought side-by-side with on occasion. I couldn't be anything but honest with him. Instead, I asked, "How's Jennica doing?"

Beyan sighed, suddenly looking worn. "She still hasn't woken. She's so thin now, too, even though we're doing our best to keep her fed. But the Royal Healer says it has nothing to do with her body. I think ..."

"What? What is it?"

Beyan sighed again. "I should never have agreed to it. But Coran's our first child, and he's the Crown Prince ... and Jennica said it would be completely harmless. A mere formality."

He looked away for a moment, at something I couldn't see. When he turned back, unshed tears shone in his eyes, and I realized he must have answered my call in their bedchamber. Of course—he would want to spend every possible moment by Jennica's side.

"There's a Calian tradition that binds a baby magically to its mother in its first year. For protection, and also it helps the child grow in its magical powers even before it's able to use them. Not many citizens take part in the ritual anymore—it's a bit elaborate and costly to set up—but the royal family still does it. So I said yes to it. From what I understand, the spell that was thrown in the city square weakened the tether between Jennica and Coran. She would have recovered over time though, if Coran had still been nearby. Proximity is an important part of keeping your child safe, and it's a key component of the binding.

"Jennica's current condition—staying unconscious—is a result of magical backlash, because Coran is gone from her side. If he doesn't come back … Jennica won't either."

He fell silent. Even where Farrah and I sat in our little roadside camp, it seemed like the world had gone still as well. I glanced over at Farrah, who didn't even try to stop the tears flowing freely down her face.

Thickly, I said, "Beyan. We will do everything in our power to make sure that doesn't happen."

In an equally choked voice, Beyan said, "I know, Rhyss. I know. If anyone can save my son and my wife, it's you and Farrah. I know you won't let me down."

19

—·—

CHAPTER NINETEEN

By MIDDAY, WE HAD reached the outskirts of Bomora's capital. Compared to the sprawling capital cities of the neighboring kingdoms, my home country's capital resembled a medium-sized town. A city of miscreants had no need for a fancy palace, let alone a special district for our non-existent nobles to reside. Such things would have just screamed "easy target" to the general populace anyway.

As we approached, I murmured to Farrah, "Don't draw attention to yourself if you can help it. That being said, if you notice someone following you, or sizing you up, meet their gaze directly and let them know you're aware of them. Boldness and confidence will keep you safe in this country; being demure will not."

Farrah nodded, openly curious as she took in our surroundings. Worn brick buildings lined either side of a broad cobblestone street, the main thoroughfare through Bomora's capital. A small farmer's market—rather sorry compared to the markets of Calia or Orchwell—was set up on both sides of the street.

Farrah and I dismounted. I led the way to a nearby stable, where the surly stable master eyed us warily as I handed him my horse's reins.

"How long d'you need?" he asked me.

"Just today to start, although we might need a few more days," I said breezily, aiming for that confidence I had told Farrah was necessary for dealings here. "We'll return each morning to pay for an extra day, if need be."

"A'right," the man said. He eyed us both with an openly curious—and suspicious—look. "What brings you to Bomora, anyway?"

"We're looking for the headquarters of the Emerald Order," Farrah said before I could speak or stop her.

The stable master's lips thinned into a disapproving line. "If I were you, I wouldn't ask that question so loudly. Or at all."

"Why—"

I cut Farrah off before she could continue the conversation. "Sorry to bother you, good sir. Here's some coin for the stabling." I handed over one silver coin for payment. "I believe that's the standard rate." For good measure, I tipped a few more coins into his outstretched palm. "And that's for ... other things."

The stable master's dour mood lifted slightly, as one corner of his mouth twitched in a twisted half-smile. "Thank you, sir."

I nodded in acknowledgment and steered Farrah away before she could comment on my overpayment. When we were out of earshot, she asked in a low voice, "Bribery?"

"Bribery is such an ugly way of putting it. How about, a bit of insurance," I confirmed. At her raised brow, I explained, "Otherwise we might return to find our horses have been 'borrowed' indefinitely. If we didn't give the stable master some extra coin, he'd easily find someone who will."

"Ah."

I glanced back at the stable master, who was watching us walk away with a thoughtful expression on his face. "I only hope the extra money was enough to keep him quiet, too."

"Why didn't you want me to question him? He sees people come and go all day long; he's bound to know something."

"Even if he does, we can't just inquire outright," I said. "We don't know what things are like here; if it's anything like I remember, there may be several factions at play. What we need to find out is who is in power."

"Who's in power? That's your king and queen, right?" When I nodded, Farrah looked genuinely confused. "Wouldn't even the Emerald Order be subject to and loyal to your royals?"

"On the surface, yes. But you don't survive long in Bomora without knowing what deals are being made and by whom—and by playing the underground political game extremely well. Things aren't as straightforward here as they are in Calia or in Orchwell. Or even in Rothschan."

Our nearest neighbor, Rothschan, was a strict kingdom that relied heavily on its military prowess and fearsome reputation, but even things in Rothschan were more clear cut than in Bomora. Follow the rules, obey the king and queen, and you'd be fine in Rothschan. The constant backroom deals and ever-changing loyalties in Bomora made our political system about as clear as mud—and just as dirty.

To pass the time—and to maybe get lucky and learn something—Farrah and I wandered through the farmers' market, such as it was. Five ramshackle wooden stalls with sorry looking fruit did not really make a market.

After passing a stand boasting partially rotten fruit, Farrah asked, "I know you said Bomora relies on the sea for food, but surely their farmers could do better? Or is the land here just not good for farming?"

I dubiously eyed a stand of wilted vegetables. "Actually, this seems really odd to me. I know it's near the end of the season, but I remember the local farms always had good produce to sell. Then again, it's been a long time. Maybe my memory is faulty."

"It's not your memory that's faulty, lad," said the vegetable seller. I winced, embarrassed at being overheard insulting her produce. The wrinkles at the corners of her eyes crinkled as she smiled at us, revealing a crooked grin that was missing teeth in a few places.

"Forgive me, madam. I didn't mean—"

She waved away my paltry apology. "Never apologize for speaking the truth. Because, in truth, our farms have suddenly been failing. Started maybe three years ago, just producing less and less, until this year, we barely had any harvest to speak of." She pointed at her stall. "Even though I know this isn't fit to eat, it doesn't stop me from trying to sell it anyway."

Despite how pathetic her produce was, I couldn't help but smile. Spoken like a true Bomorran.

"Do you know what caused it?" I asked. "Drought, or perhaps pests?"

The vegetable seller shook her head. "Neither." She lowered her voice. "I'm not a superstitious sort—we make our own luck here in Bomora—but I think our farms' malady is magical in nature. And I'm not the only one."

She glanced up and down the street, making sure no one was paying attention to us. She lowered her voice even more. "There seem to be odd doings at the place the Emerald Order calls home. There always were, but it's gotten more frequent lately. And sometimes, late at night, there will be funny lights and sounds coming from Glidhaan's Grove, just outside the city. My grandson went once to spy on the Order—" a bit of pride crept into her voice at the word 'spy' "—and he said he saw all sorts of weird, otherworldly creatures at the Grove,

mingling with the Order." She shuddered. "A bad business all around,
if you ask me."

Farrah and I exchanged loaded looks.

"Interesting. Thank you." I handed her a coin in appreciation for
the information, but she waved at her stall again. I picked out a sorry
looking squash and thanked her again, then Farrah and I hurried away
from the market and deeper into the city.

"What do you make of that?" Farrah asked when we were out of
earshot.

"It's interesting," I repeated. "Whether or not it's true ... I guess
we'll find out."

Farrah looked down the main street, shading her eyes against the
midday sun. "Where's the royal palace?"

"Bomora doesn't have one."

She frowned. "But this is a kingdom, right? You just said Bomora
has a king and queen to rule it."

"Yes," I said, "but—"

Farrah grabbed my right arm. "Wait. Don't look now, but I think
someone is following us."

"Remember what I told you?"

She turned around halfway and leveled a gaze across the street,
toward a darkened alley. Two people in dark clothes peeled themselves
from the shadows and started moving briskly toward us.

"I thought you said that would stop whoever was following us, not
invite them to join us!" she hissed as I turned to face the pair.

"It'll be okay," I said as calmly as I could. I was glad Farrah was
gripping my arm, and not my sweaty hand which would have betrayed
my nervousness.

As they drew closer, they became two distinct men, their faces lined
and weathered from years of being at sea. Outfitted in loose-fitting

dark brown shirts over equally baggy black trousers, the pair approached us, the grim set of their mouths and eyes showing that they had business with us.

Possibly unpleasant business.

"Hello, gentlemen," I said congenially. Beside me, Farrah released my arm and straightened, not wanting to appear uncomfortable in front of them.

"Hello yourself," the older of the two responded. "You're newcomers to Bomora, aren't you." It wasn't a question.

"Why should that matter?" I asked.

"And you've been asking questions about the Emerald Order," the man continued, as if I hadn't spoken.

I groaned. "I knew I should have given the stable master more money."

Farrah and I looked back at the stable master, who was far enough away that we couldn't see the expression on his face. But the mocking tip of his hat as he saw us looking, combined with the deliberate turning of his back to us, was enough to set my teeth grinding in frustration.

I turned back to the two men. "All right, then. What do you want with us?"

"Not us," the leader said. "But King Addan and Queen Inari will want to meet you. Might be a few hours before they get back, though." He sighed. "Can't be helped. Come along, now."

Farrah looked like she was ready to fight the two men, but I put a restraining hand on her arm and quickly shook my head. She scowled, shaking my hand off, but understood my warning and didn't draw her weapon or cast a spell.

I nodded at the two men, trying to appear as non-threatening as possible. Starting a fight with the king's representatives would not be a good way to endear ourselves to the local leadership. And we'd get no help from anyone in the area if we did. The merchants in the market had studiously avoided looking our way during our exchange with the two men, but I knew they were already sizing us up, assessing our odds of winning, and calculating what spoils they could take from our lifeless bodies after we were soundly defeated.

"Come," the older man repeated, and he started walking down the street, away from the market and further into the city. I followed him, Farrah behind me, with the younger man taking up the rear to ensure we wouldn't run.

Around us, the buildings started to look older and more weathered. The stale, sulfur-stained smell of the sea grew stronger as we walked.

Farrah came up beside me and whispered, "Where are they taking us?"

"To see the king and queen, I assume," I whispered back. "Just like they said."

"But you told me there's no palace. So where do they live?" She gripped my arm—my left arm now, the one that was fairy-marked. As the day had worn on, the inconspicuous mark on my neck had slowly spread, a light red vine against my pale arm. I had actually felt it snake its way down my skin, an itchy, hot, tickling sensation. Fortunately, my long sleeves covered it. For now.

"Ow!" I blurted out.

"What's wrong?" Farrah looked at me, then at my arm. "You're not injured, are you?"

"Ah, no," I said, furiously trying to figure out a good excuse. "I ... I think I slept on it wrong last night."

Farrah let go of my arm. I breathed a barely audible sigh of relief.

"Sorry to hear that," she said. "If it still hurts later on, let me know. I can try a healing spell on it, if you like."

"Thanks, I'll keep that in mind." If only a healing spell would help. Farrah was a great magical talent, but even her magic would be no match against an ancient forest spirit's geas.

Farrah's brow furrowed in thought. "Wait a minute. You were sleeping sitting up against a tree, weren't you? How could you have slept on your arm wrong, then?"

"Well, I—"

Fortunately, whatever outlandish lie that nearly escaped my lips was cut short by a satisfied shout from the man leading us, who had stopped briefly to survey the area ahead. "Ah, good! Let's step it up, then."

He quickened his pace, forcing us to move faster to keep up with him.

We had reached Bomora's harbor, which was as old and weathered as the city we had just walked through to reach it. Our little group made our way to the docks and passed by several ships that were currently moored: two small fishing vessels, three merchant ships, and an eye-catching, impressively large red-and-gold warship.

Farrah made a sound of surprise as we walked right by the warship. "Wait," she whispered to me. "I thought we were going to meet Bomora's king and queen."

"We are," I whispered back.

"But ..." She craned her neck around to look back at the bright and garish ship we had just passed. "Aren't they—?"

Our little group stopped in front of a nondescript merchant vessel at the edge of the harbor. In the wake of the other ships, it was easy to overlook. Indeed, the old and creaky ship looked like it would fall apart at the slightest puff of wind. The paint boasting the name of the ship had faded away, leaving a random "c" and then "s" on the hull.

Our leader stopped, calling out to someone who was busy on the deck. "Ho, there! Is that you, Baz?"

The man on deck stopped what he was doing and peered over the railing at us. "Tarek! Well met, man! What brings you out this way?"

Tarek nodded his head at Farrah and me. "Brought some new-comers to meet Their Majesties."

Baz chuckled as he looked us over. "You're lucky they're in a good mood today. Otherwise they'd throw you two into the sea and be done with you. Well, then, come aboard. I'll let them know."

The four of us made our way on deck while the man named Baz headed toward the stern of the ship, presumably towards the captain's quarters.

While we waited, Farrah commented, "It's impressive that your royalty takes an interest in all your citizens, from all walks of life, instead of only paying attention to the upper classes." She nodded toward the gaudy warship we had passed earlier.

Tarek quirked an eyebrow. "And what do you mean by that, exactly, miss?"

Farrah shrugged. "Just that it isn't the usual way of things in other kingdoms. Take Rothschan, for instance. I doubt their royals would deign to visit the crew of a ship like this one—" she waved her hand expressively, encompassing the entire sorry ship "—nor would the leaders of my home country, Shonn. King Beyan and Queen Jennica of Calia would, but they're more hands-on than most of the other leaders in the Gifted Lands."

Tarek smiled. "Ah, I see, miss. Well, what you need to under-stand is—"

He stopped talking as Baz reappeared. Baz nodded at Farrah and me. "They've been granted an audience. Come with me, please."

"Wait," Farrah said, as Tarek and the younger guard turned to go. "What were you saying?"

Tarek smirked. "It's no matter, miss. I daresay you'll understand soon enough." With that enigmatic statement, the two men left.

Farrah and I followed Baz to the captain's quarters, where he rapped smartly on the slightly open door. A deep, velvety voice said, "Enter."

Baz bowed slightly and stood in the doorway, just blocking our view of who was inside the room. "I bring the travelers that Tarek delivered."

"Very good, Baz. You may see them in."

Baz opened the door further and stepped aside to allow Farrah and I entry. She shot me an apprehensive look, but entered the room. I followed after her. Baz bowed again and shut the door. I didn't hear his footsteps walk away, and I knew he was standing just outside the cabin, within earshot, ready to act if there was trouble.

Across the room, a man sat behind a wooden desk, idly twirling a shiny, sharp-looking dagger in one hand. His long, dark brown hair was tied back with a satin ribbon that matched his tresses. Nearby, a raven-haired woman perched on the edge of the desk, her long hair similarly tied back in a practical manner.

The man stood up, still playing with the knife. His eyes, the same rich dark brown as his hair, grazed over us appraisingly.

In a sudden, swift motion, he twirled the dagger one last time, then thrust the blade firmly into the desk. Both Farrah and I flinched at the abrupt, loud thunk as metal met wood.

"Welcome to Bomora, strangers. I would know your names, so you are strangers no more."

"This is Farrah, formerly of Shonn, now of Orchwell." I indicated Farrah, then put my hand on my chest. "And I am Rhyss. I, too, live in Orchwell, although Bomora is where my family and I originally resided."

The man's gaze sharpened. "Ah, so not quite a stranger then."

Farrah cleared her throat. "And may we know who you are?"

The man raised an eyebrow in surprise, then smiled. The smile didn't quite reach his eyes. "But of course, my dear lady. This—" he motioned toward the woman sitting on the desk's edge "—is Queen Inari. And I—" he gave us an ironic bow "—am King Addan, ruler of Bomora and the Aentin Sea. At your service."

20

—·—

CHAPTER TWENTY

FARRAH GAVE A SLIGHT gasp, and fell into a hasty curtsey. I followed suit to show my respect, bowing to the royal couple. I knew Farrah's surprise was entirely my fault; after all, I hadn't warned her ahead of time what to expect.

Even though I had had ample time on our journey together to tell her.

I braced myself mentally, knowing that once we had a moment alone, Farrah would—understandably—have many, many questions for me. And probably some other choice words as well.

King Addan nodded at a small navy blue couch set against one wall. "Please, sit."

Farrah and I sank down into the velvet cushions. I gave a quick glance around the room.

The captain's quarters—or royal suite, I reminded myself—was elegant but functional. Besides the desk and plush couch, there was a bed, just large enough for two, across the room. A large wooden chest lay at the foot of the bed.

The room's real personality shone through in its decorations. A rich red silk tapestry displayed on the wall hinted at an exotic adventure, as did the smooth wood-and-ivory masks hanging next to it. A built-in shelf displayed a few more trinkets and treasures from the royal couple's travels. My mind reeled. Farrah and I were both very well-traveled, thanks to our work with various Seekers, including King Beyan when he used to Seek dragons. But our travels, so far, had been restricted to the Gifted Lands. The idea of exploring beyond the continent was novel. And intriguing.

"Welcome to the Starchaser." King Addan opened his arms wide proudly.

"It's a beautiful ship," Farrah said politely.

"We'd like to think so. After all, it's our home."

"Oh?" Farrah couldn't hide the surprise lacing her tone.

Queen Inari laughed. "That's a common response for people who aren't from our fair country and are unfamiliar with our unconventional ways. Unconventional, that is, to those who are restricted by their traditions."

I smirked at the slight emphasis she gave the word 'fair' — while the surrounding environs were beautiful, I don't think any of Bomora's citizens would call the people-inhabited part 'fair'.

"After all, we are the rulers of both Bomora and the Aentin Sea," the queen repeated her husband's words.

Realization dawned on Farrah's face. "Oh! You're—"

"Pirates?" King Addan saved Farrah from finishing her sentence. Her eyes grew wide, and her cheeks turned pink from embarrassment. "It's all right, my dear. We rather enjoy the label."

"Reputation is everything," Queen Inari agreed.

Farrah opened her mouth, then closed it quickly, too polite to blurt out the questions we all knew she desperately wanted to ask.

The king laughed. "It's all right," he repeated. "Perhaps after you answer our questions, we'll favor you with some answers of our own."

He strode around to the front of the desk, leaning his tall, lanky form against it with the same casual air his wife, still perched on the edge of it, exhibited.

"To business, then, now that we are no longer strangers to each other," the king said airily. But despite his easy tone, I could sense the steel underneath. "What brings you to our fair kingdom? Especially you, Rhyss formerly of Bomora." He turned his appraising eyes on me. "Those who leave here rarely choose to return."

Queen Inari laughed, a silvery sound. "Then we must be the rare exception, darling."

King Addan gave her an affectionate look. "You, love, are always the exception. And exceptional."

The queen smiled, fond exasperation in her tone. "You're only saying that because I saved your skin on our last voyage. Again."

He laughed. "What would I do without you?"

"Ah, darling, let's pray you never have to find out."

Now that I could see the king more closely, I noticed the gray beginning to show at his temples and the lines in the corners of his eyes, either from years of squinting in the sun or from laughing. Quite possibly both.

The queen's feet didn't quite touch the floor from where she sat on the desk's edge, leading me to think she was much shorter than her fairly tall husband. A few wisps had escaped from her pulled-back dark hair to frame a lovely, heart-shaped face. She openly assessed Farrah and me with her bright blue eyes.

The royal couple were dressed similarly to Baz and Tarek in loose-fitting, dark-colored outfits. Which made sense, given their seafaring life.

The king turned back to me. "Well? Your reason for coming to Bomora?"

When I didn't respond immediately, the king smirked. "Know that my men are trained to listen and watch for certain things. If they brought you to us, then I have a fairly good idea of why they did so."

"Plus it's always nice to meet new people," Queen Inari said. While her words were pleasant, there was a veiled threat underneath.

I could feel Farrah tense beside me, ready to defend us with magic if need be. Despite the tension in the room, I sighed. It wouldn't help baby Crown Prince Coran—or his home country of Calia—if we got into an altercation with the leaders of Bomora. "We're here in your country to find the Emerald Order."

Farrah hissed in warning, but I ignored her and continued talking. "Farrah and I are representatives of King Beyan and Queen Jennica of Calia, hoping to recover that which was taken from them by the Order."

"Oh?" King Addan raised one dark eyebrow. "And what would that be?"

I hesitated, not wanting to spread the news of Prince Coran's kidnapping unnecessarily. But the shrewd appraisal from both King Addan and Queen Inari told me they would know instantly if I was lying or withholding information from them. Neither option would endear them to our cause. So I said simply, "The Emerald Order kidnapped the newborn Crown Prince of Calia."

A long silence followed my words. I resisted the urge to shift my weight, not wanting to appear uneasy, but behind my back I clenched my hands together in two tight fists.

Finally, from King Addan: "And do you think we—" he nodded at his queen, then pointed to himself "—have anything to do with it?"

Oh dear. I would have to tread carefully. Were the royals of Bomora working with the Emerald Order? If that were true, then Fararh and I would be lucky to make it off this ship alive.

"We have heard nothing that would lead us to believe that Your Majesties are a part of it," I said slowly. "But anything that happens in Bomora falls under your purview."

The unspoken implication hung in the air. King Addan and Queen Inari silently stared at Farrah and me. We met their gazes, not backing down, just shy of a challenge.

Then King Addan sighed heavily. "Would that statement were true."

The slight catch in his voice made me look at him sharply. Queen Inari covered her husband's hand with her own and gave it a brief squeeze. The king looked at his wife, and some quick, unvoiced conversation occurred between them. He gave a slight nod, then turned back to Farrah and me.

"I would appreciate it if what I am about to say does not leave this room," the king said. "As a courtesy from one kingdom's leader to another."

"As official representatives of King Beyan and Queen Jennica of Calia, we vow that anything you say will remain in confidence, nor will it be used to betray your country in any way," Farrah said. An undercurrent of magic laced her words, and all of us could feel the magic binding us to each other. King Addan looked slightly startled at the unexpected spell, but Queen Inari turned an appraising look on Farrah.

"Thank you for that," the queen said. "We have our own way of creating a covenant, but your way works as well."

"Very reassuring," the king agreed. "And less messy." At Farrah's quizzical look, he explained, "Our way involves a bit of bloodletting."

Ah. Of course. From my home country, I would expect nothing less. Maybe I had been away from Bomora too long, but for me, at least, Farrah's way was definitely preferable.

"Well, now that we have your reassurance ..." The king's voice trailed off. He cleared his throat and straightened. "Do you know much about the Emerald Order?"

Farrah and I both shook our heads. Farrah said, "We only learned about them when they kidnapped the prince. Since then, it's just been little bits of information. We know they want to introduce magic into Bomora by starting a war between the Fae and the Gifted Lands."

The king nodded. "The Emerald Order was established well over a decade ago, but for a long time no one, least of all the queen and I, took it seriously. It seemed to be more of a pseudo order than any serious organization. So, the Crown maintained a hands-off, look-the-other-way policy when it came to them. As long as they weren't doing anything that truly threatened the Crown or the kingdom, we weren't going to bother with them. Although the Emerald Order has always been on the fringes, in recent years it has gained more influence in Bomora.

"Seven years ago, Queen Inari and I were blessed to welcome a beautiful baby girl into the world. Our little princess, Jianne, was the exact image of her mother, perfect in every way. Our kingdom of misfits rarely bands together for anything, but I do not lie when I say the kingdom rejoiced over Jianne's birth.

"Last year, the queen and I decided to leave our daughter in Bomora while we sailed the Aentin Sea. We always stay in Bomora during the winter when the waters are rough, but come spring Jianne would sail with us until it was time to return home in the fall. We thought Jianne would benefit from staying in Bomora for an entire year, to see how things are run. So we left our daughter in the care of Chancellor Theodore Tayend until we could come home."

The king took a shuddering breath. "When we returned, the princess was gone. Not kidnapped, or run away. But ... traded. To the Emerald Order. By the chancellor."

The king didn't say anything for a long while. Our breathing seemed overly loud in the confines of the captain's quarters. Finally, Farrah said gently, "For what purpose, Your Majesty?"

The king clenched and unclenched his fists, his gaze locked on something unknown across the room as he relived the horror of finding his only daughter missing. "For the chancellor? Power. For the Emerald Order? To this day, I'm still not sure. Whatever they wanted the Bomorran heir for, it can't have been good."

"Where is your daughter now?" I steeled myself, knowing the answer would most likely be a sad one. Farrah and I hadn't seen any sign of a child when we came aboard the Starchaser, although it was possible she was elsewhere on the ship.

The queen took up the tale. "We tried to get her back. We immediately went to the Emerald Order's headquarters, forced our way in, tore the place apart trying to find her." Her voice broke as tears sparkled in her eyes. "But it was too late. When we found Jianne, she was dead."

"We're sorry for your loss, Your Majesties," Farrah murmured. I nodded in agreement.

"Thank you."

"What happened to the chancellor?" I asked.

"He went into hiding. We didn't find him that day at the Emerald Order's place, and our spies haven't been able to track him down either. If he's still in Bomora, he must be hidden by a very strong glamour."

"And if he's still in Bomora, then his life is instantly forfeit," King Addan said savagely.

"Understandable," I said. Farrah gave the royal couple a gentle smile in sympathy.

"So, as you may guess, we are no friends of the Emerald Order. We want nothing more than to see that group dismantled, their headquarters burned to the ground, and their leader in power no more. Dead or alive, I don't care. Although once I find out who exactly hurt my daughter, I'd like to bring them to justice personally." The ferocious glint in the king's eyes made me feel almost sorry for the person or persons responsible for the little girl's death. Almost.

"We want nothing more than to recover Prince Coran—safely—from the hands of the Emerald Order. If we have to do all that you want to befall the Emerald Order to make that happen, then we will. The prince's safety is our utmost concern."

King Addan gave me a long, measured look. "Queen Inari and I can no longer ignore the Emerald Order's actions, but they've grown too influential in Bomora and our position has become too weak for us to move against them. It's hard to unite the citizens of Bomora in anything, and the Emerald Order covered their tracks too well. They made it seem like Chancellor Tayend acted on his own, despite the fact that Jianne was found on the Order's property. Kidnapping the citizens of another kingdom—especially a royal heir—could be considered an act of war. And while we'd do our best to defend ourselves, Bomora has survived this long mostly by keeping to ourselves and staying out of the other kingdoms' notice."

He raised his hand toward me, palm up. "We were too late to save our Jianne. But you have our full support to save your Prince Coran." His face turned fierce. "And if you can bring down the Emerald Order while doing so, then you have only to name your reward, and if it is in our power to give, it is yours."

I grasped his extended hand, sealing the agreement between Bomora and Calia.

"All right, then." Releasing my hand, the king moved back around his desk and opened a drawer. "Let's discuss how you're going to infiltrate the Emerald Order's headquarters and put an end to them once and for all."

He rummaged around briefly, then pulled something out and held it up. A gold disc, a little larger than the coins I carried in my bag, glinted in the light streaming through the cabin window. A small hole had been drilled on one side so a worn leather cord could be threaded through it. Etched in the gold circle was a picture of a crown and a macaw, the symbol of a Bomorran pirate king. King Addan smiled proudly when he saw the shining royal symbol.

"Take this. There's someone you need to go see."

21

CHAPTER TWENTY-ONE

FARRAH AND I MADE our way through the twisty cobblestone streets of Bomora's capital. In the deepening twilight, the ramshackle buildings began to blend together, but I wasn't worried. Although it had been some time since I had wandered this city, I could still recall where most things were. Besides, Bomora hadn't changed much over the years.

Bomora wasn't as wealthy as its nearest neighbors. The magical kingdom of Calia in the north had always been a draw for visitors, and now, with its Academy of Magical Arts recently founded by Calia's Queen Jennica, those visitors were becoming permanent residents. Orchwell, to Bomora's east beyond the Hwisprian Woods, also attracted visitors who sought the services of one of the country's famed Seekers. The Seekers alone kept the country's coffers full, but there were some non-Seeker tradespeople who called Orchwell home. Even Rothschan, to the south, had more money to throw around than Bomora, although I always had the impression that their riches were due to their rulers' extreme frugality, with few exceptions. If anything, Rothschan's income went right into maintaining their impressive military.

Since Bomora mainly served as an outpost for the unwanted criminals of the Gifted Lands, most of its citizens were too busy hoarding their own wealth to want to share it with their kingdom. I suspected Bomora became a country only because the veneer of respectability that came with being an official kingdom helped turn scrutinizing eyes away from how Bomorrans really made their living.

Once Bomora organized itself into an actual kingdom, certain rules fell into place. The kingdom didn't have an official set of laws, but even thieves have some honor. One of the unspoken codes in the kingdom was in regards to who, exactly, one could rob. Since it was considered bad form to rob your neighbor, and Bomora bordered the Aentin Sea, most people turned to piracy.

Rulership usually went to the strongest person who could hold the throne, either through guile or bloodshed. Sometimes both. King Addan came from a line of Bomorran kings who had held the kingship for a surprisingly long time—at least several generations—solidifying his rule both by birthright and by strength.

And strength was something that Bomorrans respected. If you were strong enough and smart enough to take the throne, then in the eyes of a Bomorran citizen, you were worthy of their undying loyalty. Which is why the king's tale of Chancellor Tayend's betrayal particularly disturbed me. If his most trusted advisor was willing to betray him, and the death of their beloved child princess hadn't roused the country into finding and bringing Chancellor Tayend to justice, then it meant King Addan might be losing favor with his people.

All of this history and conjecture I quietly regaled Farrah with as we made our way through the city streets. I didn't want her blindsided again. And I needed to assuage my own guilt for not having given her warning earlier.

Farrah didn't interrupt, just nodded every so often as we walked. When I finished, she asked, "But if Bomorrans are so loyal to their rulers, then why wouldn't King Addan just go to the Emerald Order and burn it to the ground? Those who follow him would condone his actions, especially since the Crown Princess had been killed."

"The Emerald Order has been around for several years, and I'm guessing its roots are too deep now to be plucked out safely without breaking Bomora in two. They must be offering something that the Crown can't give the people." We turned down a side street that ended at a stone wall. A few rats scurried away at our approach.

"But what? What do you think it could be?"

I shrugged as my steps slowed. "I have no idea."

We stopped in front of a plain wooden door. Patches of the brown wood had faded from years of use and exposure to the elements, and the metal handle, while sturdy and serviceable, was worn smooth from constant use as well. Near the top of the door, about eye level, was a small indent where a knocker must have once hung.

"This is it."

Farrah frowned. "Are you sure?"

I surveyed the darkening alley, counting the doors we had passed before stopping at this one. "Five doors in. Yes, I'm sure. This is the place King Addan told us to go to."

"Okay, then." Now it was Farrah's turn to shrug, as she gave in to my judgment.

I just hoped my judgment was correct.

I rapped lightly on the worn door, around the spot of the missing knocker.

"Do you think he'll talk to us?" Farrah asked while we waited for someone to open the door. "After all, he doesn't know we're coming."

"I hope so," I said. "We don't have many other leads to go on."

We heard an inside bolt unlock, and then the door slid open a crack. A suspicious eye peered out at us. A man's crotchety voice sounded from somewhere below the eye. "Whaddya want?"

"We're looking for Yorath Flynton," I said.

"Oh, yeah? And who's 'we'?"

"I'm Rhyss, and my friend here is Farrah."

"Never heard of either of you," the man spat out. "Now go away." He began to close the door.

I wedged my foot in between the door and the frame before he could shut it fully, ready to throw my full weight against the door to keep it open if need be. The man reacted quickly, pushing against the door, heedless of my poor, rapidly-getting-squished foot. Little pokes started peppering my foot and then my ankle; he was either kicking at my foot, trying to force it backward, or was jabbing at my foot with some unknown object.

From under my shirt, I fished out the small gold medallion that King Addan had given me. I dangled it from its leather cord at eye level with the mysterious man inside the building. The final bits of fading daylight caught the raised part of the disc, also catching his attention. He stopped his onslaught against the door and my foot. "Where did you get that?"

"You recognize this, then?"

"Where did you get it?" the man repeated, although his resigned tone told me he knew exactly where the necklace had come from.

"Can we come inside?" I glanced around the alley, uncomfortable with the surrounding darkness now that the sun had sunk below the wall at the end. "Our business isn't something we'd want curious ears to hear."

The man hesitated, but a second look at the medallion dangling from my hand decided him. "One moment." He looked down. "If you wouldn't mind?"

I removed my foot from the door, flexing it in its boot as I tested out movement. It was sore from the little altercation; there would definitely be bruises later. I grimaced, glad Farrah couldn't see my pain. She had offered some healing magic, if we had time. At the rate I was going, I would definitely have to make the time.

The man closed the door completely, and we heard a chain slide back. Then the door opened again, wider, and the man who I presumed to be Yorath Flynton stepped back and beckoned us inside.

I slipped inside, Farrah right on my heels. As she shut the door behind her, our curmudgeonly host said, "Lock it too, would ya?"

Farrah obliged. Both of us stood by the door, waiting for the man to give us more direction. We were in a small sitting room of sorts, with a fire crackling in the hearth across the room from us and two chairs and a low couch scattered in front of it. A staircase, half hidden in the shadow just out of reach of the firelight, yawned up to the house's second floor. A darkened doorway on our level hinted at other rooms beyond ours.

The man waved a gnarled hand at the chairs by the fireplace. "You're here now. You might as well sit."

Farrah and I exchanged glances, and then both moved toward the indicated seats. The man gave a satisfied grunt. "You want something to drink?"

Without waiting for an answer, he stumped toward the dark doorway. The sound of his uneven gait caught my attention; I noticed he walked with a pronounced limp, using a cane to support his weight. That cane must have been the source of the foot poking I had felt earlier. At the door, he leaned his cane against the door frame and walked heavily into the dark room. The sound of a match striking the wall sounded, and then a light appeared somewhere at head level; he must have lit a wall lamp. Farrah and I looked around the room while trying to politely ignore the mutterings and grunts from what must have been our host's kitchen. A slight clatter sounded, and Farrah started to rise.

"Can we help you with anything?" she called out.

A growl met her gesture of kindness. "You'll help more by staying out of my way."

Farrah sank back down, her mouth a thin line, her eyes flashing.

Eventually our host came back, moving slowly as he balanced a tea tray against his uneven walk. Our eyes met. "Don't you even think about it, young man. You stay right where you are."

I leaned back in my chair, palms up to show I wasn't going anywhere. The man made his way to where Farrah and I sat, putting the tray, with its ceramic teapot and cups, down heavily on a nearby table. The cups rattled a bit, and I reached out a hand to steady the tray, which I quickly drew back when the man scowled at me.

The man sank down on the couch, his energy clearly spent. Farrah leaned over and poured out three cups of tea for all of us, handing me one and silently holding one out to our host. She pretended not to notice his labored breathing, just waited until he had settled down a bit.

He took the cup and took a long sip. To pass the time, I sipped my tea as well. The sound of my signet ring clinking against the ceramic cup caught our host's attention, and he looked at my hand.

He snorted. "That's an interesting ring. I've seen some other people around town wearing the same kind of thing. Must be the fashion these days."

I held out my hand to him so he could see the ring better. "Really? Does everyone shop at the same jeweler's then?"

He took my outstretched hand and stared more closely at the signet ring. "Must be. Same cut, even the same cheap material." He rubbed his hand over the smooth, flat top of the ring. "I don't know why anyone would want to wear fake gold, or buy such a plain ring with no designs on it, but at least if it's fake and ugly, it keeps the thieves away."

He dropped my hand and took another sip of tea. Farrah gave us both an appraising look, but didn't comment.

The man sat back and turned his own shrewd gaze on us. "All right, Rhyss and Farrah who I've never heard of. What's your business with me?"

"I take it you are indeed Yorath Flynton, then?" I asked him.

"You don't see anyone else here, do you?" He sighed. "Yes, I'm Yorath."

"The Master Builder of Bomora," I stated, wanting confirmation.

He snorted. "That title means nothing anymore. I haven't designed anything for His Majesty since ..." His voice trailed off.

"Since the death of the princess?" Farrah said gently.

"Yes." His face was stone. "It was my fault, you understand? That little girl would still be alive if it hadn't been for me. The king was right to dismiss me."

"I don't understand," Farrah said. "King Addan said you could help us."

Yorath stared into his teacup as if it held all the secrets of the universe. When he looked up, unshed tears shone in his eyes. "You don't know what I used to do, do you, girl?"

Farrah eyed me, then Yorath. "King Addan told us you used to be Bomora's Master Builder, a position he appointed you to years ago, and that you would be the best person to talk to about infiltrating the Emerald Order's headquarters."

"Most of what the king told you is true," Yorath confirmed. "I did hold that position once, a long time ago. But the title 'Master Builder' is misleading. I didn't create the buildings in the city, but I enhanced them."

"Enhanced them?"

"Many of our important buildings needed deterrents against thieves or assassins. This is Bomora, after all. If you were lucky—or perhaps unlucky—you might find secret passages to get you from one place to another quickly and quietly; traps to make you want to turn back or stop you in your tracks, depending on how stubborn you were; hidden rooms to keep you safe, your family safe, your treasure safe—or provide a convenient place to stick an intruder so they'd never be found again. And those were just the basic designs. That was what I did, my dear. I designed those extra features, for the right amount of coin or clout. And I was very good at my job."

Farrah said, "The king said you could help us. Can you, then?"

He didn't answer her question, instead pointing a gnarled finger at me. No, not me. My necklace. "May I?"

I pulled the leather cord from around my neck and handed him the medallion. He turned it around and around in his hands, rubbing the pads of his fingers over the raised symbol. He sighed. "Perhaps I was too good at what I did."

Now that he had begun talking, his words tumbled over each other, like a dam finally bursting. "King Addan paid me handsomely for my services, but he never begrudged me taking other, outside jobs. As long as I saved my best work for the royal family, it didn't matter to him. Besides, this is Bomora. A little bit of intrigue would be good for everyone, right? Kept you on your toes.

"But I got prideful. I was the best in the land, and I knew the secrets of every trap, every puzzle. So when the Emerald Order wanted me to design their headquarters, I accepted the challenge. And I outdid myself. The building was practically impenetrable. But it was fine, it didn't matter, because—along with my patrons—I would know how to get past every defense. So I didn't mention this special commission to the king.

"Except that, the day the work was completed, the Emerald Order ... detained me in their new fortress. And wiped my memory with their cursed magic. I still didn't think it mattered, except then they stole the princess and King Addan and Queen Inari tried to rescue her, nearly losing their lives in the process. In the wake of grieving their dead daughter, I had to tell them what I had done ... and King Addan rightfully stripped me of my title and banished me from his presence."

A tear slipped down Yorath's face. "I don't blame him. I loved the little princess like she was my own daughter. She was such a sweet little thing. I grieved her death as well. I'm lucky that the king didn't do more to me. He could have called for my execution. For years I couldn't sleep, I'd jump at every shadow. I was convinced he had sent an assassin after me."

He looked around at his shabby abode, then down at his mangled leg. "Sometimes I wish he had."

Silently, I handed Yorath a crumpled handkerchief from my pocket. He wiped his eyes, sniffling.

"So if you designed the secrets within the Emerald Order's head-quarters, then you can help us," Farrah insisted gently.

Yorath shook his head. The tea in his cup threatened to slosh over the edge with the movement. "No, I can't. The Emerald Order erased my memories, remember?"

"What about the people who helped build the traps?"

"They were either members of the Order who were spelled to secrecy, or they are dead." The flatness of his voice warned us from pursuing that matter more.

After the silence grew unbearable, I said, "Do you have a map of the building, diagrams of the traps, anything?"

Yorath shook his head. "My maps, my drawings, are in the Emerald Order's possession. Part of our deal included that I turn those over to them. They paid me quite a bit for that privilege, as I have always kept my creative materials."

"Oh." I couldn't hide the disappointment in my voice. Why would King Addan send us to this man, a complete dead end?

Farrah's face reflected my thoughts. Carefully, she put her barely touched teacup down on the tray and started to rise. "Thank you for your time, Master Flynton. It's getting late, and we won't take up any more of your time—"

Yorath waved the medallion at Farrah, then at me. "Sit down, young lady. I didn't finish."

"But you just said—"

"I said that I no longer have my exact maps and drawings of my creations for the Emerald Order's headquarters. But I've been designing these hidden features for a long time, remember. They didn't confiscate everything, just the items directly related to them. All the things I designed for them had a basis in something else I had created before."

He placed his teacup back on the tray, and motioned toward his cane, still leaning against the wall leading to the kitchen. "Could one of you be a dear and hand that to me?"

I jumped up and grabbed the cane, handing it to its owner. Yorath got up, a bit wobbly, and moved toward a bookshelf lining one wall, shoving the king's medallion in his pocket as he did so.

"Now, where did I ...?" He muttered under his breath while he perused the various book spines. He ran the fingers of his right hand over the dusty books while leaning heavily on his cane with his left. His questing fingers stopped at a volume I couldn't quite see from where I was sitting. "Ah, here it is."

He pulled out a plain brown leather journal and blew across the top of it, sneezing at the dust that flew off. Mumbling something about needing to hire a housekeeper, he stumped back to his seat and opened the book. He looked carefully at one page, frowning in thought, before thumbing to the next one and studying that page with equal gravity.

I tried not to be too obvious as I slightly craned my neck to see what it was Yorath was poring over. I could see penciled drawings, with notes scribbled in the margins, and arrows highlighting various points of interest. I couldn't quite make out what exactly the drawings were of, or what the notes said, but I realized that the book in Yorath's hands was some sort of reference. Perhaps an early journal of his work?

Yorath turned another page and studied the drawing on it. A smile broke out on his face. "Ah! Here's one of them!"

He turned the book around to show us what he had found. It still looked like random scribbling to me, but from the enormous grin on Yorath's otherwise surly face, whatever he was showing us was something important.

"Is this one of the traps at the Order's building, then?" Farrah asked, her own face lit up in response to Yorath's smile. "Can you tell us where exactly this is, and what we need to do to get by it?"

Yorath's face fell a little. "I can give you some idea, yes. But it won't be completely accurate. Every trap, every passageway I designed for the Emerald Order was based on an older design, but I had tweaked or enhanced things for them, and the notes on those changes were confiscated. I only know that this is one of the Order traps because of this."

He pointed at a mark he had made in the bottom right hand corner of the page. "I had marked the designs I wanted to use in this, my original workbook. And then I had copied out the pages into a different journal, along with the changes. It's that second journal that the Emerald Order took from me. So while these might not be the most up-to-date designs, it should at least give you an idea of what you will encounter."

"Some knowledge is better than no knowledge," I said, and Farrah nodded her agreement.

Yorath smiled a little at our encouragement.

"I'll always blame myself for how I made this whole wretched affair come about. But you two give me hope; perhaps you can right the wrongs I so foolishly made years ago. Pull your chairs up to either side of me so I can explain these diagrams to you. While my mind is on fire at the thought that finally the Emerald Order will get what it deserves, my poor old bones can't take the excitement."

22

CHAPTER TWENTY-TWO

YORATH, FARRAH, AND I spent the next few hours poring over the delicate, yellowed pages of the journal. Yorath detailed each trap for us, making our heads spin with the myriad of ways a person could get lost, disoriented, or die in one of his secret passages or hidden aspects. Spending some of my formative years in Bomora, I had heard of some of these devices, but fortunately had never found myself the victim of their design. I found it fascinating to learn about this intriguing but somewhat sick history of my home country. Farrah found it interesting as well, declaring at one point that she would probably never trust a Bomorran building again.

At one point, Yorath said, "I never did ask. What is it you're wanting to do, once you get in the Order's headquarters?"

I told him about Prince Coran's kidnapping. Yorath merely responded, "Ah." His eyes grew misty, and I wondered if he was thinking about poor Princess Jianne.

Evening had already been approaching when we had called upon Yorath. By the time we were done going over his journal—and listening to his stories of how he created the traps, and his tales of the unfortunates who found themselves in them—it was near midnight.

When the stories finally wound down, Yorath graciously offered to let us stay for the night, rather than have us risk trying to find a room at an inn at such late notice (and possibly getting pickpocketed or worse for being on the streets so late at night). Gratefully, Farrah and I accepted his offer.

Yorath pointed up the stairs with his cane, saying, "You'll have your pick of two rooms up there. They should be fairly fresh—I have a lady who comes every other week to give the place a thorough cleaning. It's a bit of a luxury for me, but it's not as easy as it used to be for me to get around." He shook his cane for emphasis. "Anyway, have a good night, you two, and I'll see you in the morning."

"But what about you?" Farrah asked. "Isn't one of those bedrooms yours?"

Yorath shook his head. "Used to be. Not anymore. These days I just sleep down here instead of trying to get up and down those stairs. I've got bedding in the corner, there." At the foot of one of the bookshelves, I noticed a large wicker basket full of neatly folded linens, with a pillow placed on top to one side.

Over our host's protests, I picked up the tea tray, now full of empty, dirty dishes, and headed to the kitchen. We had drunk the pot dry and gone back multiple times for more. Farrah hastily followed me, calling up a light spell as she went so we didn't need to bother lighting the wall lamp.

After we cleaned the dishes, Farrah and I made our way upstairs while Yorath banked the fire and made himself comfortable on the couch. Farrah's spell light accompanied us, illuminating the hallway just enough for us to see the doorways to our two rooms.

Farrah stayed long enough for me to find a candle on the bedside table and light it, then she continued on to the next room. In the dim light, I could see normal bedroom furniture—a bed, the nightstand where I had found the candle, a dresser on the wall opposite the bed. And above the dresser, a medium-sized picture hung.

I held the candle closer to the picture, curious. It was a painting of a group of three people—a man, a woman, and a dark-haired young girl, who looked to be in her mid-teens. I didn't recognize the woman or the girl, but the man looked like a younger—and happier—version of Yorath. But he hadn't mentioned a family of his own, and no one else was in the house but him.

I wondered at the story the painting hinted at. Settling into the bed, I blew out the candle. The last thing my eyes saw before the darkness hit them were the watchful eyes of the trio across the room.

I awoke early the next morning, partly because I hadn't drawn the curtain shut before I went to sleep, so the sun poured into my room—and on my bed—at full blast. And also because as soon as it was light out, Farrah was knocking politely but insistently at my bedroom door.

Groaning, I called out, "Give me a moment, would you?"

The knocking stopped. For maybe a minute or two. Then, when I apparently hadn't moved fast enough to suit Farrah, it started up again.

"Ugh. Hold on."

I tumbled out of bed, yawning and stretching as I moved toward the closed door. I yanked open the door, interrupting Farrah mid-knock.

"Aren't you dressed yet?" she asked me.

"Good morning to you too," I grumbled. "No. I just woke up. How would I have time to get ready?"

"You've had so much time," Farrah insisted. "I've been awake for hours." At my raised eyebrows, she amended, "Well, not hours. But for long enough that I'm dressed and ready to go."

"Some of us aren't morning people."

"Some of us can see that." She giggled. "You should see your hair."

I groaned again, running my hand through it. "How bad is it?"

Her grin grew wider as she chuckled. "It's pretty bad. It looks like a—"

She stopped mid-sentence, frowning at me. "What happened to your arm?"

"What? What do you mean?"

Farrah pointed at my arm, which was halfway raised to smooth my hair down. "That. What happened?"

I glanced over at the spot on my right arm that she indicated. And silently cursed myself at my stupidity.

The long, loose sleeve of my shirt had fallen back, exposing my pale, freckled arm. Which had a mess of angry red vines growing on it, twisting around each other so that it looked like they were moving. The odd markings were too grotesque to be more freckles. As the magic slowly spread over me, I had gotten used to the dull pain and the constant itchiness to the point where I had nearly forgotten about the curse.

Until now, when Farrah discovered it.

It was now the second day since my encounter with the Heart of the Hwisprian Woods, and I was halfway to being completely cursed if I couldn't retrieve her magic from the Emerald Order. Her magical mark was slowly spreading across my body. Pretty soon I wouldn't be able to conceal it.

"Oh. Uh. I ..." I couldn't think of a plausible reason for why my normally smooth, unblemished skin suddenly sprouted an odd, body-length birthmark.

Farrah stepped closer to me, grabbing my arm and pulling it toward her.

"Ouch!" I protested, but she ignored me as she studied the markings.

"It's really nothing," I said, trying to pull my arm back. But she held on, a grim look on her face as she muttered under her breath. The red welts darkened and glowed dully. My skin felt prickly and hot. Farrah ran her fingers lightly up my arm, then gasped in pain and drew her hand back. The red glow brightened slightly, as if mocking her. Farrah looked down at her hand. A drop of blood had appeared on her fingertip, bright crimson against her ebony skin.

"Are you all right?" I asked Farrah. "Let me get something for that."

She let go of my arm then, and I turned away to rummage in my pack, which I had tossed at the foot of the bed last night. Although I knew Farrah was hurt, I took a little longer than necessary to search for bandages and some salve, taking the time to surreptitiously check out the slowly-growing curse vines on my skin.

Whatever magic Farrah had done had no effect on the magic taking over my body. The glow had faded, and the earlier itchiness was gone too. I flexed my fingers, noting that fairly soon even my shirt sleeves wouldn't be able to cover the magic.

I grabbed the items for Farrah and straightened up, holding them out toward her. She waved away the salve, taking only the cloth and blotting her finger with it. "It barely hurts, now. It will probably stop bleeding soon. It's not very deep."

Now that that was taken care of, she unfortunately turned her full attention back to me. "So, answer me. What is that?"

I briefly debated coming up with some random reason for the markings on my skin—sunburn? a new tattoo?—but knew she would see through that immediately. This was Farrah, after all. One of my oldest and closest friends. Besides, the last thing I wanted was Farrah mad at me.

I sighed. "That night in the Hwisprian Woods, when you thought you saw something and I went to investigate? Well, I found the creature you saw." I described the encounter I had had with the Heart of the Woods, including the geas she had placed upon me. I finished with, "At least I still have two days left, including today."

Farrah frowned. "Two days is hardly any time at all. The time will be gone before we know it. And we're wasting what's left of it. Get ready, get your stuff, and let's get going." She turned toward the door.

"That's it?" I said in disbelief.

She turned back to face me. "What's it?"

"That's all you're going to say about it?" I had braced myself for her to scold me, lecture me, something. Her non-response was more unnerving than if she had outright yelled at me.

She shrugged, but I could see the hurt in her eyes. "It happened. There's not much I can do about it now. You made a promise. We need to make sure you keep it." She turned away again, starting to walk out the half-open bedroom door.

"Farrah."

She stopped in the doorway, her back stiff, but she didn't look back at me. "I wish you would have told me. I would have trusted you with this, in a heartbeat. You're one of my dearest friends. I guess ... I guess I thought I was one of yours, as well."

She left before I could recover fast enough to respond, closing the door behind her with a quiet click that echoed loudly in my ears with its finality.

23

—·—

CHAPTER TWENTY-THREE

FEELING SUBDUED, I QUICKLY got ready for the day. Grabbing my bag, I hurried downstairs, where Yorath and Farrah were already eating breakfast in the kitchen.

Yorath's original surly demeanor had disappeared. When I entered the room, he was waving his arms about, regaling Farrah with some story about a disastrous test with one of his creations.

"... And I had distinctly told them, it wasn't finished! Yes, you could spring the trap. But you couldn't reset it! So until it was completed, no one was to go in that room!"

Farrah laughed. "So what happened to the men who were caught up in it? Were you able to get them out?"

Yorath snorted. "Eventually. But with five of them in there, they were definitely cramped. I was of half a mind to leave them in there for a while, to make sure they had learned their lesson about listening to me. But I knew they'd run out of air fast, with so many of them trapped together. So I had to get things figured out quickly. But let me tell you, I'm not sure who was crankier when they finally got out—them, or me!"

During Yorath's story, I had grabbed some bread and cheese from an open cupboard and sat down at the table with him and Farrah.

There was a jug of watered-down wine on the table, and I reached for it, narrowly missing one of Yorath's enthusiastic arms flailing at me. I poured myself some wine and took a long sip, eyeing my companions.

Yorath was happy to have an attentive audience, and Farrah seemed genuinely interested in his story. But I noticed she also carefully avoided looking my way, other than a brief flicker of acknowledgement when I sat down, and her laughter seemed a little too ready, a little too bright.

I sighed inwardly, wondering what I could do to make things better between us. Over our long friendship, we'd had plenty of disagreements, but they usually ended quickly, with an eye roll from Farrah and earnest apologies from all involved. For Farrah to barely acknowledge me ... I could feel the hurt still radiating from her.

Farrah laughed again as Yorath's tale ended. "Are you sure you don't want to come with us? It would be much easier to get through the Emerald Order's headquarters if we had you to release us from any traps that we accidentally set off."

At Farrah's mirth, Yorath smiled. "Ah, you remind me so much of my own Elaina. If my body would cooperate, I would gladly go with you, my dear, to provide what poor assistance as I may."

"Elaina?" Farrah asked.

Yorath's smile faded slightly. "My daughter. Lost to me many years ago. Like so many others, seduced away by the Emerald Order. I ... I took the job at their headquarters in part to try to get in touch with her. But she didn't want anything to do with me. My poor wife died of heartbreak shortly after that."

"I'm sorry," Farrah said gently. I murmured similar condolences.

Yorath shook his head, as if to rid himself of unpleasant memories. His eyes turned fierce. "If you find my Elaina, please ... tell her I miss her. Persuade her to come home."

"We'll do our best," I said, reluctant to promise what seemed impossible.

"That's all I can hope for." He tugged at a finger on one of his wizened hands, pulling off a small gold ring and handing it to me.

"Oh, no, we can't take this," I said, gently pushing his outstretched hand back.

"It's not payment, young man," Yorath said. "It's a family heirloom, my late wife's wedding ring. Should you come across my Elaina, hopefully she'll still recognize it, and then she'll know you and your message came from me."

I nodded as I reluctantly took the ring and placed it on my hand. A delicate band of gold with vines entwined around it, the little ring just fit on my pinky finger. My hand was getting crowded now, what with the rings of Yorath's wife and Aela's husband gracing it.

I stared harder at my hand. Speaking of vines … the magic vines of the Heart's curse had snaked down to cover most of my hand and part of my fingers. Dismayed, I looked at my other hand, only to find the same thing happening to that one as well.

"It's a lovely ring," Farrah was saying. "And I'm sure you don't want to be without it longer than you have to. We'll get it back to you, somehow."

"I appreciate that, young lady," Yorath said. "That's all I have left of my wife, now. It may be considered a bit old-fashioned, but when she died, I buried her with my wedding ring, and took hers, as is Bomorran custom."

"Oh, that's so sweet," Farrah said. "I don't think that's an old-fashioned custom at all."

Yorath patted her hand. "Thank you, my dear. I hope one day you find yourself someone who's worthy enough to partake in that custom with you."

Farrah blushed. I glanced between her and Yorath, but Farrah studiously avoided meeting my eyes. I sighed inwardly, again. Apparently she was still mad at me.

Yorath pushed back from the table. "Ah, well. As much as I'd love to keep boring you with my stories, I know you have things to do, an Order to infiltrate, and all that."

He grabbed his cane from where it was propped against the table, and stood up. He waved a hand at the table and the larder. "Just leave the dishes there. I'll clean them later. Help yourselves to whatever you need."

He stumped out, leaving Farrah and me sitting awkwardly at the table. Farrah got up and busied herself collecting the dirty dishes. I jumped up from my seat as well, intercepting Farrah before she could reach the bucket of water in the corner. Over her protests, I took the pile of dishes from her arms.

She tried to take the dishes back. "Get ready to go. It won't take me long to do these."

"I'm happy to help," I insisted, keeping them out of her reach.

She rolled her eyes at me and let me have the dishes. "Fine." She turned away, finding a rag to wipe down the table.

I smiled, happy to see some Farrah-like behavior at last. I dumped the dishes in the bucket and quickly cleaned them. By the time I was done washing and drying, Farrah had finished her task and had pulled a few rolls of bread and some cheese from Yorath's pantry. Wrapping them in a clean cloth, she said, "It was generous of Yorath to offer us this. I don't want to take too much from him."

"I think that's good enough," I said, eyeing the neat little bundle in Farrah's hands. "Farrah, about earlier. I'm sorry I—"

She cut me off. "It's fine. I don't want to talk about it anymore."

I blinked. "Really? But—"

She looked at my hands pointedly. "I mean, we'll probably have to discuss it again, eventually. But for now, I think we're better off if we just focus on what we came here to do."

"But, Farrah—"

She turned on her heel and left. Cursing under my breath, I dropped the damp linen towel I was holding and followed after her.

In the main room of Yorath's house, she was hugging our host warmly. "Thank you for everything. The information you've given us is invaluable."

Yorath pulled away from Farrah's embrace, studying her at arm's length. "It's too late for the princess, and most likely too late for my daughter. I only hope it's not too late for your little boy."

"I hope so too. Goodbye, Yorath." Farrah opened the door and stepped outside.

I shook Yorath's hand. "I'd like to add my thanks to Farrah's."

"Get your young prince out of there and away from the Emerald Order, that's thanks enough." His eyes twinkled as he looked between Farrah and me. Lowering his voice, he added, "And take good care of your young lady there. She's got spirit, same as my wife did."

I colored, feeling the blush spread instantly all over my face and neck. "Oh, uh, Farrah's not ... I'm not ..." I quickly changed the subject to cover my embarrassment. "Uh ... do you need us to bring that medallion back to King Addan?"

Yorath pulled the necklace in question from his pocket and held it up to the light. "Thank you for the offer, young man, but it's all right. I think I'm long overdue for a visit to my liege ... and an old friend."

"I think that's an excellent idea."

Farrah stuck her head back in through the still-open door. "Rhyss, are you ready to go? The day's wasting."

"Yes, of course." I hurried through the door, Yorath following at a slower pace behind me. With a last chorus of "thank you," Farrah and I waved at our host and turned to go.

Yorath called out to our retreating backs before shutting the door. "Remember what I said, young man!"

I could feel the color heating up my cheeks again. Farrah eyed me curiously. "What is he talking about?"

"Nothing," I muttered. "We should hurry."

We quickened our pace, and for a while walked in—well, not quite companionable silence. I could sense Farrah was still upset with me. But as we walked, the earlier edge of our argument wore off a bit, and we were nearly ourselves with each other again. Not quite comfortable, but close.

Locating the Emerald Order's headquarters was the easy part of our short journey. Bomora's capital wasn't very big, compared to the capital cities of the other kingdoms in the Gifted Lands. Aside from the Bomorran palace, the place the Order had chosen for their own was the next prominent building in the area.

Soon Farrah and I were standing in front of the Order's headquarters. While it was larger than most of the other buildings in the area, it wasn't ostentatious by any means. Anything fancy—be it buildings, people, or things—tended to scream "easy target" to the citizens of Bomora and didn't stay intact for long. Still, there was something dark that lingered about the unobtrusive yet imposing structure before us.

Farrah looked around. "That was ... remarkably easy to find."

"It's by design," I said. "The building may be easy to find, but it's hard to get into. Unless you're part of the Emerald Order."

Farrah grabbed my left hand and held it up. The Emerald Order signet ring glinted in the morning light. Although I was fairly sure she couldn't see it, the snake-and-butterfly symbol on my ring matched perfectly with the symbol on the door in front of us.

"Good thing you're one of them, then. Ready?" Farrah asked.

I took a deep breath. "Guess I'll have to be."

24

CHAPTER TWENTY-FOUR

FOR A FEW MOMENTS, I just stared at the door. It might have been a trick of the light, or the sleep I was still trying to shake off, but I could have sworn the animals depicted on the door started to move. The butterfly, its fragile wings flapping furiously, flitted about, trying to get away from the snake. But the snake stretched its long neck out, mouth wide, fangs bared as it reached toward it....

Even though I knew the inevitable ending, I couldn't help but hope that the butterfly would escape its potential captor this time.

As I stared at the slowly moving image on the door, the ring on my index finger began to tingle slightly. I glanced down, seeing the same image, mirrored on my signet ring, also begin to move.

A sharp poke in my side broke my reverie.

"Hey," Farrah said in a low voice. "What should we do? Knock on the door? Or maybe try to find a back entrance?"

"I'm not sure," I answered honestly. "They probably have all sorts of magical systems set in place to let them know people are coming. My guess is they already know we're here, so even if we left and tried to find another way in, they'd be warned."

"I guess it's the direct approach, then."

I nodded at Farrah's words, and knocked on the door. We waited several moments, but no one opened the door, or even spoke to us through it.

At a loss, I looked at Farrah.

"Now what?" I wondered. "Should we look for that alternate way in?"

She stared back at me, a smirk twitching at her lips. "Have you tried just opening it?"

"Oh, honestly," I said. Even as I spoke, I reached out to put my hand—the left one, bearing the Emerald Order's and Yorath's rings—on the door's heavy brass handle. It was locked. "I doubt that the door would just open—hey!"

When my beringed hand closed around the door handle, I felt a jolt in my finger, which quickly spread through my hand and part way up my arm. I jerked my hand back, flexing my fingers to rid myself of the shock.

"What? What happened?" Farrah asked.

Still shaking my hand, I said, "I got shocked by the door handle when I touched it."

"Really?" Cautiously, Farrah reached out an experimental finger. The pad of her index finger touched the metal, but she didn't react or cry out. "Huh. I don't feel a thing."

"Lucky," I grumbled. The shocking sensation had finally faded from my hand, leaving me grumpy. "Well, we tried. Now for Plan B."

"Why? Plan A seems to be working just fine," Farrah said. She indicated the door. "It's open."

"You sure?" I frowned. "It was locked when I tried it."

She pushed at the door. It cracked open a little. "See?"

"How did that happen?" I wondered. "I know it was locked."

Farrah studied my hand thoughtfully. No, not my hand. The ring of the Emerald Order that gleamed on my left index finger. "I think that shock you felt was the door recognizing you as one of the Order. That must be what unlocked it."

"You'd think Aela would have mentioned it," I said, referring to the ring's former owner.

"It's possible she didn't know," Farrah pointed out. "Or maybe she just forgot. She and her daughter had a lot of other things to worry about when we met them. Anyway, shall we?"

I sighed and pushed the door open further. Now that it had recognized me as a member of the Emerald Order, it swung open at my touch easily. I stepped inside warily, Farrah on my heels.

We stood in the lavishly appointed grand foyer of the Order's headquarters. Although it was early morning, the room was brightly lit by several sconces along the walls, as well as an impressive hearth burning directly in front of us. Two polished hardwood staircases lined either side of the hearth, curving upwards into a darkened second story. Above the fireplace was a large, gilt-framed painting of a man with striking green eyes. A bright emerald green cloak, a compliment to his equally bright eyes, was fastened around his neck and draped partway down his body, fading into the edges of the painting.

This must be Lord Indwere, the Emerald Order's founder, I mused. And then, *If my eyes were that shade, I'd wear green all the time too.*

And apparently it wasn't just Lord Indwere who favored the color green. Everything about this place was decorated in various shades of green, from the heavy velvet curtains that had been drawn to keep out the daylight, to the small fabric settee in front of the hearth. Even the lit wall sconces were some odd shade of green—I guessed they were made of copper that had developed a patina over time. The whole foyer made me feel like I was in some sort of artificial forest.

"Will you look at this place," Farrah murmured.

"You can't say they don't like nature," I whispered back.

We stood in the foyer for a few moments, wondering where to go or if anyone was going to come out and greet us. King Addan and Yorath may have warned us about traps, but none of us had counted on my ring being the key to unlock the front door. Thinking back, I was surprised Enlar hadn't mentioned it, but maybe he had thought it wasn't important since at the time none of us possessed a signet ring.

Although the time ticked by and we remained alone in the foyer, I had the distinct sense that we were being watched.

"Well, let's get going, then," I said eventually. I started toward the left hand staircase.

The instant I put my hand on the polished wood railing, the room began to turn gray and misty around us. The banister dissolved under my hand, and no matter which way I felt around me, I couldn't touch any part of the grand foyer we had just been in.

"Rhyss?" Farrah called out as the mist grew thicker.

"I'm here, just in front of you."

I felt her hand tap me lightly on my upper arm, and then it slid down and gripped my hand tightly.

The gray mist grew paler, becoming a bright white fog that pierced my eyes until I thought I must be going blind. The only sensation I was sure of was the feel of Farrah's soft hand in mine, and I held onto that feeling as tightly as I held on to her hand.

The white fog suddenly vanished, replaced by a suffocating pitch black.

"Rhyss?" I heard Farrah whisper somewhere behind me. Her hand still gripped mine.

"I'm still here," I said. But I couldn't see anything. Maybe the fog really had rendered me blind. "Except I don't know where *here* is."

"You and me both. *Illumine.*" Farrah spoke the words of the basic spell to conjure light, but nothing happened. "*Illumine.*" Still nothing. When she spoke again, her normally calm and steady voice sounded small and uncertain. "There must be wards on the place to not allow magic. But I don't know how else we'll figure out where we are."

"Why don't you just keep holding on to my hand, and reach out with your other one, see what's there? Just keep moving until you can't anymore. And if you need me to move too, just tug on me in the direction you want me to go, and I'll follow."

"That's a good idea. I'm afraid if I let go of you, I won't be able to find you again."

"Just go slowly, please."

"Slowly, so you don't trip on anything." Even in the darkness, I could sense Farrah's smirk.

"I hardly doubt the Order dumped us into a storage room," I said dryly.

A slight pull on my arm let me know that Farrah was moving further to her right. "You never know." Her glib attitude belied her nerves; her hand in mine was cold.

I took a few cautious steps to my right with her as she explored the room. It wasn't long before she said, "Hey! There's something here."

"What is it?" I waited impatiently while she carefully made an assessment.

"I think it's a wall. Brick, from the feel of it." She pulled me closer to her, putting my outstretched hand on the same material she had found.

My free hand met an uneven roughness. "I think you're right." I ran my hand up and down, side to side. "I wonder how far it goes?"

"Well, there's only one way to find out," Farrah said. "I'll go right, you go left?"

"Sounds good to me."

Heading left, I ran my hand lightly over the brick wall. Counting my steps, I estimated I had taken about seven or eight steps before I reached a corner. "Farrah!" I called out. "I've reached the end of this wall already."

From a little further away, Farrah said, "Same for me."

I kept going left, counting about fourteen or so paces before I reached yet another corner. Farrah and I would occasionally call out to each other, partly to share what we had found, but mostly I think so we didn't feel so alone in this unending blackness.

I was so busy counting steps that I forgot to keep track of how many corners I had turned, and walked right into Farrah, who was also mumbling numbers under her breath as she counted her own steps.

"Ouch!" she said, then added sarcastically, "Thanks for giving me warning."

"Sorry about that." I rubbed my arm where she had mashed it into the brick when we bumped into each other. "I didn't realize it was such a small area."

"Small room," she corrected. "Within the Emerald Order's domain. Unless you think they transported us somewhere else?"

"I doubt it. The Order doesn't strike me as the kind of group that would want to get rid of their problems by putting them far away. They'd want to keep them near and deal with them directly."

I heard Farrah sigh. "This must be the first of Yorath's trap rooms, then. He did say something about 'a convenient place to stick an intruder so they'd never be found again.' And there's no doors or windows that we could find, and no light to see if there's any trap doors or things like that. Very convenient. But if this is where they send people right away, why bother creating other traps? This place alone would do the trick. No need for other rooms."

She sighed again. "Unless you found something?" Her tone told me she thought that highly unlikely.

"I didn't come across anything when I was searching on my end."

"That's exactly my point. So, then—"

"I mean, there's nothing else in this room. If this was one of Yorath's rooms, then wouldn't there be ... um ... you know ..."

Farrah's exasperation radiated off her, even though I couldn't see her expression in the dark. "No, what?"

"Well, you know. There should be bodies, or bones, or something around here. But it's empty, except for us."

She snorted. "Maybe they like to keep this room exceptionally clean."

I sighed. "I guess we'll just have to search again, then. Why don't you—"

But before I could finish my thought, we heard a grinding sound. The wall across from us started to slide slowly to one side.

"Did you find a switch or something?" Farrah asked, confused.

"No." My voice came out equally confused. "I thought maybe you did."

As the doorway opened wider, a bright light from beyond it shone into the room. I blinked rapidly, temporarily blinded—after being in total darkness, my eyes couldn't adjust that fast.

My vision finally came back. I blinked again, sure I was imagining things.

The person who—I presumed—was responsible for our unexpected freedom stood in the opening, silhouetted by the light. They stepped forward, solidifying into the form of a young woman with long, straight dark hair and an open, intelligent face.

She frowned as she looked at Farrah and me. "Well? Are you coming? Or would you prefer to stay here?"

"Who are you?" Farrah asked warily.

"I think I should be asking you that first, as you are the newcomers here."

"That's fair," Farrah conceded. "My name is Farrah, and this is Rhyss."

"Well met, Farrah and Rhyss. I am Elaina Flynton."

25

CHAPTER TWENTY-FIVE

MY MOUTH DROPPED OPEN. Next to me, Farrah wore a similar expression of disbelief.

I thought there had been something slightly familiar in the way the woman spoke, her vocal inflections similar to Yorath's, except in a younger, higher tone. And she did look like an older version of the picture of Elaina I had seen in Yorath's house.

And Yorath had mentioned his estranged daughter was part of the Emerald Order.

But still—it seemed extremely convenient for her to just appear, right when we needed help.

Elaina ignored our lack of manners and said, "Come along, then."

She turned on her heel and started to walk away. Farrah and I exchanged a quick glance, then hurried after her.

The bright light that had blinded me earlier dimmed into several burning torches perched high along the dirt-and-rock walls of the strange cavern we found ourselves in. Four passages branched off from the room we were in.

Behind us, the door to our dark cell slid shut. Startled, I stopped walking and whipped around to stare at the nearly seamless door. Farrah stopped and looked back as well. Seeing that we had both stopped following, Elaina stood in the center of the cavern impatiently, arms crossed as she regarded us.

"What was that?" I asked, indicating the room we had just left.

"An oubliette," Elaina said.

I frowned. "An oubliette? But I thought—"

"That they'd fallen out of fashion? Hardly."

But that's where you're wrong, I thought, remembering our hours-long conversation with Yorath the previous night. However, I knew better than to say that aloud to Elaina, who was still an unknown element. Oubliettes *had* fallen out of fashion in the other kingdoms of the Gifted Lands at least a century ago; if a palace was old enough to have one, the archaic room had most likely been boarded up or converted. Or forgotten completely—which was the point of an oubliette, anyway. Very rarely did any other building besides a palace have one—they just weren't rooms considered necessary to a noble's home or a merchant's business.

Although Yorath had warned us he had designed several around Bomora. And when we had fallen into it from the Order's fake foyer, Farrah had described our oubliette perfectly.

It was just—in all my traveling with Farrah and Beyan around the Gifted Lands, I had never heard of an oubliette that someone accessed by magic, instead of through a trapdoor.

There's a first time for everything. Unfortunately.

"Funny," Farrah said deliberately. Her next words could have been plucked straight from my thoughts. "Your father didn't mention anything about a magical oubliette. Or perhaps I assumed they were only accessed by mundane means."

Elaina stiffened. "You know my father?"

"A lovely man, once you get past the grumpiness."

Elaina didn't respond. Instead, she started walking again, toward one of the middle passages.

"Wait!" I called out. "Where are we, and where are we going? And why did you come for us?"

She stopped, turning slightly to call over her shoulder. "You're at the true entrance of the Emerald Order's headquarters. There's a timed spell on the foyer to transport any who enter to this place. Newcomers start in the oubliette until we can be certain of their identity. If we aren't, then ...." She shrugged, her casualness at those unfortunates' implied fate somehow more chilling than if she had said outright what happened to them.

She pointed at my ring. "That permits you entry to the true building. You may have found a way to enter without it, but you would never have left the oubliette if you didn't bear one of our rings. I am here to guide you. Now come."

Without waiting to see if we were following, she picked the second passage from the left and disappeared into the darkness.

"I don't like it," Farrah said in a low voice. "I can feel the magic oozing out of this place; they must have spent a fortune on something this elaborate. And then to maintain it?" She shook her head. "I can't even imagine the cost."

"So we're somewhere underground or just outside the building, and all roads will lead us there?" I looked at the passage Elaina had disappeared into. "Or just one road?"

"It's hard to know," Farrah said. "I think, since the time Yorath built some of the trap rooms for them, they've made changes. Many of them. There is much more here than he told us to expect." She looked around, frowning, her arms spread wide as she turned in a slow circle. "For one thing, he hadn't designed any magical traps. Just improved on his original, mundane designs."

"So, should we follow?" I pointed at Elaina's passage.

Farrah shook her head. "I don't trust her. It seems too convenient."

"I agree. So, which way?"

"Uh ... that way." Farrah pointed at the fourth passage, the farthest on the right, and we hurried down it.

The light from the main cavern behind us grew dimmer. Farrah opened her hand. "*Illumine.*" She smiled in satisfaction as a cool ball of silver light blossomed above her palm. "Glad to see that things are working as they should."

We continued on in silence for a while. Despite Farrah's magical light, the darkness of the dirt-and-rock passage around us felt oppressive, barely kept at bay by the bobbing spell ball.

The passage was just large enough that Farrah and I could walk side by side. I kept a wary eye out for anything that might remotely resemble a trap, but nothing seemed untoward. We kept moving forward.

Farrah stopped, frowning. "What was that?"

"What was what?" I looked around, but didn't see anything.

Farrah waved a hand behind her experimentally. "I felt something just now, while we were walking. Something very subtle—like we were stepping through a thin curtain or a cobweb or something."

I looked at where Farrah was waving her hand in the air. "I didn't feel anything, but since I can't use magic, that doesn't mean anything."

Farrah held up her spell light to the area we had just passed through. "I can't be sure ... but it looks like the air here shimmers just a little bit." She muttered a spell under her breath, putting her hand to the area she was examining. "I can't tell. Why can't I tell? If there is magic here, whoever created it must be a master magician. It's so subtle as to be nearly undetectable."

"What does it do?"

"I have no idea. If I can barely sense it, I can hardly analyze it." Her frown deepened as she studied the area. "I feel like I lost something."

I quickly took stock of myself. My pack was still tightly shut, secured against my back. My sword and dagger hung at my belt, and nothing had fallen out of my pockets. "I haven't lost anything. What did you lose?"

Farrah shivered, staring at the invisible barrier. "I'm not sure. Let's go."

She hurried away. I followed.

We walked on—faster than our original pace—in silence for a bit more. I could tell the unknown spell curtain bothered Farrah, but there wasn't much I could do to help. Talking about it would only highlight the fact that she couldn't comprehend it, which would just make her mad.

Instead, I said, "I wonder how long it will take Elaina to realize we aren't following her."

"I wonder what she'll do," Farrah said. "With three other passages to choose from, it might not be worth her time to come after us."

"Even if she does, we should be able to hear her coming. It's not like—"

A muted thump sounded somewhere in the passage behind us, followed by another set of footsteps. I stopped, as did Farrah.

"Did you hear that?" I whispered.

Farrah nodded. "Run, or fight?"

I quickly surveyed the surrounding passage. Ahead lay pure darkness—we had no way of knowing if the passage we were following would open into a larger area, or branch off. The passage itself provided no places to use as cover—or for us to hide.

Throwing my pack to one side where it would be out of the way, I drew my sword. "Have we ever run?"

Farrah grinned as she threw her bag to be with mine and sent her spell light to bob above our heads. It cast a weak glow several feet ahead of us as we turned to face whatever was coming our way. "It's not our style. Although, I do recall that one commission, involving that nest of earth dragons ..."

"It was one time! And it was one of our first jobs, if you recall that as well!"

She laughed, and then there was no more time for talking.

Our mysterious followers were upon us.

26

CHAPTER TWENTY-SIX

"OH MY GODS! IT'S *us*!"

That was the only warning I could give Farrah before my doppel-ganger swung his sword at me. My surprise at seeing my mirror image caused me to barely raise my own sword in time to deflect his blow.

It was uncanny, looking at—and fighting—myself. Or, I should say, a construct that looked like me. Matched in height, he—it?—had the same shock of red hair and smattering of freckles across its face and neck. It wore the same cream-colored linen shirt and dark brown trousers I was wearing, and I could even see the magical vines of the Heart of the Hwisprian Wood's fairy geas running down its arms and spreading over its hands.

My opponent lunged, but I dodged his attack, following with a strike of my own. He parried that easily and renewed his attack. I stared at his expressionless face, his eyes devoid of any spark of humanity. Somehow, that lack of feeling made him even more frightening to me. He was cold, as cold as the magic that had created him, with only one express purpose.

To kill me.

As we were evenly matched, our fighting had become fairly rote. Neither of us got a hit, but neither one of us backed down either. If anything, I'd most likely fall to my doppelganger; eventually my energy would flag, but he seemed to have unending stamina.

I noticed the tip of his tongue sticking out in the corner of his mouth, something I tended to do when I was concentrating on something. Funny how even his mannerisms were exactly mine. *Is that really how I look when I do that? I look so stupid....*

"Argh!"

While my thoughts had been wandering, my mirror image had gotten past my guard long enough to graze my upper arm with his sword. Pain bloomed immediately somewhere near my shoulder, and I hissed—partly at the pain, but mostly at my own stupidity. One more slip up, and he would skewer me without a second thought. My sword arm, already growing tired, now felt even weaker with my new injury.

A quick glance at Farrah told me she was having the same problem I was. Her dark forehead glistened with perspiration, and her wild eyes only grew more desperate as she shouted spell after spell. Locked in a magical battle with her doppelganger, she too could not outsmart or overpower her opponent. How would you be able to outthink your own self?

"This isn't working!" I called to Farrah.

"Tell me about it!" Frustration laced her voice as she held her hand out toward her mirror image. Purple light, just a few shades darker than Farrah's hair, lanced toward her opponent, bouncing harmlessly off a magical ward just in front of the Farrah construct.

"Now what?"

"What about—?"

I cut her off before she could voice the thought. Already I was slightly panicked, wondering if our copies would instinctively know our intent. "Yes! Let's do it!"

With a shout, Farrah quickly raised a ward of her own with her left hand, turning her right hand—with all its deadly magic—at my doppelganger. At the same time, I pulled my dagger and hurled it toward the Farrah doppelganger. The Farrah construct didn't react in time to change her partial ward to a full shield. My knife sliced through the air and lodged in her throat, effectively cutting off whatever spell she would have conjured. Blood spurted from the wound as she fell to her knees.

Meanwhile, the Rhyss construct turned at Farrah's shout. I felt his confusion more than saw it cross his face.

He took the full blast of her magical attack to the chest. Purple light washed over his upper body, then spread to cover him completely. His sense of confusion changed to alarm—well, as much alarm as a magical construct can feel—when he realized what was happening. But by then it was too late, not that he could have countered anything. Farrah's magic did its gruesome work on my doppelganger, seeping into his skin and then dissolving him in an explosion of purple sparks.

I ducked, expecting magical backlash, bits of exploding construct, or both. A few heartbeats later I straightened cautiously, amazed that neither had happened. I looked at where my opponent had been.

He had completely disappeared, as if he had never even existed.

I examined the area. Nothing. Even his sword, which had looked exactly like my own, was gone. I sighed in disappointment. My sword was a replica of the Sword of the First King, Calia's most prized historical treasure and a fine weapon. I would have enjoyed having two Swords of the First King, if just to confuse Queen Jennica and King Beyan.

The Farrah image had fallen over on her side, my dagger protruding from the bloody mess of her neck. As I reached over to grab it, the construct disappeared. I raised my knife to the spell light that still hovered above our heads. The blade looked like I had just pulled it from my belt—a shiny silver, free of any blood. While I was glad to be spared the tedious task of cleaning it, the fact that our two doppelgangers had vanished so easily—and bloodlessly—made me uneasy. They had definitely looked, moved, and fought like real people. And if they had slipped a blade in between my ribs or hurt Farrah with magic, that would have felt all too real as well.

Visibly shaken, Farrah stared at the spot where her other self had fallen. "I'm glad that worked. I was beginning to think this was going to be my last fight ever."

"Same here. I'm glad you and I were thinking the same thing."

She raised her eyes and gave me a wobbly smile. "When you've fought side-by-side with someone as much as we have, you develop an instinct about how to support each other. Good thing, too."

I nodded. "Definitely a good thing."

She started to say something else, then swayed on her feet. Instantly, I dropped my sword and sprang to her side, just catching her before she hit the hard ground.

I lowered her gently. "Farrah, are you okay?"

She groaned. "I will be, in a day or so, if I can get some rest. I think I expended too much magic in that fight. I'm so ... tired."

She closed her eyes. I froze in indecision, afraid of moving her, but also knowing that we couldn't stay here for too long. Who knew if more doppelgangers—or other things—would come from the darkness to attack us?

Light footsteps crunched from the direction of the passage entrance, igniting my fears. Quickly, I propped Farrah against the wall and grabbed my sword, moving in front of her to meet whatever was walking toward us.

A shadow emerged from the edge of the darkness. Coming closer, it solidified into the form of Elaina. And she looked angry.

"There you two are! Why didn't you follow me?" Without waiting for me to answer, she took in the scene and said, "And what happened to your friend, there?"

Before I could say anything, she answered her own question. "You passed through the veil and set off the trap, didn't you." Her pointed tone told me she already knew the answer.

"Farrah needs help. Healing, perhaps. Rest, definitely," I said.

Elaina snorted. "Well, she won't get either down here. She can rest for a little bit, and then we should get moving."

She leaned against the wall opposite from Farrah and stared at us. Figuring I might as well use the time wisely, I sat down next to Farrah to take a short break myself.

"How did you know where we were? And do you know what happened?" I asked Elaina.

She snorted again. "With the ruckus you two were making, it wasn't hard to figure out which passage you'd taken. Disarming the magical trap took some time, though. I had to do that first before I could come after you."

"You disarmed the trap?" I repeated hopefully.

"For myself," she clarified. "It's been awhile; I had nearly forgotten the proper spell to disable it. But I needed to make sure nothing nasty would eventually follow me while I was looking for you. I'm afraid I can't say the same for you two, though."

I shuddered. "So you mean more doppelgangers will be on the way?" I glanced down the dark passage, straining to see if anything else was coming toward us.

Elaina shrugged. "Eventually. The trap takes a bit of time to reset. And most people don't survive the first wave of magical constructs anyway. That's why I said your friend can't rest too long. We definitely want to be out of here before the second wave comes."

"But wouldn't the second wave just follow us out of this passage and into wherever we end up?"

"No. Once someone's cleared the passage proper, the magic stops creating doubles."

I vaguely remembered Yorath telling Farrah and me about a similar trap design, one that involved a mirror and one's own reflection stepping out with evil intent. But something like that would have been obvious; you could hardly ignore an oversized mirror in your path. Then I recalled Farrah's earlier statement: *I feel like I lost something.* That *something* must have been the magical veil pulling part of her essence from her to make a copy. I hadn't felt it, simply because as a non-magician, I don't sense it being used either. But the veil had obviously stolen part of me as well to create my duplicate.

I shuddered again. Yorath had said the Order had taken his designs and improved upon them. Unfortunately for Farrah and me, we had wandered right into one of those improved situations.

I looked at Farrah. The magical light she had conjured was still glowing above us, but dimmer now. She was keeping it going, just barely. Her breathing came shallowly, and I worried at even that little effort she was expending.

Elaina muttered a spell under her breath, and a ball of light appeared, brighter than the one currently floating in the air. "Save your strength," she said to Farrah.

Farrah's light immediately winked out. Maybe I was just being hopeful, but it seemed like she was breathing easier already.

Elaina studied Farrah. "A few moments more, and then we should go."

I nodded. Even though Farrah didn't acknowledge Elaina's words, I knew she was grateful for the additional time.

We fell into an uncomfortable silence. I tried to observe Elaina without being obvious. Then, from Elaina: "All right, ask your question."

I looked away, embarrassed at having been caught staring. "I don't have a question."

She raised an eyebrow. "You've already deceived me once, by abandoning my guidance and picking a deadly passage, forcing me to pursue you and give you assistance. Let's not add to your sins with more lies. What is it you want to know?"

Slowly, I said, "Well, as you know already, we met your father, Yorath—"

"—And you want to know why I chose the Order."

We stared at each other. She sighed.

"Fine. I'll tell you."

27

Chapter Twenty-Seven

"I DIDN'T LEAVE BECAUSE things at home were bad, or because I was bored and needed a change," Elaina began. "No, I joined the Order for the most cliché reason of all: I fell in love."

"Your father did say you were seduced by the Order," I said. "I assumed he meant it figuratively."

"In a way, he's right. Their promise of power definitely drew me in. But the bigger lure was Millan." She sighed. "We were classmates, and friends. I'd always had a thing for him. When I realized he felt the same way, it was the happiest day of my life.

"Although the Emerald Order had been established years before I had been born, by the time I was in my mid-teens, it had grown into the mighty entity it is today. And for a child of Bomora who wanted a sense of respectability and stability, it was extremely attractive."

I studied Elaina, who looked to be near my age. Perhaps a few years younger.

"I can imagine," I said. Bomora wasn't rich, compared to the other kingdoms in the Gifted Lands. Violent crimes were frowned upon, but thievery was practically a national pastime. There were a few respectable merchants, farmers, or other citizens who earned their money by lawful means, but if you wanted to earn an actual living, you learned from a young age the real route to making money. And it wasn't usually the honorable route.

"Can you?"

"Yes. I'm from Bomora, originally. Although my family moved when I was young, when I was thirteen or so."

"Ah." Elaina nodded. "Then you understand how it works here."

At my nod, she continued. "Millan's father was a woodworker, a craftsman who made furniture and did repairs. Beautiful work, but hardly enough to keep his family fed. So when the Order showed interest in Millan, not only was Millan eager to join, but his family practically pushed him into their arms. I was a bit more skeptical, but I decided to join the Order as well, mostly to keep an eye on Millan. And to be with him."

She sighed. "Over the years, Millan became more entrenched in the Order and their ideals. As did I. We were both rapidly rising stars in the Order, and there were even rumors that Millan was being considered for leadership. We were ecstatic."

A few minutes ticked by while I waited for Elaina to continue. When she didn't seem inclined to, I prompted, "And then what happened?"

She sighed again, her eyes haunted. "And then the Order kidnapped Princess Jianne, and in the ensuing fight between the Order and King Addan and Queen Inari, Millan got killed. As did the princess. I'd already felt uneasy about Princess Jianne's kidnapping, and then when Millan died … so did my unwavering devotion to the Emerald Order."

She straightened suddenly, her eyes afire. "You know what they're doing, right?"

"I-I'm not sure," I stammered. "I was told they're trying to undermine Valdonne's Treaty, but—"

"The Order created a black market by selling human babies to the Fae, since the treaty outlaws the stealing of human children and the substitution with changelings. But the Fae need those humans to ultimately survive—it's their ties to humanity, however wrongly obtained, that allow the Fae to ground their magic in nature and grow in power. Without any connection to humankind, Faerie magic would ultimately untether from the Gifted Lands and fade away. Before, when relations were better between Fairiekind and humans, humans would go to the Fae willingly, but in the last few decades humans have been warned away from trusting the Fae.

"But it's not just having humans in their lands that help Fae magic. Birth matters too. Which is why the Order took Princess Jianne—more power for both the Order and the Fae. And why—"

"The Order wanted Prince Coran," I finished, realizing. "A human baby born of a union between a powerful, shapeshifting magician and a former Seeker, who comes from a long line of skilled Seekers. That's a lot of latent magic packaged neatly in one child."

Then something else Elaina had said hit me. "Wait—what do you mean, more power for the Order? How do the Fae pay for the stolen children?"

"Faerie magic is more useful to the Order than money. With each child sold, the Fae have promised a bit of their magic in return—allowing the Order to tap into an ever-growing deep well of magic, and tying both of our groups ever closer to each other."

I recalled Enlar's words from back in Calia. *Their goal is to tie all of the Gifted Lands closer to the Fae. Publicly, they say their purpose is to strengthen relations with the Fae, but their true aim is to steal the magic from the lands of Faerie until there is nothing left.*

Suddenly, everything made sense. The Order, through their black market ties to the Fae, were able to use Faerie magic. And when the time was right, the Order could use that connection to wipe out the Fae completely.

Once, of course, they felt there was enough magic to sustain them for a long, long time.

With belated realization, I looked around and said, "Speaking of which—should we be worried that anyone in the Order can overhear us?"

She shook her head. "No. It's hard to explain exactly, but where we are is somewhere outside of the Order's reach, although it's also part of the Order's headquarters and eventually leads you into the building." She smirked, a hint of her former sassiness showing through her sadness. "If you pick the right path, of course."

I chuckled. "Of course." I paused. "So, I take it you're no longer as enamored with the Emerald Order as you once were?"

Her smirk faded. "After seeing what happened to the young princess, and my beloved ... No. I don't want to be a part of the Order anymore, but it's hard to get away once you're in it." She sighed. "And now that they have another young captive, that baby prince ..."

As Elaina and I had been talking, that odd sense of familiarity had been creeping over me again. I had thought it was from Elaina's connection to Yorath—after all, I had seen a picture of her younger self hanging in my room last night.

But it was more than that. It wasn't just her face that was a little familiar.

It was her voice.

I gasped and jumped to my feet, drawing my sword. I stepped in front of Farrah to shield her. "You're the one who kidnapped the prince! You broke into my room at the Blue Pony and tried to kill me!"

Behind me, Farrah groaned and moved slightly, but didn't try to get up. Elaina didn't draw her weapon, just held her hands out in a gesture of peace. "Let me explain."

I drew my sword up until the tip was level with her exposed neck. "Please do. And if I don't like the explanation, I'll kill you immediately."

Elaina held herself stiffly, afraid to make a move that would accidentally draw her blood. "I did participate in the kidnapping of the prince, it's true. The Order sent three of us—Aela, me, and a man, Raithe—to go get the prince. But I knew Aela was going to try to run, and I wanted to run away with her. I thought this mission would be the perfect time to leave the Order, permanently. I was hoping to talk to Aela while we were on the assignment together, but I never had a chance. Raithe never left me alone for a single moment, and then when Aela missed our rendezvous ... I tracked her down, but it was you I found instead of her. I thought something bad had happened to her."

She sighed. "At that point, I had no choice but to return with Raithe and the baby to Bomora."

Slowly, I lowered my sword. Even though I had no good reason to trust Elaina, I somehow sensed she was telling the truth about her aversion to the Order and wanting to leave. I sighed. "Thank you for telling me. I ... we're here to take the prince home."

She pursed her lips but didn't say anything. Then, finally: "I don't like it. It's one thing to try to tap into the magic of willing adults, but I don't agree with what they've been doing lately. Innocent children. Babies. It might be too late for me, but I'll do my best to make sure it's not too late for your prince."

"Thank you."

She shrugged uncomfortably. "It's the least I can do."

I tugged at the delicate gold ring on my pinky finger and held it out to Elaina. "Your father wanted us to give this to you. To let you know you can always go home."

Elaina took her mother's wedding band from me, turning it this way and that in the cool light, rubbing her finger over the pattern as if she wanted to memorize it by touch. She slipped it onto her right hand's ring finger, where it fit like a perfect promise. Even in the dim light, I could tell she was trying to blink back tears.

"Thank you." Her voice was thick with emotion. "I—thank you."

"Of course."

She sniffed and swallowed, wiping her eyes with the back of her hand. She waved at Farrah. "Is your friend feeling better? We should go."

28

CHAPTER TWENTY-EIGHT

THE BRIEF REST HAD done Farrah some good, although I could tell from her demeanor that she still felt shaky and weak.

We made our slow, careful way down the passage. Our halting progress worried me, and the occasional glances Elaina would shoot back the way we had come let me know she was worried as well. But she didn't say anything, just continued to hurry us along the passage as fast as we could go without taxing Farrah further.

It felt like the passage would never end, but eventually it started to grow lighter ahead.

I sighed in relief. "Finally! I thought—"

Whatever thought I was going to share with Elaina and Farrah was drowned out by the sound of heavy footsteps coming quickly from the dark behind us. As one, we all stiffened and started moving faster.

"You may have had that thought too soon," Elaina said.

"Should we—"

"No. Run!"

Farrah and I did as Elaina commanded. Well, sort of. I ran. Farrah, still exhausted, tried to run but settled into a quick, uneven limp. Elaina took up the rear, ready to defend us. As I was unwilling to outpace Farrah, we didn't move very fast.

I glanced over my shoulder, trying to ascertain how far away the new doppelgangers were. Elaina hissed, "Don't worry about it, just go!"

The light at the end of the tunnel solidified into a shimmery veil of magic before us. It covered the entire length and width of the passage, like a semi-opaque door. Beyond the white veil, I could make out the vague outline of what looked like a sitting room.

"Farrah, go!" I put her in front of me and pushed her toward the veil. The noises behind us grew louder.

"She won't be able to get through unless she has a signet ring from the Order, or is holding on to someone who does," Elaina said.

I grabbed Farrah's hand and, with a final burst of energy, jumped through the veil. I heard Farrah cry out, but whether it was from the sudden movement or from my vise grip on her hand, I couldn't tell. We tumbled into the room I had glimpsed, landing hard on the carpeted floor, just as I heard the crash of metal on metal behind me.

I looked up. Through the veil I could see a hazy outline of Elaina fighting off two beings similar in size to Farrah and me—the new wave of constructs. Her left hand, with her own Emerald Order signet ring, punched through the veil, with the rest of her following suit not long after.

Unlike Farrah and me, Elaina kept her balance, only stumbling a bit as she passed through the magical doorway. She kept her sword at the ready, but the two figures on the other side didn't follow.

Instead, they slammed up against the veil in a final attempt to reach us. The sight of Farrah's and my faces twisted in hatred, slightly blurred through the veil, caused my blood to run cold. With one last snarl, the two figures disappeared in a shower of sparks.

Elaina sheathed her sword. "Well, I'm glad to see the magic still holds."

Was she being sarcastic? I couldn't tell. I decided not to comment.

Farrah and I got to our feet. Fascinated, Farrah poked at the shimmery veil. Her hand went through it, a hazy ebony appendage on the other side of the magic doorway.

"It's a two way door if you're coming from inside the Order's headquarters, but one way if you're coming from inside the passage," Elaina explained. "Although why you'd want to leave through the passage is beyond me."

Satisfied that we were truly out of danger—for now—Farrah and I looked around. We were in a near-replica of the original foyer that we had entered earlier. While it still had the furnishings and rich green colors of the first room, it seemed to have faded somehow. The first area had been perfectly polished, gleaming with impressive wealth. The Emerald Order's true foyer spoke more of genteel poverty than anything else. Threadbare, sun-faded curtains hung limply over the windows. Unlike in the other room, no fire burned in the large hearth here. The wall sconces gave off some light, but overall the room was much gloomier and darker than the first. Shadows swallowed the room's corners, and even Lord Indwere's painted face seemed to be stern and scowling, instead of bearing the proud, haughty face he had worn before.

Perhaps the majority of the Order's funds went to maintaining their magical defenses rather than building upkeep.

"That's correct. We have more important things than fancy furnishings to spend the group's limited supply of money on." Elaina answered my question, and I realized belatedly that I had spoken my thoughts aloud. "The only people who see this room are those true members who've either made it past the magical traps or know how to bypass them. So there's no need to impress them."

She waved her arm around the depressing room. "Welcome to the Emerald Order."

I smirked. "Thanks." I sighed. "Now what?"

"Follow me." Elaina moved to the right-hand staircase—made of wood, like the previous one, but much dirtier and worn in the middle than the other had been—and started upstairs.

I shrugged and followed. A few steps up, I realized Farrah wasn't behind me. Turning, I saw she was still at the magical entry, poking at the veil and muttering to herself.

"Farrah!" That got her attention, and she turned. I nodded toward Elaina's retreating figure. "You coming?"

She nodded, and with one last curious look at the veil, she hurried after me. "I could study that all day," she muttered.

"Maybe you'll get a chance later, on our way out," I said. Farrah didn't respond, but I could feel her skeptical grimace boring into my back.

Elaina waited for us at the top of the stairs. Closed doors lined the hallway on both ends, but Elaina walked a few steps to a door just left of the staircase, directly above the great hearth in the foyer below.

"This is our leader's office," she said in a low voice. "Give me a moment to let him know you're here."

She knocked on the door. A deep, muffled voice called from within. "Enter."

Elaina opened the door just wide enough for her to slip through. Her body blocked the crack in the office door, so Farrah and I could only get vague impressions of the room beyond: rich mahogany bookshelves lining the walls, a plush dark red carpet covering most of the hardwood floor, several lit sconces placed high in various intervals around the room. Like the foyer, the room had seen better days, but it was still impressive.

Elaina said, "There are some visitors here to see you, sir."

The deep voice, much clearer now, spoke. "Hmm. I wasn't expecting anyone today. How did they get in?"

Elaina neatly sidestepped the question—or at least, the details. "One of them wears a ring of the Order."

"Interesting," the voice said. "Well, then. I would like to meet this person who carries our seal, yet somehow is unknown to me. Send them in."

Elaina nodded her head, once, then turned and opened the door wider to let Farrah and me enter. Farrah walked in first, her hands moving surreptitiously behind her back as she soundlessly mouthed something. Her lips barely moved; someone who didn't know Farrah very well wouldn't have caught her movements. But I knew what she was doing—she was checking the magic in the room, trying to gauge how much was in use and what spells there might be.

I followed after Farrah, stepping to her side. In front of us was a heavy mahogany desk, a perfect match to the bookshelves. Behind it sat a man who was shaking his slightly shaggy salt-and-pepper hair back from his face. Even though he seemed as worn and faded as everything else in the Order's headquarters, he still carried himself with an air of power and dignity.

Even though it had been over a decade since we had last seen each other, I recognized him immediately.

Elaina gestured at us. "May I present Farrah and—"

The man stood up as he got a good look at me. His eyes widened. "Rhyss." He couldn't disguise the shock in his voice.

I sketched a short, ironic bow. "It's been a while, Magnus. What a pleasure to see you again."

29

— · —

CHAPTER TWENTY-NINE

MAGNUS FROWNED. "AM I just 'Magnus' to you now? You used to call me 'Uncle Magnus' readily enough. Indeed, your father told me you always looked forward to my visits. Couldn't stop talking about it, before or after."

"Uncle?" Farrah said, her frown an imitation of the one Magnus wore.

"A courtesy title," I explained, not taking my eyes off the man standing behind the desk. Who was eyeing me just as warily. "Magnus was my father's best friend, a close friend of the family's."

"Was?" Magnus echoed. "I know it's been a while—"

"At least ten or more years, I believe."

"But surely your father still counts me as one of his dearest friends."

"I'm sure he would." It wasn't a total lie. "If he was still alive, that is."

Magnus gasped, putting his hand to his chest as if I had physically hit him with my matter-of-fact statement. He staggered back slightly, the stern frown on his face replaced with genuine sadness. "No. Say it's not true."

I nodded. "I wish it weren't, but both he and Mother passed away years ago in a fire."

"Oh. What horrible news." He straightened up, walking around the desk toward Farrah and me. "Well, thank the gods you're still here. I'm sure Markus and Bianca are watching over you with pride."

He threw his arms around me in a big embrace. I yelped, surprised at the little pinpricks I felt along my arms, back, and chest from the pressure. *The curse.*

Magnus pulled away, holding me at arm's length. "Are you okay, Rhyss?"

I tried to laugh it off, giving him a brief, weak hug back. "Just took me by surprise, that's all."

Magnus beamed at me. "My goodness, the last time I saw you, you were all limbs and elbows. I'm glad you're here, my boy. Now I can do right by my best friend's son."

He clapped me on the back, then turned to Farrah. "And who is this lovely young lady?"

Elaina introduced Farrah to Magnus, who was just as jovial and charming as I remembered him being from my childhood. Farrah was polite but wary, taking her cue from my less-than-warm reaction to the leader of the Emerald Order.

Magnus turned to Elaina. "Are there any available rooms?"

Elaina paused, thinking. "Pen and Frenna are still away, so there's at least two."

"Good. Would you see that those rooms are made ready for our guests?"

"Actually, I believe they should be ready already."

"Oh, we wouldn't want to impose—" I started to protest.

"No imposition at all, Rhyss," Magnus said, in a voice that, while sounding cheerful, also brooked no argument. "You and your friend will be my guests, for as long as you'd like to stay. Elaina can show you to your rooms, and then I would be honored if you would join me for dinner."

Although I was sure both Elaina and Farrah desperately wanted to know about my history with Magnus, we kept the conversation light as we walked down the hallway to our rooms. While I didn't necessarily want to stay at the Emerald Order one moment longer than I needed to, I couldn't deny that Magnus's generosity would allow Farrah and me a convenient excuse to poke around and try to locate Prince Coran.

"Magnus has proven himself a very capable leader. Before, the Order—" Elaina paused mid-sentence and looked at me, concerned. "Are you all right? You seem to be having trouble breathing."

The itching and poking of the curse vines had come back with a vengeance, and I had practically been panting as I tried to keep pace with Elaina and Farrah. I tried to get my breathing back under control. "I'm fine. Just the excitement of the day."

Elaina accepted my excuse and continued talking about the history of the Order. Farrah, however, raised her eyebrows at me. I definitely couldn't fool her.

Near the end of the hallway was a large picture window, its threadbare green curtains drawn back to let the day in. Elaina opened one of the doors, revealing a functional room with plain, worn furnishings—a bed, a desk and chair, a single dresser, and a small, square mirror—but devoid of any personality.

"Most of the members prefer to stay in their own homes around Bomora. We encourage it, actually." Elaina's voice took on an ironic tone. "It's much easier to recruit people if you live among them."

Farrah gave Elaina's shoulder a sympathetic squeeze. Elaina smiled briefly, then said, "The room next door is the same as this. I'll let you two get settled in, and come back later to bring you to dinner."

Farrah murmured our thanks, while I simply nodded. Elaina turned to leave, and Farrah immediately whirled on me, most likely with the intent to quiz me about what had happened in Magnus's office. "Rhyss, why didn't you—"

Elaina turned back around, her expression and tone serene. But her eyes flashed a warning. "I'm sure, after the eventful day you both have had, rest is probably the best course of action."

She reached up a hand to brush her hair back from her face and tuck it behind her ear, very slowly and deliberately.

Her hand lingered a little too long on the curve of her ear, before she cocked her head toward the nearest wall.

A warning, then. *The walls have ears.* With Magnus in his office just a few doors down, it probably wasn't wise to talk about anything important right now.

Farrah settled down, although both Elaina and I could tell she was bursting with unanswered questions. "A good idea, Elaina. Thank you. I'm sure we'll all have plenty of time to talk at dinner."

"Indeed." This time Elaina did leave, her boots making soft noises on the hardwood floor as she walked away. Farrah and I stood there in an awkward silence.

"I guess since both rooms are the same, I'll just take the other one," I said.

Farrah just nodded.

"Okay, then." I shifted my bag on my back and went to the room next door. As Elaina had said, it was an exact copy of Farrah's room.

Dropping my bag on one side of the bed, I sank down next to it, fully intending to follow Elaina's suggestion and take a nap. I leaned over and started undoing the laces on one of my boots, gladly pulling it off my tired foot and tossing it to the side. My back cracked from the effort. I straightened slightly, stretching to release more tension.

And then I got a look at myself in the mirror hanging on the opposite wall.

Since we had left the Hwisprian Woods, we hadn't stopped at any place where I would have been able to view my reflection. I had known, from Farrah's reaction, that the Heart's curse was spreading all over my body. But now I was able to see how much it had taken over me.

In addition to the vines snaking down my arms, chest, and legs—all of which I was already aware of—the curse vines now spread upward, like a reverse tattoo of tree roots creeping over my neck, chin, and the bottom part of my cheeks. I stared at my face in dismay. It wouldn't be much longer now before the curse took over me completely and killed me. From the looks of things, I worried that the one day I had left to find the baby Prince Coran and the Heart's soul, then return to the Hwisprian Woods, wouldn't be enough time.

Only one day left.

If I was lucky.

30

CHAPTER THIRTY

Knock, knock.

I groaned and turned over on my side, as if turning my back to the door would make the sound go away.

Knock, knock, knock.

The knocking at the door was growing more frequent and more insistent. I fought my way to wakefulness and sat up, groggy and with a slight headache.

"Rhyss?" Elaina's muffled voice came through my closed bedroom door. "Are you awake?"

I groaned again. I had only slept for an hour or so, but I felt like I could have happily kept sleeping for several hours more. "Yes," I called out. "Give me a minute, I'll be right there."

"Of course," Elaina said. "I'll be waiting out here in the hallway."

I nodded in response, even though she couldn't see me, and forced myself to get out of bed. I had fallen asleep sprawled on the side of my bed where I had been sitting earlier. I must have been more tired than I thought: not only was I fully clothed, not even taking the time to remove my coat, I hadn't bothered to remove one of my boots. My right leg felt slightly sore from the weight of the boot dragging it down while I slept.

I scrubbed my arm over my eyes and grabbed my left boot from where I had tossed it at the foot of the bed a few hours ago. Running my hands over my clothes, I tried to smooth out the wrinkles, to no avail. Oh, well. Magnus had only mentioned Farrah and me joining him for dinner—he hadn't specified how we needed to look. Hopefully, it would just be the three of us—four, if Elaina was allowed to stay—and I wouldn't have to worry about being impressive.

Besides, Magnus knew me well. Or, at least, he had at one point. While I had changed much from the gawky, hero-worshiping boy he remembered, I hadn't changed in one of the ways that had always caused my parents great embarrassment: my lack of care for my appearance.

I opened the bedroom door to find Elaina and Farrah quietly chatting in the hallway. Farrah, as usual, looked impeccable, although I was sure she was still recovering from the day's earlier fight against our doppelgangers. She looked much better, though. The color had returned to her cheeks and her eyes weren't so glassy.

"I see you got some rest," I said.

"I did," Farrah said cheerfully. "And apparently you did too."

I yawned. "Not enough, though. It's never enough."

She laughed. "The only thing I can think of that you like more than sleeping is food. Come on, I'm starving."

That was a good sign; it meant her body was beyond the initial shock of magic overexertion, and now just needed food to help her recover her magical stores completely.

Elaina led us down the stairs and back into the green foyer. "If Magnus approves, I can take you on a more complete tour after dinner. Or he might even want to show you around himself. But, for now, the dining hall is this way ..."

We followed her into a dining room that looked like ... a regular dining room. In it was a large wooden table, serviceable chairs, and a lot less shades of green than the foyer. Plain white dinnerware was already laid out on the dining room table. I had half expected green dishes or even green silverware—and if the latter had been true, I definitely would have resorted to eating with my hands. Forget about table manners.

Magnus was already seated at the head of the table. He waved at the other chairs nearby. "Please, sit."

I surreptitiously noted the place settings. Four. So Elaina was to join us, then. Good. Unless Magnus had some surprise guest who was slated for the fourth seat.

Farrah and I took the places to the right and left of Magnus. After a quick glance at Magnus for confirmation, Elaina sank down into a chair next to Farrah.

Three servants clad in the dark green reminiscent of the Order's distinctive cloaks put several dishes on the table in front of us. While the Order didn't seem to use their funds toward building upkeep, they certainly didn't skimp on their food. I counted roast fowl, stewed vegetables, salmon pie, and honey cakes among the dinner dishes. There was also a plate piled high with various cheeses and breads, and a generous jug of wine.

Magnus picked up a large knife and began cutting into the fowl. "Help yourselves."

I exchanged a look with Farrah across the table. She shrugged and smiled. I mirrored her gesture, and then reached over to cut myself a slice of pie.

Once we had all served ourselves, Magnus sat back and surveyed the table. His eyes landed on me. "Rhyss, my boy. It really is a wonder to see you again after all these years."

I finished chewing the bite of carrot I had just popped in my mouth and took a long swallow of wine before answering. I had a feeling I was going to need some liquid fortification to get me through this dinner.

"Agreed," I said. "Truthfully, I didn't think I'd ever return to Bomora."

"What brings you here, anyway?" Magnus asked, looking between Farrah and me. Across the table, Farrah's eyes flashed briefly in worry.

"Before they died, my parents mentioned they still had holdings here in Bomora," I said, the lie springing to my lips easily. "I came back to settle their affairs here."

Magnus looked puzzled. "I thought they sold off all their property and settled all their debts before moving. Or sent money back, if they weren't able to take care of it before they left. That was the word on the street, anyway."

I shrugged, hoping my faked nonchalance would fool Magnus. "That would make things easier for me, although if it's true, then we traveled here for nothing. But, to be fair, if they did have any open debts or issues here in Bomora, I left it way too long. I'd be surprised if anyone remembers any money owed to them after so many years."

Magnus smirked. "If there's one thing Bomorrans have, it's long memories. A country of cutthroats and thieves wouldn't forget any outstanding debts, no matter how long it's been. If Markus had owed anyone money, they would have tracked him down and made him pay it back, either in coin or in blood."

"True." Not wanting to continue this line of conversation, I started tucking into my meal.

Farrah spoke up. "Forgive me, sir, but ... I know you know Rhyss, but I'm afraid I don't know *how* you know him. If you don't mind telling me the story?"

Magnus laughed. "Call me Magnus, my dear, please. You mean to say that Rhyss hasn't told you about me?" Farrah shook her head. "Hmm. I almost feel a little hurt at that. Then again, it has been a long time, as he keeps reminding me."

Magnus took a sip of his wine before continuing. "Rhyss's father, Markus, was my dearest friend growing up. We lived next door to each other, went to school together. We were always getting into trouble together, too."

"Father loved telling me about that time you two released a greased pig into the school," I interjected, laughing. "I think I heard that story at least once a week. I always thought there were easier ways to get out of going to class."

"But none as fun," Magnus said, laughing as well. Farrah chuckled too, and even Elaina cracked a smile.

"So you and Rhyss's father were close," Farrah prompted as the laughter died down.

"Yes," Magnus confirmed. "I stood in his wedding, and I was the first one to meet Rhyss after he was born—after Markus and Bianca, of course. And when they asked me to be Rhyss's godfather, of course I said yes."

"You're Rhyss's godfather?" Farrah asked, giving me a sharp look.

"I sure am, although I never thought that I would be called upon to actually take care of Rhyss." Magnus frowned. "I wish you had sent me word when your parents died. I would have taken care of you. It may not look like it, from the look of this place, but I am quite well off."

"I'm sure you are," I said. "But it's all right. When they died, I was already close to my majority. And I hired myself out to help a Seeker during his commissions. He had steady work for several years. So I was never in any danger of starving."

"Still, though." Magnus's frown deepened. "I'm sure grief clouded your mind, but I'm also sure your father would have wanted you to contact me."

"It did take me several years to come to terms with their deaths," I said, sidestepping the second part of his statement. Because one thing I distinctly remembered, shortly after my family had moved to Orchwell, was my father warning me never to have any contact with Magnus, ever again.

Farrah drew Magnus into another topic of conversation while I continued to eat and surreptitiously observed him. Magnus seemed to be the same jovial "uncle" I remembered from my childhood, completely unaffected by any talk of the past, except for the brief flash of sadness he showed upon learning of my parents' deaths. Didn't he remember the falling out that he and my father had had before my family left Bomora? Perhaps with all the time that had passed, he had moved on. Forgive and forget. He certainly seemed to have forgiven my father's memory.

But had he forgotten?

I was finishing my meal when Magnus's words drew me back into his conversation with Farrah. "So you're able to use magic, then? How fascinating."

"It comes from my background," Farrah said. "I'm part Fae."

"Fascinating," Magnus repeated. "As a fellow magician, I'm always interested in meeting other magic users and learning about their process. I find Fae magic particularly interesting."

Was it just me, or was Magnus looking at Farrah a little too intently? Not just with the gaze of a fellow colleague, but something more intense.

Something hungry.

"I'd be happy to discuss it more at length with you," Farrah said. "Although I'm not sure how helpful I'll be. My magic, being innate, comes to me instinctively. I once tried to teach the current queen of Calia, Queen Jennica, how my magical process works. It didn't go too well."

She laughed. Magnus laughed too, but his laugh sounded a little too bright to my ears. Like he was trying too hard to make Farrah trust and like him.

"Well, my dear, then I'm sure you'd be interested in taking a tour of the Order after dinner," Magnus said. "Most of the rooms are boring in their functionality—such as this dining room, the kitchen, the bedrooms—but we do have one room that I'm particularly proud of. Our library."

"A library?" I said. I didn't remember Magnus being a bookworm, but people could change.

"The Emerald Order's library boasts the largest collection of books on magic and magical history in all of Bomora." Magnus preened. "It took years to amass such a collection, and you wouldn't believe the amount of money I personally spent and all the favors I called in to get a lot of them. But it was worth it."

"We'd love to see it," Farrah said quickly.

"Of course, my dear, of course." He threw his napkin down on the table and stood. "Shall we?"

"But you've barely touched your plate," I said. Elaina, Farrah, and I had finished our meals. Magnus had been so deep in conversation with me, then Farrah, that he had hardly eaten.

"It's all right. I'm so excited that you two are here, and it's hard for me to eat when I'm excited." He laughed. "I'll just have the servants hold onto it for me for later. Come, come."

We pushed back our chairs and followed Magnus to the entryway. As he walked through, he waved at a waiting green-clad servant nearby, who sprung immediately into action and began clearing the dirty dishes from the table.

"I'll take you right to the library, since it really is the best room in the place," Magnus said. We passed the kitchen and went down a hallway, passing some empty rooms that looked like classrooms or meeting rooms. I marveled at how big the place was. From the outside, it didn't look nearly as spacious, and I said as much.

"In the beginning, the Order really wasn't much," Magnus agreed. "Just the size of a modest mansion—" inwardly, I snorted at the idea of a "modest" mansion "—and most of the rooms did double duty. But as we grew in numbers, we also grew in funding—and ability. So many of these rooms are magical add-ons."

"Wait." I stopped as the magnitude of what he was saying hit me. "You mean, this entire wing is all a magical construct? As well as the illusion that Farrah and I encountered when we first entered, that fake fancy foyer? And the passages and the traps in the 'other' region? Which, if my guess is correct, also uses magic to lead you to the Order's true location?"

Farrah and Elaina had stopped with me. Either they were as awed as I was, or—more likely—it was because I had been walking in front of them and was now blocking the hallway.

Seeing that we were no longer behind him, Magnus stopped walking as well and came back to us. "Well, yes." He sounded surprised at my surprise, as if I had stated, *What do you mean the sky is blue?* or, *What, grass is green?* "The Order is founded on the study and acquisition of magic. I don't see why that's so amazing."

"Because of the sheer amount of magic it would take to keep all of this going," I said, thinking of my conversation with Elaina in the cave. "I don't know much about how to use magic—that's Farrah's specialty—but I've been around enough magic users to know that to do all of that would require a lot of magic. A lot of continuous magic. There might be ways to shortcut, but not for very long. And not for all that the Order is using it for. I don't think even the mages of Calia could keep something like this going for more than a few days."

Magnus shrugged casually, but his face was unreadable. "While I can't say the Order's magicians have the same formal training that the Calian magicians do, we've found our own unique way of doing magic. If the results are anything to go by, it's working, isn't it?"

He resumed walking, pushing open a door on the right a few feet away from our group.

"It certainly is," Farrah murmured, eyeing me sidelong as we followed Magnus.

We reached the doorway Magnus had disappeared through. And stopped in awe.

Magnus hadn't been lying when he said the Emerald Order's library was impressive. Bookshelves lined each of the four walls in the room, reaching up several stories high—definitely past where the actual ceiling should have been. Now that I knew this wing had been created by magic, contemplating this room didn't hurt my head as much as it normally would have.

Looking around, there wasn't an empty spot on any bookshelf. The room also had an oversized hearth, currently unlit, on one wall, and various tables and chairs for reading or studying. The room was a scholar's dream, although it would take several lifetimes for any scholar to read through all the volumes on the shelves.

Farrah crossed over to a shelf and started looking over the titles. "*The Gift of the Gifted Lands: A History of Fae Magic*," she read aloud. "*The Perils and Processes of Enchantment. Necromancy, or Why*

Immortal Beings Choose To Engage With the Dead." She walked down the length of a few shelves, examining a few more books, before turning wide eyes on Magnus. "This is amazing. Some of these books are extremely rare."

Magnus smiled broadly. "As I said earlier, I'm very proud of our collection."

"As you should be." Farrah turned back to the shelf and plucked a slim red volume from it. "May I borrow this book?"

"Of course, my dear," Magnus said. "But only for the duration of your stay here at the Order. We don't allow any of our books to leave the premises. You understand."

"Of course," Farrah echoed. She clutched the book to her chest somewhat possessively, making me wonder what she had found.

We spent a few more minutes looking around, making polite noises about the size and scope of the library's collection and how comfortable the room looked. But I've never been much of a reader—I like to say I'm a man of action, although Farrah would argue that it's more often *in*action—and Farrah seemed impatient to get back to our rooms and start reading the book she had borrowed.

Magnus was in the middle of describing how they chose which books to keep, when I let out a huge yawn. "Sorry," I said sheepishly.

He laughed. "It's alright. It's getting late, and you've had a long day. You can come here whenever you like to look around, you don't need me getting in your way."

As we left the library and stepped into the hallway, a cry pierced the air.

A cry that was distinctly a baby's wail.

31

CHAPTER THIRTY-ONE

As the unseen baby let out another loud wail, a tired-looking woman hurried down the hallway toward us. Her somewhat tangled, messy hair and wrinkled skirt and blouse made me think she either didn't care about her appearance, or—more likely—was too busy to tend to it.

As she approached, I could hear her muttering something about "just a few moments for dinner." When she saw us, she stopped short. "Oh, hello! Hope the baby's crying didn't bother you, I'm on my way to feed him." She gave a little chuckle. "He's got quite the appetite. Seems like I can't step away for a second before he wants to eat again."

Magnus waved her away. "It's quite understandable. We won't keep you."

With a brisk "thank you," she hurried away past us, disappearing into a room just a few doors down from the library to the left.

"Baby?" I raised an inquisitive brow at Magnus.

"My newborn son," he replied. "Born just a few weeks ago."

"Oh! Our congratulations, then." I looked down the hallway where the tired woman had gone. "When she's not so busy, we'd love to meet your wife."

"My—oh!" Magnus said, realizing who I meant. "That wasn't my wife. My dear wife unfortunately did not survive the birth. The woman you saw is a wet nurse I hired from town to take care of my son."

"I'm sorry for your loss," I said, as Farrah murmured similar condolences. I studied Magnus carefully. It could have been the fading light, but he didn't look like a man who was grieving his late wife. While my father had been stoic, reserved with his thoughts and feelings, the Magnus I remembered had usually been very open with his emotions—quick to anger, but just as quick to be generous or jolly. "I didn't know you were married."

"Yes, but unfortunately our time together was short. We had been married less than a year when I lost her."

I nodded in feigned sympathy. Behind him, Elaina caught my eye and shook her head slightly.

So my guess was right, then. Magnus was lying about his dead wife—and his supposed son.

Magnus said, "Speaking of my son, I'd like to spend some time with him now that he's awake for a bit. Elaina can show you back to your rooms, if that's alright with you both?"

"Of course," Farrah said.

"Tomorrow, I can take you to meet some of our members who live in town, or we can just relax here if you like," Magnus said. "Whatever you prefer."

"We can find ways to keep ourselves occupied," I said. "If you have work to do—"

"Work? Bah," Magnus said, winking at us. "I have no work while you're here! It's no bother at all."

I murmured my thanks, then Farrah and I followed Elaina back down the hallway while Magnus disappeared into the baby's room.

The three of us walked in silence until we reached the foyer and the staircase leading upstairs.

"You know that's not truly his son, right?" Elaina said in a voice so low I could barely hear her. At our affirming nods, she said, "Listen. Magnus plans on delivering the prince to the Fae at Samhain, since magic will flow more freely between the two worlds at that time."

"Samhain?" Farrah breathed. "But that's in two days!"

"Actually it's tomorrow night," Elaina corrected. "The exchange usually happens just after midnight, when the holiday officially begins. Just Magnus, as the Order's leader, attends. Sometimes he brings other members, but not often. It's a very secretive event; those who are privileged enough to attend don't talk about the details, just that it involves the Fae. But for the first time ever, the entire Order is expected to attend this event. If you ask him, I'm sure he'd be willing to bring you both along. This might be your best chance to steal the prince back. He'll be away from the magical wards on this place, although there will be a lot of people surrounding him."

Hmm. We didn't have a lot of options. Judging from how freely the Order used their magic, my guess was the wards here were very strong indeed. Or we could try to take him in the midst of a crowd where he was being constantly watched by both the Order and the Fae. Since the Order's headquarters had been fairly deserted tonight, I didn't have a good sense of how many people would be in attendance.

And dealing with the Fae would be worse. We would have to contend with whoever was at the event that we could see—as well as those creatures who were small or skilled enough to hide in the area.

I bit my lip, thinking. Not only did we have to figure out how to smuggle Prince Coran away—I would prefer that instead of an outright fight against unknown numbers of humans and Fae—but we also had to somehow bring Magnus back to the Heart of the

Hwisprian Woods to fulfill my promise to her. I somehow doubted Magnus would come with us willingly.

I nodded slowly. "He seems delighted to see us, particularly me. I think I can convince him to take us along."

"Good." Elaina pointed up the stairs. "You know where your rooms are. Goodnight."

She opened the front door. The lamp lit streets of Bomora lay beyond, with a scattering of stars overhead.

"Wait, where are you going?" I asked. From Elaina's story, I thought she stayed permanently at the Order.

She lifted her hand, where her mother's gold wedding band shone on her finger. "I know it's a little late to go visiting, but ..." She shrugged, a shy smile on her face. "Better late than never, right?"

Farrah smiled warmly, and I felt an answering grin cross my face. "Right."

32

CHAPTER THIRTY-TWO

ELAINA SLIPPED OUT INTO the night, closing the door quietly behind her. Farrah and I headed upstairs to our rooms. But to my surprise, instead of going into her bedroom, Farrah followed me into mine.

"Farrah, what—"

She closed the door behind her and locked it. There was an indecipherable look in her eyes, and I found my heart pounding wildly. I stood stupidly in the middle of the room as she walked over to me. Just inches away, she looked up at me. Some of her lavender hair had fallen out of its hair ribbon, forming a cloud around her scowling face.

"Why didn't you warn me about Magnus?" she asked me quietly.

I sagged, all the breath pouring out of me in a heavy sigh. "Because I didn't think it would ever come up. It's been years, and after my family left, I never heard from him, or about him. I thought maybe he had died, or moved away."

Farrah sank down on the bed, tugging me down with her so we could continue our quiet conversation. "So what's the story? Your side, I mean. Not the one Magnus told me tonight."

I looked down at my hands, which I had been unwittingly clenching tightly together. "You know my family moved to Orchwell when I was just thirteen, right?"

She nodded.

I continued, "Magnus was the reason why. The Order was formed when I was a child, and Magnus had been a part of it from almost the beginning. At first, my father thought it was just something fun and silly for Magnus to get involved in. After all, Magnus was single with a lot of time and energy to spare, while his best friend was married with a family. But as the years went on, and the Order grew bigger and more powerful, Magnus changed. Whenever they'd meet, or Magnus would come over, he'd always talk about the Emerald Order and its ideals and how it was the future of Bomora and the entire Gifted Lands."

Farrah frowned. "But even if Magnus was a little too ... enthusiastic ... about being a member of the Order, what did it matter to your family? I mean, everyone has things they're passionate about, and it's easy to get carried away by that passion."

"The problem was me." I grimaced. "I worshiped Magnus. My mother had no siblings and my father wasn't particularly close to his brother. Magnus was the uncle I always wanted. Part friend, part mentor, part big brother. We were extremely close as I was growing up. I mean, you heard him. My parents even named him my godfather.

"As Magnus got more entrenched in the Order, my parents worried about his influence on me, that I might also choose to get involved. Especially since there were rumors that Magnus was being primed to be the Order's next leader. I'd already begun attending meetings with him, sneaking out so my parents wouldn't know.

"The Order would hold these annual raids. Magnus told me the raids were intended to round up unwanted babies—the ones living in squalor in the streets, children of the homeless or of prostitutes—and find good, stable homes for them. Better than the kingdom's orphanage, which is little better than a workhouse. Giving a poor child a better home? It seemed like a good idea to me.

"But Father caught me sneaking out, making me miss my rendezvous with Magnus. The next day word came that children had been taken—but from the homes of the wealthy, or those who had publicly spoken out against the Order. And if that wasn't horrible enough, several people had died trying to protect their children from the kidnappers.

"Father immediately started packing up our house, selling things off, settling any outstanding debts. He found us a place in Orchwell so quickly, I sort of suspected he had been planning on leaving Bomora all along. The raid just made him move faster."

Somewhere during the course of my tale, Farrah's hand had found mine. Or maybe mine had found hers, for comfort. I wasn't really sure. She now squeezed it in sympathy, encouraging me to finish my tale.

"So your family moved to Orchwell," she prompted.

I shrugged. "That's pretty much it. We moved to Orchwell, and since Father had settled his debts in Bomora before we left, or soon after, no one from here felt compelled to find us to collect. Which would have let Magnus know where we were. The first few years, my parents constantly worried that Magnus would show up in Orchwell and try to charm me away. Eventually, they relaxed and just focused on life in our new kingdom."

"As did you. Until today."

"Until today," I echoed. Now that my secret was out, I felt incredibly weary.

Farrah's fingers had been gently rubbing mine, and one of them caught on the signet ring that snugly fit on my index finger. She lifted my hand, holding it toward the lit candle on my bedside table. She squinted at the ring, nearly going cross-eyed with the effort. "There's something more you're not telling me."

"What do you mean? I—"

"Yorath called this ring a cheap piece of jewelry, plain and ugly. His eyes may be old, but he would have said if he could see the design in it. The one both you and Enlar are able to see. The one that Enlar said that Bomorrans could see, but if Yorath, who is from Bomora, couldn't see it ... then I don't think that's it." She looked at me, eyes accusing. "It's something only true members of the Order can see, isn't it? And you're a true member." Her eyes widened as she thought of something else. "And that's why we were able to gain entry into the Order's headquarters, isn't it? It had nothing to do with the ring."

I sighed, knowing it was pointless to lie. "Yes, you're right. In a way. We did need a ring to get in, but only a true member would be able to use it. I think we ended up in the oubliette because you, a non-member and potential threat, were with me. But once I entered the building, I would have been recognized by the building wards—my guess is, once the wards were alerted, Magnus probably sent Elaina to fetch us from the oubliette."

I sighed again, twisting the ring around and around on my finger. "And I did get inducted when I was younger; I thought it was just something fun and exciting to participate in. But my parents found out, and they started keeping a close eye on me. That's why my father caught me the night of the raid."

Farrah eyed my second-hand signet ring. "If you were a member of the Order, where's your ring?"

I grimaced. "My father paid an underground Bomorran mage to sever the binding between my ring and me. As mages in this kingdom are very rare and largely self-taught, you can imagine how painful it was to undergo his spell—it felt more like a magical experiment, honestly. My signet ring was part of his payment."

Farrah frowned. "Why didn't you mention any of this, back in Calia? From the minute you saw the seal on that letter, when Coran was taken? We could have—"

"Could have what?" My voice came out in a harsh whisper. "Coran was already gone by that point. Jennica was already unconscious. What good would the knowledge have done Beyan, or you?"

Farrah shook her head. "I don't know. But at least—"

"When we left Bomora, I was glad to leave that part of my life behind. I was scared for a long time that it would come back to haunt me, and I was lucky that it took this long for it to happen. It's not a part of me I'm proud of, Farrah." I dropped my eyes. "And if you found out ... I didn't want you to think less of me because of it."

Somehow, during all of this, Farrah had never let go of my hand. Or maybe I had never let go of hers. She didn't say anything for a long moment, just continued to rub her fingers lightly over mine.

Then, softly: "I'll admit I'm upset that you kept things from me, like the Heart's geas, or the fact that you knew more about the Order than you let on. I'm not happy about it, but I understand why you didn't want to tell me about them. But I would never think less of you because of stupid mistakes from your past. It's the person who you are today that I care about."

"I'm sorry," I said. "You're right, I should have trusted you with that information."

"We're a team, Rhyss. Always."

I opened my mouth to say more. *Thank you for being so understanding*, or *I care about you, too*. Instead what came out was a jaw-cracking yawn.

Farrah giggled. "I can take the hint."

She stood up, releasing my hand. I found myself missing the warmth and comfort from her small gesture. "I want to do some reading before bed, anyway."

"Oh, yeah," I said, remembering the red book she had picked out in the Order's library. "What book did you get?"

She grinned, holding up her selection. The title was spelled out neatly in gilt letters: *Mixing Magic: How Human Mages Can Tap Into the Magic of the Fae.*

"But you don't need to know how to do that," I said, confused. Farrah's half-Fae, half-human heritage meant she was born with Fae magic. She knew a little of how human magic worked, but she never really relied on it.

"I don't," she cheerfully agreed. "But I'm interested in learning more about those who do."

33

CHAPTER THIRTY-THREE

I WOKE UP THE next morning to sunlight streaming through my window, directly onto my face. I groaned and covered my eyes. It seemed like no matter where I went, I was destined to sleep in places that liked to arrange their beds so they faced east. Very annoying.

I got up and got ready for the day. Although Magnus had insisted that Farrah and I relax and sleep in, I also worried that I'd miss him if I took my time. Hopefully, I could catch him at breakfast.

I hurried downstairs to the dining room. I was in luck; Magnus was finishing his morning meal, reading over some documents. Neither Farrah nor Elaina were in sight, although I did see a few other green-cloaked people at the other end of the table, eating and talking in low voices.

"Rhyss!" Magnus looked up and greeted me, then waved toward one wall. "Grab some breakfast and come join me, my boy."

I looked over to where Magnus was gesturing, seeing a generous spread of cold food on a long wooden buffet. I grabbed a plate and started loading it up, then joined Magnus.

"Good morning, uncle," I said, figuring I might as well start the day turning on the charm. Magnus grinned at my calling him uncle. "Did you sleep well?"

"Sure did." He pushed his papers to the side. "Which is good, because it will be a late night tonight."

"Oh?" I pretended ignorance, although, thanks to Elaina's warning, I knew what Magnus meant.

He leaned forward conspiratorially. "Remember that raid I was going to take you on, all those years ago?"

"A little bit," I said noncommittally. Honestly, how could I forget?

"Well, since then, we've gone further afield," Magnus said. The fire in his eyes was either passion—or madness. "There are poor souls all over the Gifted Lands that need good, loving homes. And there are parents who have the means to provide the world and more for them."

"That's wonderful."

"Isn't it?" He sighed, his face turning thoughtful. "I often think about how generous your father and his parents were toward me. Even though I was old enough to take care of myself when my parents died, they were kind enough to take me in, and be my second family."

Oh, that's right—I had forgotten about that part of Magnus's history. His parents—both accomplished thieves—had died in a botched housebreaking when he was sixteen, and although he was certainly able to take care of himself, my father's parents had taken him in. My grandparents had been part of one of the few respectable merchant families in the kingdom, and, if I remembered my family lore correctly, hadn't wanted their son's best friend to end up in one of the unsavory trades so common in Bomora. They had hoped to be good influences on Magnus, and counted on their son Markus's friendship with him to help Magnus rise above his origins.

But I suppose old habits die hard, especially if they were family traditions. If only my grandparents had known what Magnus would become one day....

"Every orphaned child should have a chance at a better home, the best home possible," Magnus continued. "Don't you agree?"

The gleam was back in his eyes—and it was definitely madness. I refrained from saying, *But your Emerald Order is the reason these poor souls are "orphaned" in the first place. And I don't think giving them to the Fae is giving them the "best possible home."*

Instead, I just nodded as the excited words poured out of Magnus.

"Well, tonight, we will be presenting one such child to a very powerful family. I'd be honored if you could come to the event tonight. Bring your friend Farrah, too. It will be such a celebration."

Well, that was easy. Too easy? I decided not to worry about it. "Thank you. We'd be glad to join you."

Magnus leaned back, satisfied. "Good. Glad that's settled. What do you and Farrah have planned for today?"

"I'm not sure. Do you have any suggestions?"

Magnus started to speak, but right then Farrah entered the room with Elaina on her heels. "Good morning, everyone," she said cheerfully.

The two women grabbed some food from the buffet and joined us at the table. Elaina didn't waste any time on small talk, just tucked right into her breakfast, but Farrah gave us all a charming smile. "So, what's everyone's plans for today?"

"We were actually just discussing that," I said. "Magnus invited us to a special presentation of some sort tonight."

Brows raised, Elaina nodded approvingly. "Wonderful."

"So, then, back to the original question," Magnus said, looking between Farrah and me. "Is there anything in particular you two want to do today?"

He waved at the people at the far end of the table. "I'm afraid I have some things to do to prepare for tonight, but we have a few members who would be happy to show you around Bomora and help you with anything you need."

He smiled at me. "Although you probably don't need a guide. Bomora hasn't changed that much since you left."

I smiled back. "It's been a long time. It would be nice to look around, get reacquainted with some of my favorite spots. But you're right, I don't need a guide."

"I'll go with you," Farrah said. "Although I might not be out with you the whole day. I want to spend some time in the Order's gorgeous library."

"Great," Magnus said. "We'll see you tonight, then. Make sure you're back here no later than an hour or so after sunset. It will take a while to prepare everyone and get over to the meeting area."

"Where is that?" I asked.

"Glidhaan's Grove, just outside of the capital. It's one of the oldest and most sacred places in the area."

Glidhaan's Grove. I met Farrah's eyes across the table. The vegetable seller in the market had mentioned odd goings-on at the grove, related to the Emerald Order. It seemed that tonight we'd get to learn the truth behind her speculation.

Then something occurred to me. "Do we need the members to accompany us? Or are we able to get back in?"

"You should be able to return to the true building, instead of being put through the magical tests, as long as you have your ring," Magnus said. "Since it's now been recognized by the Order's wards, it should permit you entry."

"Good." I didn't really want to have some strangers tagging along with us, listening to every word Farrah and I said.

With our plans settled, we finished eating and left. Farrah and I soon found ourselves back on the streets of Bomora. The capital city was slowly waking up—the types of jobs most Bomorrans had did not lend themselves to getting up early—so there weren't too many people walking about.

"Which way?" Farrah asked.

"I do need to stock up on supplies," I said. "And I'd love to look at some weapons."

Farrah snorted. "You say that in every city we visit, but the day you actually replace that old rusty blade of yours, I'll ... I'll concede that your cooking is better."

"My cooking *is* better. Nothing to concede. And anyway, it's my favorite weapon. My trusty knife. We've been through a lot together. Also, it's not rusty anymore."

"It still looks like it's one fight away from breaking."

I shook my head, chuckling at our familiar argument. "Where would *you* like to go?"

Farrah peered off into the distance. "I'm fine with shopping. But I think we should also visit King Addan and Queen Inari, let them know what's happening. Perhaps they can also send reinforcements for us."

"Good idea."

We started toward the docks. The day promised to be beautiful—the marine layer that usually coated Bomora's streets in the morning had already burned off, revealing a clear, sunny sky. Which was good—hopefully there would be no rain tonight. I couldn't think of anything more miserable than standing in the rain, in the dark, while trying to steal back the prince and leave quickly.

To my dismay, I moved slower than I normally would have if I had been curse-free. Every step was painful now. I felt like I was walking on knife tips, and the slightest brush of my clothes against my skin felt like fiery brambles. Farrah was kind enough to ignore my labored breathing, but I knew she was thinking about it from the constant worried glances she'd give me when she thought I wasn't paying attention.

After a few moments, I said in a low voice, "Do you hear that?"

Farrah cocked her head and concentrated. Then she gave a short nod. "Someone following us?"

"I believe so."

She stopped abruptly, pretending to look at a sign just above a closed shop. Fortunately, we were just on the outskirts of the Merchants' District, so it didn't seem unusual for her to do so. She turned back to me. "It's the people who were sitting at breakfast earlier. The guides Magnus volunteered."

She shook her head in disbelief, half joking, "What's with evil uncles running secret organizations? First Kaernan's, now yours ..."

"Actually, Magnus isn't my uncle," I pointed out, remembering our first commission with the lost loves Seeker. "And Kaernan's uncle wasn't really evil."

"Well, Magnus was your late father's best friend. It's close enough."

I glanced around quickly. No crowds to lose them in. No convenient alleys to duck down, and the majority of the shops weren't even open yet. "How are we going to lose them? Farrah, I've got nothing."

She grinned savagely, and I almost felt sorry for our followers. "Don't worry, I do. Let's get going. Cover me."

She started walking again, in a direction away from our true destination. As we walked, she muttered a spell under her breath while surreptitiously making some arcane gestures with her hands. I kept up a cheerful chatter about our shopping trip, pretending we hadn't noticed the Order members following us and trying to distract them from what Farrah was doing.

She finished her spell, and then in one quick movement, turned around and flicked her fingers at the two green-cloaked people who weren't even trying to be unobvious.

They didn't react fast enough to ward off or counter her spell, and both were hit full force by it.

Their purposeful walking slowed, and then the pair stood stupidly in the middle of the street.

Farrah walked up to them and snapped her fingers in their faces. Neither one reacted. "Good. Let's go." She began walking back toward the docks.

I caught up with her. "What did you do to them?"

"Temporary confusion spell," she said. "It clouds their minds so they won't remember their purpose, or how they ended up standing in the street. Eventually they'll recover their memories, but it will take about a day for the spell to completely wear off."

"Nice," I said, impressed. Then I frowned. "Please tell me you've never used that spell on me, for any reason."

She laughed. "No need. You get confused enough as it is."

"Hey!" I gave her a playful shove, which only made her laugh harder as she shoved me back.

At the docks, I recognized Baz from the royals' ship. "Back again?" he said.

"We have news for Their Majesties," Farrah said.

"Come." He led us back to their ship, knocking on the door to their private cabin. Cracking it open slightly, he said, "Your Majesties, please pardon the intrusion. Your visitors from the other day are back, with news."

"Send them in," came King Addan's voice from within.

Baz opened the door wider to permit us entry, then closed it behind us. I didn't hear his footsteps move away, and guessed he probably was guarding the door.

The King stood to greet us. I spied a glint of gold just hidden under his shirt—the royal medallion he had loaned us for our visit to Yorath. I was glad to see it returned to the king, and I hoped the two men had reconciled. "Well met. What news?"

"Before we begin, we'd like to call King Beyan of Calia," Farrah said. "He needs to know this information too."

"Of course." King Addan smirked. "It's about time I meet my new ally."

Farrah held out her hand, palm up, and spoke the word that would trigger the calling spell. I briefly wondered why she didn't just use the stone she had made, then realized two things. One, she didn't need it, obviously. And two, I had it; as the last person to use it, it was tucked away in my pocket.

King Beyan's face appeared almost immediately. "Farrah! Good to see you. Is Rhyss with you? What's going on?"

"I'm here," I said. "There's some people you should meet. May we present King Addan and Queen Inari, the rulers of Bomora."

The King and Queen edged in slightly, standing just behind Farrah, so they would be visible to Beyan. Queen Inari gave a little wave and then sat back down on the bed, but King Addan stayed where he was.

"Greetings, King Beyan of Calia," King Addan said. "It's an honor to meet you, although I wish we could have met under better circumstances."

"As do I," Beyan said grimly. "But with your help, I hope this ordeal will soon be over."

"For both of us," King Addan agreed. He turned to me. "Your news, then?"

I quickly explained what we had learned from Elaina last night, and how Magnus intended to bring the entire Order with him to tonight's meeting with the Fae.

Beyan frowned. "How many are in the Order?"

"I'm not sure," I admitted. "Most of the members don't live in the headquarters, so we couldn't get a good estimate."

"From what my spies tell me, I'd say there are at least one hundred members, give or take," King Addan interjected.

"One hundred," Beyan mused. "Plus the Fae. Which could easily number the same as the Order. And both sides have magic as well."

"We'd be happy to send our guards in," King Addan said. "They won't provide brute force, but sometimes a little stealth is better than a direct approach anyway." He smirked. "After all, this is Bomora. We have a reputation to uphold."

Everyone laughed, easing a bit of the tension in the air.

"So that's ... how many?" Beyan asked.

"About seventy," King Addan said.

"A good amount, but not enough to outnumber either side." Beyan frowned. "I could contact my father-in-law, Joichan, but if he left Graenir now, it would put his ambassadorship—and our relations with that kingdom—at risk. Still, for Coran ..."

King Addan sniffed. "I fail to see what your father-in-law can do that my men cannot."

"He can turn into a dragon," Beyan said matter-of-factly.

King Addan blinked. "Oh."

"It can't hurt to contact him," I said. "Have him on standby. But as a last resort."

"Maybe if he explained to the Graenir leaders what's going on?" Farrah said. "Surely then they'd let him leave, without penalty."

"Perhaps." Beyan looked thoughtful. "I'll call him as soon as we're done here. If only Jennica could go too."

My heart sank. So Jennica still wasn't better.

"If Joichan can help," I said, "and assuming all goes well, should we give him Prince Coran?"

Beyan shook his head. "If—*when*—you secure the prince, head straight back to Calia. Joichan can follow you after, but don't risk the prince's safety by sticking around."

"So, my seventy men and a possible dragon," King Addan said. "That evens the odds somewhat. But what about the Fae? And what about the magic?"

Farrah had a thoughtful gleam in her eye. "I think I have an idea of what to do about that."

King Addan looked like he wanted to argue, but Beyan, who knew Farrah well, perked up. "If you have an idea, Farrah, I trust you."

"Thank you."

"So I'll send my men to Glidhaan's Grove just after sundown to be in place for the midnight meeting," King Addan said. "But if we need to get in touch, how shall we do so?"

"That's no problem," Farrah said. "I can infuse an object with a calling spell that anyone can use. Just like the one I gave you, Rhyss." She nodded at me.

"Perfect," Beyan said. "I'm glad we have some semblance of a plan, although I'm worried about how much of it relies on us being lucky."

"You know from our many adventures together, Beyan, just how lucky we are." Farrah smiled. "And speaking of luck." She turned to me. "Guess you won't have to listen to me nag you about that knife after all. Have fun shopping without me."

34

— · —

CHAPTER THIRTY-FOUR

AFTER ENDING THE CALL to Beyan, Farrah enchanted King Addan's medallion with the calling spell and instructed him on how to trigger it. We said our goodbyes to the king and queen and left. As we opened the door, Baz stepped to the side to let us pass.

"Have a good day, friends," he said.

"You as well," I said. "Although I'm sure we'll see you later."

He raised a brow. "That's the way of it, is it?"

I grinned. "Hope you don't mind."

He grinned back. "Nah. I could use some action."

As we hurried away, we could hear King Addan call Baz into the room, no doubt to tell him to gather the king's men. Although it was only mid-morning, they'd have a lot to do before tonight if they wanted to be prepared.

As did I.

"Are you sure you don't want to walk around the Merchants' District with me?" I asked Farrah.

She shook her head. "It would be fun, but I need to get back to the Order. And that library."

"Ah. Okay, then." While I was glad Farrah had seen something in the Order's library that could perhaps help us tonight, I knew better than to get into a discussion about magic with her. I could already feel the headache forming just thinking about it.

"Oh, dear."

"What is it?"

Farrah frowned. "I just realized, I won't be able to get back in. I don't have a ring."

I tugged the Order's signet ring off my finger and handed it to her. "Here, take it."

"Then how will you get back in?"

I felt in my pocket for the calling stone, reassured to feel its weight in my hand. "I'll use your fancy, handy calling stone, of course."

She slipped the ring on her finger. "All right. I'll see you back at the Order, then."

I pointed out the path she should take, and then stood there for a moment watching her go. She hadn't even gone two steps when a tall, thin person emerged from an alley and began following her. I started after them, worried.

Then I saw the person recoil as if stung. They grabbed their head, doubling over in sudden pain. Farrah continued on her way, not even bothering to turn around.

I smiled to myself. No need to worry. She would be just fine by herself in Bomora.

I wandered into the Merchants' District. By now, all the shops were open and the streets were more crowded than they had been earlier.

While I did buy some supplies for the return trip home, I found myself drawn to a shop window that featured ... baby items. Well, the mission to recover Prince Coran was the reason I was here, after all. Still, that didn't mean I had to stop and look in the shop window, which featured two handmade wooden cradles, some carved wooden mobiles, and little wooden toys and blocks.

And I didn't have to open the door and actually go inside.

A musical voice greeted me. "Welcome to my shop, sir! My name is Nima. Is there anything special you're looking for today?"

The shop owner bustled over to me. Nearly as tall as me, her dark brown hair was tied back and peppered with little bits of wood. As was her apron. I looked around the shop. It was filled with all sorts of wood carvings—not just the cradles and toys in the window, but also chairs, small tables, bowls, trinket boxes. A beautifully intricate blonde-and-mahogany chess set was displayed on one table. "This is your shop?" I asked. At Nima's proud nod, I added, "These are amazing."

"Thank you." She beamed with pride. "I do all sorts of woodcarving, but I like to display the items in the window by theme." She winked at me. "First time father, eh?"

"Oh. I'm not ..."

Nima laughed. "No need to be shy about it. Becoming a father scares many a man, but it can be quite rewarding. Once you get past the fear, of course."

She pointed at the cradles in the window. "Made from the strongest wood, guaranteed to keep your new baby safe."

"Oh, I'm not ..." I started to say again, then stopped. I finished lamely, "From around here."

"Oh?" She quirked an eyebrow. "Then you probably don't want something so big and bulky to have to carry with you. A little toy for the new baby? A trinket for the mother?"

"Ah. I really shouldn't—" Randomly, I found myself wondering what Farrah might like.

"I understand. It's better to shop with the woman's input." She winked, then bustled over to the shop counter, where a big bowl filled with small carvings sat. She pulled something from it, then handed it to me. "Here you go."

I took it automatically, puzzling over it for a few seconds until I realized what I was holding. A pacifier.

"I found a very soft, but durable wood to use for these," Nima explained. "Best for calming your baby down so you can get some sleep."

Huh. Something like this might actually come in handy tonight. "How much?"

Nima winked again. "Free of charge, sir."

"Are you sure? I'm happy to pay for it." Coming from a Bomorran merchant, usually as devious and cutthroat as the rest of the kingdom's citizens, it was an extremely generous offer.

"I'm sure," she said. "You just go and enjoy spending time with your new baby."

"Wow. I ... thanks."

She waved away my words with a smile. "Just come on back when you're ready to outfit your baby's room. And bring the missus!"

I smiled back and exited the store. Putting the pacifier in my pocket, I decided to head back to the Emerald Order.

35

— · —

CHAPTER THIRTY-FIVE

THE REST OF THE day passed uneventfully. Farrah spent her time studying in the Order's library, while I ate a late lunch and then took a nap. I figured I'd need it to get me through the night.

I woke up as the sun was setting. Heading downstairs to check on Farrah, I saw green cloaks everywhere. There were some people conversing in the foyer, while others were moving about, preparing for the meeting. Someone was passing out little jars of salt, and many people were pinning finger-length twigs of rowan to their clothing. I even saw several people sharpening some iron knives and swords.

But even with how crowded the Order had suddenly become, I realized I was seeing just a portion of the membership, and wondered, not for the first time, if our plan was going to work.

The one place that was free of any people—save for Farrah—was the library. I breathed a quiet sigh of relief as I slipped inside.

Farrah sat at one of the small tables, hunched over an open book. A small stack of additional volumes was piled on the desk to her left, while two books lay open on her right. Some wisps of her lavender hair had fallen out of her ribbon, forming a cloud around her ebony face. She didn't even look up as I entered, lost in her studies.

I pulled up a chair across from her and sat down. "Hey, Farrah."

She startled, and her finger skimming the page skidded across the paper, causing it to pucker. She frowned and tried to smooth the paper out. "You could give me some warning."

"I did," I pointed out. "Find anything good?"

"Actually, yes, I have." She picked up one of the open books and handed it to me, pointing at a specific passage. "Look at this."

Following her pointing finger, I read:

…. And whilst one may not consider themself a true practitioner of Faerie magic unless one is born of Faerie, there are some ways a human can share in the magic of the Fae. As tradition is considered of utmost importance to the Fae, these ways include rituals of request (this proves particularly potent on special holidays in which the Veil between the two worlds is the thinnest) or by aiding the Fae in some of the practices against humans for which they are best known: changelings or the offering of adults for either sport or servitude. One does not even have to have a blood bond with the baby or adult which is being offered, as power and dominance sometimes provide a stronger tie than even blood may. Through such a bond, one may access Faerie magic continuously, and can continue to strengthen their ties to the Fae and use such magic with subsequent offerings. Interestingly, while humans can tap into Faerie magic, and also share each other's powers, the sharing of power only works one way. The Fae can—and often do—share power amongst themselves, but cannot access human magic, as its nature is too foreign to the Fae to use properly.

And yet the Fae need humans, lesser beings though they be. For the one thing humanity holds over the Fae is the fact that the power of the land of Faerie will fade without any ties to humankind.

I looked up from the book. "This all seems really interesting, but I can't make any sense of it."

Farrah chuckled. "I know, I know, you're not the scholarly type. Basically, what diPera is saying here is that those kidnapped children are the conduits for the Emerald Order to have Faerie magic. But the magic only flows one way—into the Order, from the Fae—and the Order can share that magic amongst themselves."

I frowned, trying to figure out where Farrah was going with this. "The Order has been turning over kidnapped babies to the Fae for at least ten or more years by now. And who knows? Maybe they've even given the Fae some human adults." That was a lot of power, stored up over time. "And if all the members are sharing power—"

"Which we know is possible. We've seen it first hand," Farrah said, calling to mind the confrontations we'd had over the years with two power mad former knights of Rothschan stealing magic from their own citizens, as well as the people of Calia. "The Order may be doing something similar, or perhaps have figured out a less .... gruesome ... way of acquiring power."

"Okay. So they're getting more magic with each offering ..."

"Continuously." Farrah jabbed her finger at the text. "Fae magic is about nature. It may wax and wane over time, but each season renews it in some capacity. And it only goes one way."

I thought about the copious amounts of magic the Order was using for its traps and glamours. They obviously had built up their magical stores where they had magic to spare.

Enlar's voice echoed in my head. *Their true aim is to steal the magic from the lands of Faerie until there is nothing left.*

The Heart of the Hwisprian Woods had said that her forest was dying, its bleeding magic flowing straight into the Order through her stolen soul.

And every member of the Order would be in attendance at tonight's presentation of Calia's Crown Prince Coran to the Fae, when normally only Magnus, their leader, would go with a limited number of people.

Speaking of all the Order's members ... my mind raced over all the things I had seen on the way to the library.

And suddenly, I knew what the Emerald Order planned for tonight. For the prince, and for the Fae.

I gasped. Farrah's grim face told me she had already come to the same conclusion.

"It will be Samhain in just a few hours," she said. "One of the sacred holidays for both humans and the Fae, when magic will flow strongly between our two worlds. When the Order gives Prince Coran to the Fae, there's a brief moment when he's of both worlds. The Order already has enough magic behind them that they could launch an assault on the Fae, but if they kill Prince Coran at the right moment, they can use that world duality to decimate the Fae that are present. From there, it would be easy enough to keep the portal open and kill off the rest of them. They'd be too weak to fight back, anyway."

"So what do we do?"

"We just have to make sure we get Prince Coran out of there before the ritual transfer begins. Otherwise, none of us will make it out of there alive."

36

CHAPTER THIRTY-SIX

OUR HORSES' HOOVES MADE soft footfalls as we led them into the moonlit area. Glidhaan's Grove was only about a half hour's ride outside of Bomora, and perhaps we were even early, for the wood seemed empty.

Empty of the Fae, I mean.

The full force of the Emerald Order, some on horseback as well, but mostly on foot, had gathered in the open area ringed by the tall, dark trees.

Elaina dismounted and went to Magnus to help him. He passed Prince Coran to her, then dismounted himself. For a brief moment, while Elaina was holding the prince, our eyes met, and I thought, *This is perfect! We should take the baby and run!* but Magnus instantly reached for the baby prince, and the opportunity was gone.

Besides, this wasn't the right time. I only hoped I would know the right time when it came.

I scratched at my neck where the clasp of my green cloak lay. Magnus had gifted both Farrah and me with green cloaks of our own for the occasion.

"Finally, Rhyss, you're one of us! Well, you've always been one of us, but now you look like it!" Magnus had said proudly as he had handed me the heavy cloth.

Although the cloak looked elegant, it chafed at my neck. But it did provide good cover for my traveling bag, which was hidden underneath. Farrah had brought hers as well. We both knew that whatever happened tonight, we would not be going back to the Order's headquarters.

When Farrah had seen me dressed in the green cloak, she had given a short laugh. "With that cloak, and those vines running down your arms and over your face, you'll blend in just fine in the forest."

I had laughed along with her, but inwardly I was worried. This was the final night of the Heart's curse. By dawn tomorrow, if I hadn't either killed or brought her Magnus, I'd be dead.

You'll probably be dead regardless, a voice inside me said matter-of-factly. I didn't know what bothered me more: the fact that the voice was probably right, or the fact that it was so calm about it.

As I scratched, I glanced around. In the darkness, I couldn't tell if King Addan's men were in place, but I hoped they were. It hadn't seemed wise to contact him again once I returned to the Order, what with all the people around.

I looked to the nighttime sky. The full moon shone coldly overhead, a scattering of stars adding their own lights against the darkness. I didn't see any large shadows overhead, and wondered if Beyan had gotten in touch with Joichan. If Joichan was even coming.

I shivered, even though the heavy cloak excellently kept out the cold night air. *I really, really hope we're not on our own.*

And then all thoughts fled my mind as, across the grove, the Fae came.

A pale light seemed to blossom from the ground, illuminating the figures that had started walking toward us. Tiny pixies flitted about, weaving around the heads of their larger Fae companions. Their giggles echoed across the grove. Several lithe women stepped out from the trees, their hair long braids of green and gold and red, their dark brown skin boasting various whorled patterns. Squat little men wearing pointy red hats followed on the women's heels. These must be the dryads and gnomes of Glidhaan's Grove, I realized.

And then the light grew bigger and brighter, until it seemed it was practically daylight in the wood. Through the light, I could see glimpses of a world beyond: daytime in that world's forest, showing off the bright reds and deep oranges of an autumn similar to ours. And yet the leaves had an otherworldly perfection to them that spoke of a realm steeped in dangerous, ancient magic.

This must be a portal between our world and the land of Faerie. Samhain was here, and the Veil between the worlds had thinned enough to allow more of the Fae into the human realm.

The beings now stepping into our midst from that other world were even more beautiful, if that were possible, than the gorgeous, deadly land they had just left. And they were just as deadly in their perfection.

A tall man with long raven tresses stepped through the portal. Clad in an icy white tight-fitted jacket and breeches, he glowed with an inner light. At his side walked an equally tall and stately woman, her jet black hair piled high on her head and pinned in place with elaborate diamond-studded combs. Her bright white fitted bodice dress boasted elaborate embroidery and more white jewels, offset by the white fur-lined cloak she clutched around her gown.

If I couldn't have guessed they were Fairie royalty from their look and bearing alone, the crowns they both wore would have tipped me off. These impressive figures must be King Finvarra and his Queen, Oona, the long-reigning royals of the Seelie Court of Faerie.

As they approached, Farrah and Elaina dipped low curtsies, while I bowed to the royal couple. Magnus merely nodded his head, possibly because he held Prince Coran in his arms.

Or possibly because he considered himself equal to the Faerie royals.

Hmm. Interesting.

"Magnus." King Finvarra's voice, rich and resonant, rang out over the grove. "I see you brought us a new offering, as promised. But who are all these others you bring with you?"

"Greetings, Your Majesty," Magnus said. He waved one hand to indicate the entirety of the Emerald Order. "This is the group I lead, the Emerald Order."

"Ah. Lord Indwere's pet project," the Faerie king said. He surveyed the people behind us. "Impressive how much your numbers have grown in such a short time."

"Well, it has been over a decade since Lord Indwere was with us," Magnus pointed out delicately.

The king blinked once, his only indication of surprise. "Indeed? Has that much time passed?"

Queen Oona said, "Time doesn't have the same weight to us as it does to you humans."

"Of course," Magnus said. He lifted Prince Coran higher so the Faerie royals could see the baby's face. Surprisingly, despite all the moving and jostling, Coran stayed fast asleep.

King Finvarra waved a hand over the baby, and Coran started to glow, soft and golden. The king's own hand started to glow as well. A satisfied smile spread over the Faerie king's face. "Perfect. Absolutely perfect."

Both the king and Magnus looked overhead, marking the moon's position in the nighttime sky.

"It is time. Give me the child."

Magnus started to transfer the sleeping child to King Finvarra's outstretched arms. Prince Coran just barely touched the king's eager fingers, still partially supported by Magnus.

And then I spied the glint of moonlight on metal.

37

—·—

CHAPTER THIRTY-SEVEN

I THRUST MY HORSE'S reins into Farrah's hands.

Unresisting, she took them from me. And gasped as she spied what I had already seen. "Rhyss! There—hurry!"

But I was already moving.

Magnus had handed the baby cradled in his left arm to King Finvarra. In his right hand, an iron dagger had appeared. While the Faerie king was focused solely on his new acquisition, Magnus thrust the dagger directly into the king's chest.

The king gasped and staggered back, grabbing his chest.

Prince Coran started to slip from his grasp. Finally, the chaos proved too much for him, and he woke up, wailing.

I rushed forward and grabbed the baby just before he could hit the ground.

Horrified, Queen Oona rushed to her husband's side, easing him to the ground. Blood rapidly flowed from his wound, staining his once pristine white jacket a bright crimson.

Magnus pulled another weapon from his belt—an iron sword—and raised it high. Time seemed to slow as, wide-eyed, I watched Magnus attack the unarmed Faerie queen. A gasp barely had time to escape her lips before his sword sliced across her neck.

The gruesome sight shook me out of my trance. I ran back toward Farrah. "Come on, let's go!"

She quickly mounted her horse, then reached out her hands to take Prince Coran from me so I could get on my horse as well. I shook my head, not wanting to let go of the little prince.

Behind us, Glidhaan's Grove erupted with the sounds of battle. The Emerald Order, iron weapons at the ready, charged at the Fae. The Fae countered with their own magical attacks.

Farrah spurred her horse into a run. Before I could do the same, a handaxe whizzed past my ear.

"Don't even think about it."

Magnus stalked toward me, his iron sword raised. Blood dripped from the blade. With a sinking feeling, I quickly glanced behind him. Queen Oona lay slumped over the unmoving body of her husband, King Finvarra.

Magnus leveled his sword at me. Even though I was on horseback, with his height, he still had enough reach to injure me. "Don't make me hurt you, boy. Give me the child."

I debated the wisdom of pulling my sword while holding Prince Coran. My hand crept to my side. Magnus and I looked at each other for a long, measured moment.

Even though his dark eyes were now completely mad, all I could see was the jovial "uncle" who had spent countless hours as my friend and mentor. The man who my parents had once trusted with my life. Although I knew I had to fulfill the geas to deliver him, dead or alive, to the Heart of the Hwisprian Woods, I also knew I wouldn't be able to hurt him, let alone kill him.

My hand dropped away from my sword.

I felt the finality of my future close in around me.

An arrow whizzed out of the darkness, catching Magnus's shoulder blade. He yelped and dropped his sword.

"Go, go!" Elaina's voice yelled at me from the direction of the shot.

I obeyed, prompting my horse into a gallop. Farrah, seeing that I hadn't been following her, had turned back. We now both headed for the forest, going as fast as we could, while I tried desperately to hold on to Prince Coran.

Although the cries of the injured and dying, both human and Fae, echoed throughout Glidhaan's Grove, one anguished cry stood out over the others.

"Elaina!" Farrah said, halting her horse.

"We can't go back," I said.

"I know," she said, but she looked torn. Reluctantly, she spurred her horse into moving again, away from the battle.

At the edge of the grove, I chanced a look back. Many of the Fae lay slain, their beauty marred by the gruesome deaths the Order had inflicted on them. It looked like the Order had the upper hand.

But then a group of ragtag men emerged, screaming, from the darkness behind the Order. King Addan's men, there to put an end to the Emerald Order once and for all.

And in the dark sky, a bright orange flame blotted out the stars in the sky. The wind picked up, and the battle stopped momentarily as both the Fae and the humans turned as one to look up at the sky.

Joichan, father of Queen Jennica of Calia and grandfather of Crown Prince Coran, had arrived.

He landed in the grove with a thud, causing the ground to ripple with the weight of his arrival. Another breath of fire burst from him, upward into the sky, a warning to the Emerald Order.

Both Fae and humans alike scattered, screaming. The brave—or maybe foolish—ones who hadn't left the grove turned to face this new and potentially common enemy.

Joichan started to reach out toward the nearest green-cloaked figure with a sharp, wicked-looking claw. The white light from the still-open Faerie portal illuminated each flowing emerald-colored cloak, providing easy targets for Joichan to identify his enemy.

I wondered if any of the members of the Order would be smart enough to realize they should remove their cloaks before it was too late.

Oh well. Definitely not my problem.

I turned and rode after Farrah.

38

CHAPTER THIRTY-EIGHT

AFTER PICKING OUR WAY out of Glidhaan's Grove, we found the main road out of Bomora and headed east. We rode steadily through the night, stopping only long enough for me to make a makeshift sling out of my green cloak to carry Prince Coran in. The baby prince had settled back down, happily sleeping in the sling nestled against my chest.

I looked down at his peaceful face. He gurgled in his sleep, a little smile spreading over his face.

As we rode I kept an uneasy eye on the full moon overhead. Daylight would soon be here—in fact, we should reach the Hwisprian Woods right around sunrise. And I would re-meet the Heart with nothing to show for it. I could already feel the magical vines tattooed on my skin growing thicker, wrapping themselves around my heart, ready to squeeze my life away.

At another point, we made a quick stop to eat something and let the horses rest. We sat on two fallen logs, wolfing down some hard rolls while the horses grazed.

The thorns pressed into my neck, making it hard to talk. "I think ... you ... should carry the prince."

I carefully lifted the sling over my head, gritting my teeth against the sensation of hundreds of tiny knives scraping against my skin as I did so. I passed the baby to Farrah.

"Me? Why? He's doing just fine with you," she said.

"Just … please."

She shrugged and took Prince Coran from me, putting the sling around her body. "You'll have to get over your fear of babies, you know. You're his godfather, after all."

I stayed silent, unwilling to tell her that it wasn't a fear of babies that made me give her the prince. It was more that I was afraid for his future safety if he stayed with me.

Food finished, we got back on the road. We were making better time than I had expected. Although the sky was beginning to lighten with the purple of morning twilight, we could see the edge of the Hwisprian Woods just ahead.

"Do you think it will be okay, when you meet the Heart again?" Farrah whispered as we drew closer.

"It will … have to be. I have no proof … that Magnus is dead." I sighed. "And, back there … I can't kill him. No matter … what he's become."

"I understand." She sighed as well. "I hope the Heart will understand that, too."

The sound of thundering hoofbeats behind us made us both turn.

An arrow hit me high in the shoulder, just missing my heart.

I gasped for air as I slumped forward. The pain radiating from my shoulder made it hard to breathe, as did the tightening grip of the cursed vines. I could feel their solidness now, thick and binding, twisting around me as they slowly dug their thorns in.

My horse whinnied in fear and bolted forward. Farrah galloped after me, grabbing the reins of my runaway horse just as we disappeared into the darkness of the Hwisprian Woods. Soothing my mount, she got the beast under control, while desperately trying to keep the prince secure in his cloth sling.

"Who shot you?" she wondered, but I couldn't answer her through my wheezing. Not that I had an answer for her, anyway.

She looked around, then at me. "You're not in a condition for us to try to outrun whoever that was. And I need to tend that wound. Let's find a place to hide."

We veered off the road, heading deeper into the forest. In the faint purple light, we found a spot that allowed me some measure of comfort while still keeping us fairly hidden. Farrah dismounted quickly, a bit awkward with Prince Coran strapped to her. I tried to dismount as well, but had to lean heavily on Farrah to avoid completely tumbling off my horse. She helped me lie down, head propped against a fallen log.

And not a moment too soon. We could hear the hoofbeats of my unknown assailant entering the Hwisprian Woods. I strained to listen over the rushing in my ears. It sounded like a lone rider, thank the gods. Farrah and I were definitely in no shape to deal with multiple attackers.

The rider picked their way down the leaf-strewn road, passing our position. The hoofbeats faded off into the distance. But just as I thought perhaps we were safe, we could hear the sound of hoofbeats returning.

Farrah and I silently exchanged glances. The mystery person seemed to know vaguely where we were. If we could just wait them out....

The whole forest seemed to be frozen in silence.

And then Prince Coran, who had somehow slept through all the earlier commotion, woke up and started to fuss.

Farrah frantically began soothing him, crooning to him in a barely audible whisper. It didn't seem to make a difference. He was most likely hungry or something, and any moment now he'd probably start crying....

"Left ... pocket," I whispered hoarsely to Farrah.

She gave me a puzzled look, but obligingly reached into my left pocket. When she fished out the wooden pacifier, she smiled and nodded. She popped it into Prince Coran's mouth, smoothing back his hair, just as the start of a cry escaped his little lips.

The hoofbeats from the road, which had been slowly *clop-clop-clopping* back and forth, stopped.

I sucked in a breath. The dull pain from my shoulder was getting worse, and the sharp thorns pressed in deeper. How was I not bleeding all over already? I clenched and unclenched my fists, trying to focus on something else besides the pain.

Farrah reached over and smacked first her mount, then mine. The horses ran off into the forest, whinnying loudly as they left.

Immediately, we heard a third set of hoofbeats following them.

"Good," Farrah whispered, coming to my side. She touched the arrow still protruding from my shoulder. "Oh, dear. This is going to hurt."

"It can't be any worse ... than I'm already feeling," I said, breathing heavily. "But ... it hardly matters. In just an hour or so ... I'll be a dead man anyway."

Footsteps crunched over the fallen leaves that led to our hiding spot. The tip of a sword touched my throat.

"That's right," a new voice said. "You *will* be a dead man."

Magnus.

Slowly, I turned my head just enough to look up at him. Farrah stayed where she was, her arms wrapped protectively around Prince Coran.

Magnus looked a bit worse for wear, bruised and bloodied from the battle at Glidhaan's Grove earlier in the evening. His clothing was a bit charred, and parts of his hair and eyebrows were singed, suggesting he had gotten caught in Joichan's fire.

I hoped Joichan was all right. And Elaina.

Magnus looked down at me, scorn radiating from him. And something else.

"You were like a son to me," he whispered, the hurt in his voice making him sound like a little boy, and not the leader of a secret magical organization. "When your father took you and your mother and disappeared, I lost the only family I had ever known. And then to have you return ... I thought you knew how much that meant to me."

His voice took on a manic quality. "You should have been mine, you know that? Markus got everything ... the beautiful girl, the strapping son. The chance at getting out of the cesspit known as Bomora and a chance at respectability. While I had to make do as a second-rate thief, laughed at by everyone, until I got my position as leader of the Emerald Order. Then all those who laughed at me before laughed no longer."

"Magnus ..." I tried to project, but I was wheezing too hard through the pain to speak above a whisper. "Uncle ..."

His eyes flashed. "You're not fit to call me that anymore. No one I would ever consider family would betray me the way you did tonight. Like father, like son. To which I say, death to bad memories."

He raised his sword to strike.

The sun peeked over the horizon, its light piercing through the trees.

And behind Magnus, an even brighter light glowed. It couldn't have been the sunrise—that was the wrong direction for it.

The light grew bigger and brighter, engulfing the silhouette of the trees around us.

The cursed vines writhing around my body hardened, and although they'd just been merely scratching and poking at me up to that point, they now chose this moment to sink their thorny little claws deep into my flesh.

And pierce my heart.

I felt another thing pierce my heart. Magnus's sword.

I screamed.

Through the haze of pain clouding my vision and the violent rushing of blood in my ears, I heard Farrah scream somewhere above me.

The light grew so bright it eclipsed everything. All I could see was white.

Magnus screamed.

And then I knew no more.

39

—·—

CHAPTER THIRTY-NINE

EVERYTHING WAS WHITE.

I blinked, unsure I had opened my eyes. No, I was fairly sure they were open. But I couldn't see anything, just an endless expanse of bright white light.

The light dimmed a little, solidifying into a familiar silhouette.

The Heart of the Hwisprian Woods approached me where I stood, dumbfounded.

"Thank you, Rhyss," she said in her low, musical voice. "For delivering the leader of the Emerald Order to me, as you promised."

"But I didn't—" I stopped abruptly. Although I hadn't personally brought him there, Magnus had set foot in the Hwisprian Woods—the Heart's domain—when he pursued Farrah and me.

I eyed the Heart warily, meeting her impassive ice blue eyes. "What happened to him?"

Her eyes flashed red. "He is no more," she said simply. "I have taken care of the blight that he was on my Wood, Bomora, and the Gifted Lands. My magic has been restored. He has paid for all of his crimes, and then some."

I bowed my head. Although I knew the Heart was in the right to reclaim her power, I also wished things could have gone differently.

Magnus, for all his madness, had at one point been part of my father's chosen family.

"Where am I?" I asked, looking around the vast expanse of white.

"You are somewhere between life and death," she said. "Your injuries were grievous. Also, my curse had just about taken hold of you, even though you had made good on your promise."

I looked at my hands and arms. My freckled skin held no more traces of the ghostly vine tattoos. Reaching up, my fingers brushed the side of my neck, finding only smooth skin. The Heart's mark was gone.

"Yes, you are free of my geas," the Heart assured me.

"What now?"

"That is up to you. You have earned your eternal rest. Or, if you wish, I can heal you and restore you to the world. I owe you a great debt for restoring my magic, after all."

Honestly, rest sounded lovely. To never feel cold, or pain, or hunger again? I could live with that. Well, obviously, I wouldn't be *living* with it, but ...

Somewhere beyond us, just on the edge of my hearing, I detected a faint sound. Someone was ... crying?

I concentrated. Words were jumbled up in between the sobs and sniffles.

Farrah's voice.

She was saying, "Rhyss, please don't go, come back to me. Rhyss ..."

The Heart watched me with her ancient, fathomless eyes. "Well? What do you wish to do?"

As much as I wanted to sleep, and just not worry about anything anymore, I found I couldn't say that. Because I *was* worried, specifically about one thing.

One person.

Farrah.

I didn't want her to be upset. I didn't like the idea that my death, blissful though it might be for me, would cause her pain. I didn't want to be the cause of her sadness.

"If you could send me back, my lady, I would be most grateful," I said.

The Heart smiled. "Your request is granted. I will heal you, but you will still require rest to recover fully. To that end, I will assist you further and provide you with a place to stay, with provisions, for as long as you need. When you are ready to leave, you have only to walk out the door, and you will find yourself on the eastern edge of my forest, on the road leading to Orchwell. I trust you can find your way from there."

"Yes, my lady. Thank you."

"It is I who should be thanking you. You have saved me, and in turn, my forest. Should you ever come this way again, you will always find a welcome here. Farewell."

She disappeared into the steadily growing white light. I shielded my eyes against the brightness, then closed them against the overpowering glow. A light breeze kicked up around me, along with the sound of rustling leaves. The wind grew stronger, bringing with it a steady rumbling noise, and then a deep cracking.

And then the wind stopped, and all was quiet.

When I opened my eyes again, everything was still white.

Something soft cradled my head and body. The weight of something warm and equally soft lightly pressed down on me. I could hear a baby crying, in the distance, and soft sniffling, just overhead.

Light touches of water intermittently hit my skin.

As my eyes adjusted and I looked around, I saw Farrah's face hovering above me, eyes downcast. The little drops of water that I had felt were her tears.

I blinked blearily and reached a weak hand out to her. "Farrah? Can you stop crying? You're getting me all wet."

She sniffed loudly, her eyes meeting mine. "Oh my goodness! You're alive!"

I groaned, starting to feel every ache and pain in my body. "Yeah. I can tell."

She grabbed my hand and looked me over. I followed her gaze to where Magnus's weapons had pierced me. My shoulder felt stiff and sore, and moving it hurt. There was a small, round scar where the arrow had hit me. Just under that, where Magnus had thrust his sword through my heart, my skin had a larger, mottled red scab. I breathed in deeply, then coughed a little. Maybe I shouldn't breathe in that deep, just yet. The Heart had spoken the truth: while she had healed the worst of my injuries, I still needed time and rest to recover completely.

"Where are we?" asked Farrah.

"The Heart said she would give us a place to stay while I healed," I said in awe, speaking half to myself as I took in our surroundings.

I was lying in a bed carved of white wood, its roughened surface with various knots and whorls a mirror of the walls in this strange, white wood circular room we found ourselves in. It gave me the impression we were inside a very large tree.

My bedcovers were a lovely patchwork quilt of red, orange, and gold leaves, and the air held a tang of earthiness.

Farrah was sitting on the bed beside me, her eyes equally filled with wonder.

"The Heart did this?" she asked, looking around.

I explained about how she had visited me, and had saved me from death after letting me choose between living or dying. But when I came to Farrah's role in my decision, I suddenly turned shy.

"But then I heard you crying, asking me not to leave, and I realized ... I couldn't leave. Not if it meant you would be unhappy."

"Why would that matter?" Farrah seemed genuinely curious, not a hint of her usual teasing snarkiness in her voice.

I took a deep breath. "Because. I love you."

Farrah didn't say anything, just stared at me. If I had any doubts that I was alive, I didn't any more—my heart was pounding so hard, I thought it would burst out of my body.

Then a slow smile spread over Farrah's lips.

"You don't know how long I've been hoping to hear you say that. Seriously, it's about time." Her smile grew wider. "I love you, too, Rhyss."

She leaned toward me and our lips met. Kissing Farrah was even better than I had imagined. As the kiss deepened, I drew her toward me and—

"Ow."

Farrah pulled back as I hissed in pain. I probably shouldn't have used my bad arm to bring her closer.

She chuckled. "I guess some things you're just not ready for yet. Lie back down, Rhyss. You've got a long way to go before you're better."

I wanted to protest—surely one more kiss wouldn't hurt—but I knew better than to argue when she went into healer mode. Instead, I reclined back against the leaf-quilt pillow.

"Where's Coran?" I asked.

Farrah looked over her shoulder. I followed her gaze. The prince was nestled in a cradle in the corner, made of the same ethereal white wood as the bed and the room. Little balls of light—tiny fairies, I presumed—floated around him. The baby was gurgling happily at his new friends, waving his arms in the air as he tried to touch them. The little Fae answered with giggles as they flitted back and forth above him.

Farrah turned back to me, smiling. "He seems to have acquired some otherworldly nursemaids. I think he's fine, for now."

"We'll need to get him back to Calia, as soon as we can."

She nodded. "We will. I'll call Beyan and let him know what's going on, and we can figure out a plan from there. In the meantime—" she gave me a stern look "—you just need to rest and get better."

"Yes, Farrah."

She softened her words with a quick kiss on my forehead. "Get some rest." She stood up and disappeared into another room I hadn't noticed before.

How big was this place? Well, it had been constructed by Faerie magic. I supposed it could be as big or as small as we needed.

While I contemplated the intricacies of Faerie magic, I fell asleep.

40

— · —

CHAPTER FORTY

FARRAH WALKED INTO MY room with a tray of food just as I was waking up. The smell of rabbit stew wafted in the air, and my stomach growled in anticipation.

Farrah placed the tray on my lap. "Glad you're awake. I didn't want to wake you if I didn't have to."

I picked up the wooden spoon lying on the tray and started eating. Around a mouthful of hot stew, I asked, "Did you get a hold of Beyan? What did he say?"

She pulled up a chair and sat at my bedside. "He was overjoyed to hear we recovered Prince Coran safely. He's sending some men to the border of the Hwisprian Woods to escort us back to Calia when we're ready. They should be in place by the time you're able to go."

She reached out and looked at my shoulder and chest. "It's looking pretty good. I can make up some potions or poultices to try to speed things up, but I don't think that will be necessary."

I flexed my shoulder experimentally. Already it felt less stiff, easier to move than it had a few hours ago. "Honestly, I'm feeling much better already. Maybe in a day or two we can get out of here."

"I hope so. I don't want the Calian soldiers to wait any longer than they have to, but Beyan is taking no chances."

"I don't blame him." I gulped down more stew. "How is Queen Jennica?"

Farrah frowned. "She's holding steady, but she's still unconscious. The sooner we can get Prince Coran back to her, the better." She looked at me sternly. "But not until you're well. So you better rest up."

I chuckled and nodded, finishing my stew. Farrah took the tray from me and left.

The hours passed uneventfully. Between tending to Prince Coran and me, Farrah had her hands full. There wasn't much I could do to help, so I slept a lot. All that sleeping must have been beneficial, because by the morning of the second day of our stay inside the large white tree, I felt good enough to travel again.

As we packed up to leave, something occurred to me. "Do you know what happened to our horses?" I asked Farrah, remembering how she had sent them away as a decoy for Magnus.

Farrah shook her head. "I don't know. After Magnus stabbed you and the Heart appeared, I stayed by your side in the woods. Everything was a hazy bright white, like an incredibly thick fog. I couldn't see more than an arm's length away from my face. Then suddenly the air shifted, and instead of kneeling by your side on the forest floor, I was sitting in this room, and you were lying in bed. I haven't left this tree since we found ourselves inside it."

I shouldered my pack and then gently lifted Prince Coran from his cradle. Holding the little prince didn't hurt my arm at all. "Well, I hope Beyan sent some extra horses along with his soldiers. Otherwise, it will be a slow walk back to Calia."

Farrah opened the door and stepped outside. Before I crossed the threshold, I turned around and faced the airy, ethereal room.

"Thank you," I said to the listening air. I felt a slight ripple on the breeze, and imagined I felt the Heart's acknowledgement of my words. Then I followed Farrah outside.

When I closed the door behind me, the door's outline melted into the tree. It looked like the doorway had never existed, and when I reached out to feel for the door handle, my hands met the smooth bark of the tree, but no cuts in the trunk where a door might have been.

Prince Coran's little Faerie companions flitted around him, making him giggle. The bobbing lights winked once, in farewell, and disappeared into the deeper forest.

Ahead of me lay the scrub and smaller trees that marked the edge of the Hwisprian Woods. Farrah waited at the treeline, where the road met the forest. She waved at me. "There you are! Come on, they're waiting for us."

I hurried along, carefully cradling Prince Coran in my arms. Reaching the road, I breathed a sigh of relief. Five mounted soldiers bearing the blue-and-white banner of Calia waited just outside the Hwisprian Woods. A young woman also rode with them, presumably a wet nurse for the baby.

Farrah was deep in conversation with one of the men. To the side of the group stood two riderless horses—the horses that I thought might have been lost to us.

The man talking to Farrah looked up. I recognized him as Kestos, the kingdom of Calia's Captain of the Guard. "Rhyss! Well met."

I nodded back. "I'm very glad to see all of you."

Although Farrah or any of the other soldiers would have been willing to carry Prince Coran, I found I was reluctant to let go of the baby. I was his godfather, after all. I wanted to personally make sure he reached home safely.

Kestos handed me a sling, much sturdier than the makeshift one I had made from my Emerald Order cloak. My arm felt better, but it still wasn't in perfect shape, so I needed help to mount my horse and then get the baby in place. So after some awkward maneuvering—"Are you *sure* you don't want me to carry the prince?" Farrah asked for the third time—I finally got settled and was ready to ride.

We headed north, stopping to stay overnight in the various roadside inns we had visited on our trip to Bomora. While the innkeepers could easily find rooms for Farrah, Coran, the wet nurse, and me, they were hard pressed to provide rooms for five more people, so the Calian soldiers camped nearby. Farrah and the wet nurse shared a room, and while I wanted the prince to stay near me, it made more sense for the baby prince to be in the women's room so it was easier for the wet nurse to feed him. Although, after the second day of seeing how tired Farrah looked from restless nights with a baby in her room, I privately was glad the women had overridden my earlier sentiment about rooming with Prince Coran.

While we rode, to pass the time, I asked Kestos if he had any news from Bomora. I hoped that perhaps King Beyan and King Addan had been in contact and Farrah and I could learn what happened at Glidhaan's Grove after we left.

But Kestos just shook his head. "I know that the two kings did talk, but I was not privy to what was said. However, Joichan returned to Calia a few days ago, and I believe he is still in the capital. So I think that is a good indication that we were victorious."

"I hope so," I said, thinking of Elaina.

The moment we rode in through the gates of Calia's capital city, the posted guards and the citizens present let out a loud cheer. Even if they hadn't heard any rumors about their beloved queen's magical malady, they would have all witnessed the prince's kidnapping. Their love for their prince and their happiness at seeing his safe return wrapped around us like a cozy blanket.

We headed straight for the palace. The impressive front doors were flung open as we approached. Beyan himself waited for us, impatient. He looked like he wanted to run right up to us, but his status as king and royal protocol kept him in place—just barely. To the side, two guards stood at attention, looking flushed and faintly embarrassed. I laughed to myself. Knowing Beyan, he probably had pushed the guards aside to open the doors himself.

We brought our horses to a halt. Before I could even dismount, Beyan was at my horse's side. "Rhyss. Farrah. I am so glad to see you back and unharmed." He reached up, arms outstretched. "Give me my son, please." A tremor of emotion laced his command.

With Farrah's help, I somehow extracted Prince Coran from his sling and passed him down to his father.

King Beyan's eyes filled with tears. He hugged his son to his chest, then tenderly kissed his forehead. The tears spilled down Beyan's face, unchecked. "Thank you. Thank you so, so much."

41

— · —

CHAPTER FORTY-ONE

ALTHOUGH I KNEW BEYAN was impatient to bring Prince Coran straight to Jennica, practicalities won out. The baby needed to be fed—and honestly, the rest of us were starving, too. After a quick bite, the soldiers dispersed, presumably back to their homes or their original duties. The wet nurse whisked Coran away to clean him up, promising to bring him straightaway to the royal bedchamber when she was finished.

So that left Farrah and me to follow King Beyan to visit Queen Jennica. We made our way to the suite of royal rooms in silence; this didn't seem like the right time for idle chitchat. When we got to the bedroom, the king entered first to assess things, then opened the door wider and waved Farrah and me in.

Joichan, the former Royal Consort and Queen Jennica's father, was in the room, as was the royal physician, Healer Pendt, who was checking on the queen. At Beyan's look, the man shook his head. "She still will not awaken, Your Majesty. But there seems to be a slight change—she was stirring a bit, whereas before she had just lain here completely still. I thought it a hopeful sign."

He looked beyond King Beyan, catching sight of Farrah and me. The weariness in his posture lifted a little. "Ah. Rhyss and Farrah. If you are here, I presume that means you were successful in recovering our Crown Prince?"

At our nods, the healer smiled. "Then perhaps that is the change I observed in the queen. I am glad to see you both back here, and well."

The healer stood and, after bowing to the king and saying his goodbyes, left the room. King Beyan sank down on the bed next to Jennica. Picking up a limp wrist, he began gently rubbing his fingers over her hand, murmuring softly to her. "Don't you worry, my love. Our Coran is back, and he's safe. Everything is fine."

I turned to Joichan. "Apologies for the delayed greeting, Joichan. It's a pleasure to see you again."

Joichan opened his mouth to say something, but no sound came out. A look of embarrassment washed over him, followed by sadness, and he slowly tapped his throat.

"I don't understand. Are you unwell?"

"My father-in-law is not allowed to speak," Beyan said from his place at the bed. "In order to be allowed to leave Graenir, and violate the terms of his ambassadorship, their royal mage put a spell of silence on him so he cannot speak while he's away. I understand it should lift once he returns."

"Oh my. I'm sorry," I said to Joichan.

He waved a hand in the air, as if he was waving my words away.

"It's a small inconvenience, if he could help Calia in our time of need," Beyan said softly. "Thank you again, Joichan."

A knock sounded at the door. Farrah opened it to find the wet nurse on the other side, holding a clean and quiet Prince Coran. She handed the baby to Farrah. "Here he is, my lady."

"Thank you," Farrah said. The wet nurse bobbed a curtsey and left. As Farrah turned back, Prince Coran in her arms, I caught the look on her face and had to bite my lip to keep from laughing aloud. Even though the king and queen had bestowed courtesy titles on us, we still weren't used to being addressed as "lord" and "lady" and found it funny more often than not.

On the bed, Queen Jennica was stirring restlessly.

Farrah crossed the room and handed the prince to his father. Beyan gently cradled his son, kissing him again on his forehead, before placing him on the bed next to his mother.

Prince Coran laughed and gurgled, stretching his fingers and toes into the air.

Next to him, Jennica stirred once more, then stilled. For a moment, none of us dared to breathe. She was so incredibly still. Had something happened?

And then the queen's eyes fluttered open.

"I had such a horrible nightmare," she whispered hoarsely. "I dreamed that ... my baby ..."

Bewildered, she turned her head to the side to see Prince Coran, still laughing and making indistinct baby noises. "It must have just been a dream."

Beyan gently brushed Jennica's hair back from her face. "I suppose it depends on what happened in the dream. Regardless, you're awake now, and our baby is back home, safe and sound. Thanks to Rhyss and Farrah."

She pushed up on an elbow slightly to look over at us and smile. "Yes. My friends. We can always count on you."

The queen was obviously still too weak for us to get into the details of our adventures—and anyway, there would be plenty of time to recount them for her later. But I had a feeling we wouldn't really need to. Perhaps, through her magical connection with the prince, she already knew everything that had happened.

"Jennica, we're so glad you're awake and on the mend," Farrah said. "Rhyss and I will leave you now, let you get some rest. We'll visit when you're feeling stronger."

"Of course," Jennica said, leaning back against her pillow and closing her eyes.

"Do you want us to take Prince Coran?" I asked Beyan.

He nodded, never taking his eyes off his wife. "The baby's room is two doors down the hall, on the left."

Farrah scooped up the baby and we left the royal bedchamber.

At Prince Coran's room, the wet nurse answered the door. The poor woman looked tired and worn, but she gamely smiled when she saw us with the baby.

"Thank you for bringing him back," she said.

"Would you like to take a break?" Farrah asked. "We can stay here with Coran for a bit."

The young woman lit up. "If it's no trouble, my lady ..."

"None at all."

She sketched a quick curtsey. "Thank you, thank you so much! I'll just go grab something to eat real quick—"

"Take as long as you need." Farrah winked at her. "If you want to sneak a nap in ..."

The wet nurse flushed. She dipped her head, then hurried out of the room.

Farrah gently placed Coran in his cradle, leaning over to coo and make funny faces at him. The sun streaming in through the big window created a halo around her lavender hair, and as she reached down once more to touch the prince's tiny hand, I was struck with a thought:

I was looking at my future.

"Farrah."

She looked at me, a question in her eyes at the unexpected urgency of my tone.

"Marry me."

"What?" She laughed nervously. Prince Coran grabbed at her outstretched finger and tried to stick it in his mouth.

I crossed over to where she stood by the cradle and grabbed her hand, heedless of the fact that it was sticky with baby spit.

"You know that was just in Coran's mouth," she pointed out. She stared deep into my eyes. "You can't be serious."

"I am serious. I love you, Farrah. Marry me."

She didn't say anything for a moment, just kept staring at me. Then: "All right. I will."

I let out the breath I hadn't even realized I'd been holding. "You will?"

"Didn't I just say that?" She laughed. "Honestly, Rhyss."

I leaned forward and kissed her. Any other questions I had for her would just have to wait. Besides, it didn't matter.

She had already answered the most important one.

42

CHAPTER FORTY-TWO

FARRAH AND I STAYED as guests in the palace while we waited for Queen Jennica to regain her strength enough to want to see visitors. We passed the time helping with Prince Coran, and also got some much-needed rest as well. While King Beyan spent most of his waking hours with his queen, he still had some kingdom duties to attend to.

One of those duties included contacting King Addan of Bomora.

Although Joichan couldn't talk about the battle, through a series of yes and no questions, Beyan had pieced together the highlights of what had happened at Glidhaan's Grove. ("It was a very long and painfully slow conversation," Beyan told Farrah and me later, privately.) The most important thing was that the Fae had not been wiped out by the Order, although their numbers had been greatly reduced. We would have to rely on King Addan to fill in the details.

So while Jennica rested, Beyan, Farrah, Joichan, and I gathered in the Great Hall to contact King Addan. His image appeared above Farrah's outstretched hand.

"As you're all in the same room, I trust you had a successful return to Calia?" King Addan asked Farrah and me.

We nodded.

Beyan said, "Thank you again for your aid, Your Majesty. We wondered if you had any information about what happened on Samhain?"

King Addan said, "My men reported that, although they tried to assist the Fae and defend them against the Order, they were sorely outnumbered. That is, until a giant golden dragon appeared in the sky."

Joichan made a small, satisfied noise.

"King Finvarra and Queen Oona of the Seelie Court were slain. The Fae held the portal open long enough to return to their own world, but sustained heavy losses. As for the Order, their numbers have been decimated, their headquarters are in ruins, and their leader has disappeared."

"Ruins?" I asked.

"It was the strangest thing," King Addan said. "Sometime during the night—towards dawn, I would say—there was a great earthquake in the city. And yet, for all the rumbling and commotion it caused, it only damaged one building. The Emerald Order's headquarters were reduced to rubble, and it looked like everything inside was completely destroyed."

"Completely destroyed?" I echoed. "But what could cause such a thing?"

A new face appeared next to King Addan's image. "It's hard to know for sure, but my guess is that the balance of magic between the Fae and the Order was upset somehow, and the backlash destroyed the Order's headquarters."

"Elaina!" Farrah and I both cried out, overjoyed to see her.

Elaina looked healthy and whole, although her right arm was in a sling. She also sported a few scratches on her cheek.

"It's good to see you, my friends," Elaina said. "I worried about what may have befallen you after you left the grove."

"We were afraid for you as well," Farrah said. "We heard you scream, and then ..."

She smiled ruefully. "As you were leaving, Magnus attacked me, and I just barely deflected his attack. But then a giant claw came out of nowhere and flicked us both aside. It saved my life, even if it did break my arm. I was thrown into some bushes and got scratched up as well."

Joichan looked sheepish.

I chuckled. "I'm sure the dragon is sorry."

"I tried to stop Magnus from pursuing you," Elaina said. She hung her head. "I don't think I succeeded."

"It's all right," I assured her. I quickly filled her and King Addan in on what happened to Magnus in the Hwisprian Woods.

"His death—and the return of power to the Hwisprian Woods—are probably what caused the earthquake," Elaina mused. She looked at me. "I'm sorry for your loss."

"Thank you." Feeling uncomfortable, I sought a different subject. "I must say, we were surprised to find you with King Addan."

Elaina laughed. "You mean, you were surprised to find me alive, and with King Addan."

King Addan interjected, "After the battle, my men tended to her wounds. I met her when they brought her back here to recover and give a report. When I realized how knowledgeable she was about the Order and their ways, I asked her to join my advisors."

"Although they've suffered a setback, there are still enough members around to cause trouble," Elaina said. "And besides, we will need to figure out what to do with all this magic. While a lot of it returned to the land, there is still enough floating around in Bomora that it, too, could cause trouble if not harnessed properly."

"Have any of the Faerie court reached out to you, King Addan?" Farrah asked.

He shook his head. "I know their leaders were slain on Bomorran land. But since the one responsible is gone—and I personally did not have anything to do with the deaths of their king and queen—I doubt they will contact me." He frowned. "Besides, I wouldn't know how to send my condolences."

"They'll need some time to recover from their losses, and elect a new king and queen," Farrah said. "But as for the rest—I guess we'll just have to wait and see."

King Beyan and King Addan talked a bit more, mostly making vows of fidelity to each other and pledging support to each other's kingdoms. Soon, we were saying our goodbyes to the Bomorran king and to Elaina, and then Farrah ended the calling spell.

Shortly after that, Joichan took to the skies to return to Graenir, to resume his ambassador position alongside his wife, the former Calian queen Melandria. We gathered in the courtyard to see him off. Watching Joichan transform into his other self—a giant golden dragon—was still amazing to see, even though, over the years, I'd seen him shift forms numerous times.

The wind picked up as Joichan launched into the air, flapping his great wings once or twice as he flew in a circle just above the castle courtyard. Beyan, Farrah, and I lifted our hands in farewell. He hovered in the air, nodding his regal golden head at us before turning and leaving. Shading our eyes against the midday sun, we watched him fly away, becoming smaller and smaller until he was nothing but a distant dot in the bright blue sky.

"I'm glad the kingdom of Graenir allowed Joichan to leave, even if it was only for a short time," I said.

"Yes," Beyan said. He frowned. "I know my mother-in-law, Melandria, wanted to come with him. Not to take part in the battle, of course, but to help Jennica. She was frantic with worry when she found out her daughter had gotten hurt. But the Graenir leaders would not allow both of them to leave." His frown deepened. "I got the impression they wanted to keep Melandria behind, as a sort of political hostage."

"Hmm." Thoughtful, I stared into the sky in the direction Joichan had flown, as if the wispy clouds overhead held some answers. "Let's hope that they take Joichan returning to them so quickly as a sign of good faith."

"Indeed."

A page approached our group. Bowing, he addressed Beyan. "Your Majesty, the queen requested that I come find you."

"Is everything all right?" Beyan asked, instantly alert.

"Yes, Your Majesty. She told me to say she's doing much better, and would like to see you." He turned to Farrah and me. "All of you, if you please."

"Tell her we'll be right in, and if she needs anything—refreshments, assistance—then make sure she gets it," Beyan instructed. The page nodded and hurried back into the palace.

"Jennica's going to be sad she missed out on all the action," Farrah said as we headed into the cool of the castle at a more leisurely pace. "There's so much to tell her, I'm not sure where to start."

We reached the royal bedchamber, where Jennica sat up in bed, propped against some pillows. She looked much better than she had when Farrah and I had been here a few days earlier. The color had come back to her cheeks, and the usual intelligent twinkle in her eyes had returned. She smiled broadly when she saw us.

"Come in, come in!" she greeted us enthusiastically. Beyan walked over and kissed his wife, then pulled the settee that normally sat in front of the fireplace over to the side of the bed. I grabbed some chairs and brought them close as well.

"You look so much better." Farrah hugged the queen, then sat down on the settee.

"I feel so much better," Jennica said. She waved at a large tray of refreshments that sat on a low table nearby. "I want to hear about everything that happened while I was unconscious. I had the page bring up a huge amount of food and drink. And if we need to get more, I'm ready." She laughed and held up a small bell, muting the sound so she wouldn't accidentally summon a servant. "So, tell me everything."

Farrah and I looked at each other. "Where should we start?"

Jennica waved impatiently. "Wherever you want. I want to hear everything."

I sat down next to Farrah and took her hand. "Well, for starters, Farrah and I are getting married."

I thought that Beyan and Jennica would be surprised, or congratulate us.

But instead, both of them burst out laughing.

"What?" I asked, looking between them both. "What's so funny?"

In between peals of laughter, Beyan said, "It's about time."

And Jennica said, "I won the bet, darling."

"Bet?" Farrah asked. "What bet?"

A giggling Jennica said, "Shortly after Beyan and I married, I told him I thought you two would be next. I said you two would be engaged within five years."

Still chuckling, Beyan said, "And I said there was no way. You two had gone this long without figuring out you were in love with each other. Why would you suddenly realize it now?"

I couldn't help but laugh. Our friends knew us too well. Probably better than we had even known ourselves.

Farrah continued to relay our adventures to Jennica, with occasional remarks from me, and then eventually Beyan. I sat back, letting the conversation wash over me. For now, things were right in Calia again, although I knew it wouldn't be long before I was itching for another grand adventure.

I rubbed my thumb over Farrah's hand. She smiled up at me. Starting a new chapter in life with my best friend—now that would be a grand adventure indeed.

Dear Reader: I appreciate you!

Speaking of grand adventures, being able to share my stories with you has been the grandest adventure ever! Thank you so much for reading *Heir of Crowns and Curses*. If this is your first time in the Gifted Lands and the world of the Kingdom Legacy series, welcome! And if you're a returning reader, I'm so honored you're on this journey with me! I hope you enjoyed this fourth book in the Kingdom Legacy series as much as I enjoyed writing it.

If you have a moment, a short review on Goodreads or wherever you like to buy books and learn about new titles would be awesome.

Want to be the first to know about new adventures? Let's be friends!

Sign up for the Newsletter: http://www.rachanee.net/newsletter

Instagram: http://www.instagram.com/rachaneelumayno

TikTok: http://www.tiktok.com/@rachaneelumayno

YouTube: http://www.youtube.com/@rachaneelumayno

Twitter: http://www.twitter.com/rachaneelumayno

Join the community on Discord: Kingdom Legacy -(https://discord.com/invite/BRXcJJ3c6f)

READ ON FOR AN EXCERPT
FROM HEIR OF SECRETS AND
SPECTERS, THE FIFTH BOOK IN
THE KINGDOM LEGACY SERIES

— · —

PROLOGUE

THE NIGHT THAT MARKED the fall of Shonn felt like any other night in the sleepy eastern kingdom.

Just like the rest of the countries in the Gifted Lands, Shonn had heard about the murder of the Faerie king, Finvarra, and his queen Oona at Samhain. And while it was indeed a terrible tragedy, no one believed the Fae would act against anyone in the Gifted Lands. After all, the man who had killed the Fae royals had been brought to justice. His followers had found similar fates, or had scattered.

Besides, Valdonne's Treaty would keep the Fae in check. Enacted generations ago—by a former king of Shonn, no less—the Treaty ensured peaceful relations between the Fae and humankind. The tricks and violence both sides used to inflict upon each other were outlawed, with severe penalties for both sides. The treaty had helped the seven kingdoms of the Gifted Lands feel easy about their magical, otherworldly neighbors, especially the kingdom of Shonn, which shared an invisible border with the land of Faerie.

The first few weeks after Samhain, all of the Gifted Lands waited in readiness, afraid that retribution would come raging out of Faerie. But fall bled into winter, and then winter started moving inexorably on to spring, and nothing happened. The humans of the Gifted Lands relaxed, sure that the Fae would not seek revenge.

But the Fae live long lives—if not quite immortal, at least far longer than any human's.

And they have even longer memories.

Midwinter came, and with it, a day of thankful celebration that the winter would soon be over. In the evening, when the festivities were done, the citizens of Shonn settled into their homes. Only when all the occupants of a home were asleep would a household Fae make their appearance, as was their nightly habit.

Usually, the brownies of Shonn took pride in keeping their chosen homes clean, and the Shonn pixies loved keeping their homes' gardens well-tended.

But this night, instead of caring for their homes, the household Fae took joy in destroying them.

Cries and shouts pierced the morning air as the sun crept over the horizon. The house brownies and garden pixies had disappeared. After that day, no one saw any more household Fae in any Shonn home.

No house escaped the willful destruction. A few even burned, from the brownies' neglect of their kitchen hearths.

While the citizens of Shonn missed their helpful companions—and wondered why the household Fae had suddenly turned against them—they soon settled into life without them. Inconvenient, to be sure, but not insurmountable.

But that was only the first, and smallest, of the horrors the land of Faerie would unleash.

— · —

CHAPTER ONE

"So, when's the big day?"

I paused, pointing my bow with its nocked arrow down at the ground. My hand relaxed slightly as I pondered Queen Jennica's question.

Truthfully, I hadn't given much thought to planning my wedding. I assumed, like so many other things about my relationship with my betrothed, that things would just fall in place somehow and I wouldn't have to worry about it too much.

I shrugged, shaking my head so the wisps of my lavender hair would fall away from my face. My hair was pulled back in its usual braid, but it had an annoying habit of coming loose and getting in the way. "I'm not sure. I mean, Rhyss and I have only been engaged for a few months."

Jennica laughed as she raised her own bow, surveying the target ahead. "It may only have been a few months, but it took you two over a decade to finally get together."

I chuckled as well. She had a point. My friend—now fiancé—Rhyss and I had practically grown up together in the predominantly Seeker kingdom of Orchwell. Our love was built on a solid foundation of friendship and exasperation, but I wouldn't have had it any other way. "You're right. We should probably get going on getting married.

Otherwise, it will be another ten years before we actually walk down the aisle."

I raised my bow again and let the arrow fly. It landed with a satisfying thud in the wooden target several yards away. My arrow landed a few inches shy of the center. I nodded, satisfied.

Jennica took a deep breath and released her own arrow, which hit the target in the top right hand corner. She smiled ruefully and wiped her brow. Some tendrils of her dark hair clung to her cheek, and she pushed them away. "It might be a while before I get to your level of proficiency, Farrah. Maybe I should just stick with magic."

"No, no, Your Majesty. You're actually doing quite well. And besides, you only just started your archery three weeks ago. I've been doing this for years."

Jennica smirked. "Okay, now I know I'm bad at this. You only call me 'Your Majesty' when you're teasing me."

I laughed. "You can always use your magic to make the arrow shoot perfectly."

The queen gave a mock gasp of horror. "That would be cheating. I am determined to learn this archery thing correctly." She giggled. "But I'll keep it in mind as a last resort."

I put my bow down on the nearby small wooden table and poured a glass of lemon-and-honey water from the glass pitcher that sat on it. A servant had just delivered the pitcher and two glasses, and I wanted a drink while it was still fresh.

"Ready to take a break?" I said, holding the full glass out to Jennica.

"Yes." She spoke so readily I had to laugh again. The archery lessons were apparently harder than the queen wanted to admit.

I poured the second glass for myself, then took a sip and looked around. King Beyan of Calia, Jennica's husband and my friend and former employer, had had a small corner of the castle grounds set up as a private archery range when his wife had expressed an interest in learning. In theory, she could have practiced with the Calian soldiers at their training grounds, and any of the guards would have been happy to instruct their queen. In theory.

Calia didn't have a standing army, which also meant they didn't have a place for soldiers to train. Wherever the Calian army—such as it was—sparred, it was somewhere outside of the kingdom's capital where it wouldn't have been wise or safe for the queen to go.

Not that Jennica usually had to worry about her safety. As a master level magician, she could hold her own against all but the strongest mages. And with her ability to shapeshift into a fire-breathing dragon, she could easily wipe out an army—and had, on the occasions when her country was threatened.

So she didn't really need to learn how to use any weapons. But when I had asked her why, she had said, "Because even magic fails sometimes, and if something should happen and I couldn't transform into a dragon ... well, it's a good idea to have a backup plan."

But now I was beginning to think she wanted to learn archery as a not-so-subtle way to question me.

"Have you begun any sort of planning?" Jennica asked, after taking a long sip of her lemon-and-honey water.

I shrugged. "Not yet. I think until we know where we're having the wedding, we can't really hammer out any other details."

"Where *will* you have the wedding?"

I sighed. "That's really the question, isn't it? Rhyss and I both live in Orchwell, but our dearest friends—you and Beyan—live here in Calia." Orchwell, the kingdom directly south of Calia, wasn't so far away that Jennica and Beyan wouldn't be willing to travel to it, but—knowing they couldn't leave their royal duties for too long—Rhyss and I didn't want them to be inconvenienced.

"Rhyss doesn't have any other family left in Bomora?" Jennica asked, naming Rhyss's home kingdom.

"No, his only family—his cousin Enlar—is here in Calia now. And after our last trip there, I don't think Rhyss is too keen to return." Recently, Rhyss and I had to travel west to Bomora to rescue Queen Jennica and King Beyan's newborn baby boy, who had been kidnapped by a power-hungry secret society. While the adventure had helped put some painful parts of Rhyss's past to rest, it had also stirred up those sad memories to begin with, and I knew Rhyss would be happy if he never had to return there.

"What about Shonn?" Jennica raised her eyebrows. "Or are there bad memories back there, too?"

I took a long sip of my sweetened water, trying to figure out what to say. Shonn, a kingdom in the far eastern part of the Gifted Lands, was where I had been from originally. Although I was young when I left, so honestly, I considered Orchwell more my home than Shonn ever was.

Still, Shonn had left its mark on me. In the form of my half Fae blood, and the innate magic that came to those of Faerie.

"Well, I just sent word to my mother back in Shonn about the engagement," I said. "I'm sure she'll have some opinions on our wedding plans."

Jennica snorted, still sounding surprisingly queenly despite the rude sound. "Fortunately, my mother was too busy with her own wedding and honeymoon to fuss too much over mine. And I think, after the Prince Anders debacle, she was just as happy to stay away from anything wedding-related."

I chuckled. A few years ago, Jennica had been betrothed—against her will—to Anders, and the match had ended in a rather spectacular fashion. "I understand he lives in Shonn now with his wife." I grinned wickedly. "If we decide to hold the wedding in Shonn, I could invite him."

Jennica groaned good-naturedly. "I'll make sure to come to the wedding in dragon form, then. And stay in it."

The idea of Jennica attending my wedding as a big golden dragon caused me to double over in laughter for several minutes. "Oh, dear. I don't know if we'll be able to find a church big enough."

Jennica grinned. "Shonn shares a magical border with Faerie, doesn't it? Maybe you should ask the Fae, perhaps their court would be willing to let you marry on their side of the border. With their magic, they'd definitely be able to accommodate a dragon."

Now it was my turn to groan as I picked up my bow. "No, thank you. I want my wedding to be as drama-free as possible."

"Tell you what." Jennica waved her bow in the air. "We'll shoot for it."

I smirked. "If you insist."

At Jennica's wave, I nocked my arrow and sighted. Taking a deep breath, I drew my bow and released the arrow. It flew straight and true, hitting the wood with a loud thump, a mere finger's length from center.

I gave Jennica a self-satisfied smile and sketched a half-bow in her direction. "Your turn, Your Majesty."

She chuckled, shaking her head at my antics. "You be careful. Pride goes before a fall, and all that."

I crossed my arms, smirking. Jennica took aim, then loosed her arrow.

My eyes widened and my jaw dropped as the smirk fell from my face.

Queen Jennica's arrow, for once, had flown just as true as mine. And it had embedded itself in the exact center of the target.

The queen turned to me, eyebrows raised and a smile quirking her lips.

"Beginner's luck," she said modestly.

"Very well done," I commended her.

Jennica laughed. "You don't have to talk to the Fae, you know. It was just a joke."

"Oh, I know." I eyed Jennica's perfect bullseye again. Even though we had made the wager in jest, I couldn't shake the feeling that I lost more than just a bet.

Farrah's story coming 2024
Sign up for the newsletter to get updates!

ACKNOWLEDGEMENTS

I HAVE SO MANY people to be grateful to and thankful for that it would probably be a book in itself, so here are the highlights:

Tom, thank you for being such a wonderful editor, and more importantly, friend. This whole book series wouldn't be here without your generosity and expertise.

Jaime, thank you for being an overall awesome person and indulging me whenever I need a coffee break (which is pretty darn often!). Those coffee walks keep me sane and that coffee (well, hot chocolate in my case) keeps me writing.

Mom, for believing in me and also loaning out my book to your entire senior community. :)

Riley, for being such a snuggly kitty whose constant need to sit in my lap forces me to sit down and finish that chapter, already!

ABOUT THE AUTHOR

RACHANEE LUMAYNO IS AN actress, voiceover artist, screenwriter, avid gamer, and amateur dodgeball player. She grew up in Michigan, where she spent way too much of her free time reading fantasy novels. She still spends too much of her free time reading fantasy, although now she writes them as novels, narrates them as audiobooks, and creates them as improv for various roleplaying campaigns as well. *Heir of Crowns and Curses* is her fourth novel, and the fourth book in the Kingdom Legacy series. She is also a staff writer for two web comics and an upcoming video game. You can find her online at her website, www.rachanee.net, or on Instagram, TikTok, or YouTube (@rachaneelumayno).

www.ingramcontent.com/pod-product-compliance
Lightning Source LLC
Chambersburg PA
CBHW021039030726
47496CB00006B/1614